BRIEF AND BITTER HEARTS

Dorothy Davies

BRIEF AND BITTER HEARTS

Brief and Bitter Hearts

The Talent
From Loyalties, by John Drinkwater
Sidgwick and Jackson, 1919

When we as ghosts inhabit history,
In reputation happy or forlorn,
Uncounted then shall all our quarrels be
As any dusty calendar outworn.

"They, with what wit they might, immortal dress
Devised for instant beauty ere they died."
So shall we live, but shall not live by less;
O brief and bitter hearts, be pacified.

From Immortality by John Drinkwater
Olton Pools, Sidgwick and Jackson Ltd.,1917

There in the midst of all these words shall be
Our names, our ghosts, our immortality.

Dedicated to the memory of Guy Fawkes,
13th April 1570 – 31st January 1606

Patriot, devout Catholic and extraordinarily brave man.

This book is also dedicated to Gene Stewart.
There are two dedications; the first is from Guy.

For Eugene, in acknowledgement of friendship, of
sharing, of caring and of trust. The time I spent with you
was valuable and cherished beyond expressing. I
dedicate this, my life story, to you in recognition and
thanks for that special time.

The second is from me:
For Gene, friend, supporter and sharer of life's problems.
You have been there for me with your calm logic and
insightful understanding more times than I care to think
about. This is a small acknowledgement of a very big
friendship.

*Any event, once it has occurred, can be made to appear
inevitable by a competent historian.*
- Lee Simonson

Guy Fawkes' comments on his story

I thought long about the way to tell you of my life. It was one of devotion, of commitment, of faith and of what they, the authorities of the time, perceived as treason. I thought hard about writing it as a story, distancing myself from the events, for they were harsh and horrible beyond imagination. I thought about it and with my trusted and beloved channel and friend, Dorothea, attempted to write it that way. But she stopped, for it came over as dry and a little dull. I agreed with her and we tried to write it from my heart and mind. I still had problems and so she invoked the help of a writer on my side of life who worked with me, gently and with great love, to bring out the best of my abilities. I am extremely grateful for his assistance and to Dorothea for arranging it for me. I would not have thought of it myself. With his guidance we turned the book back the way it was originally, the way I really wanted it to be.

And so – for Dorothea, for my friend Eugene and for you, my readers, here it is. The complete and unexpurgated story of Guy Fawkes, the man you love to hate, the figure you have burned in effigy so many times, the person who has given High Petergate in York and the village of Scotton a name to conjure with, a name to put on its inns and hotels and places of interest, a name that has survived 400 years and will continue to survive for I see, with surprise and shock, that there are even islands and places around the world named after me. Such fame has shaken me to my spiritual core. I have to do something to set the record straight about what happened then and why, to explain what drove me to such lengths, what was in my mind and my heart. So much is not known, so much is surmised. So much is mistaken by historians and as always, they seek only to read the facts and not look behind them for the man who created those facts. But then, is that not the sole reason for Dorothea to channel these books, so that we, the originators of that piece of history, as it were, can put the record straight? As His Majesty King Henry VIII rightly said in his book, there are three sources, secondary, primary and original. Which would you care to believe?

We lay much work on this one's shoulders – and fingers – in giving her this task. She patiently transcribes the words, does the editing when we go on too long, sorts out the timelines to be sure we do not stray from our path and most of all, gives us unconditional love. No spirit with a story to tell can resist such a person, such an invitation, such a project.

With those thoughts in mind, I commend to you the story of Guy/Guido Fawkes, patriot, traitor, soldier, revolutionary, terrorist, call me what you will. But do me the honour, please, of reading my story, so that you can begin to understand a little more. And, whilst I have your attention, I beg of you, do not judge me by your standards. My life in my time was very different from yours. The only thing which has not changed is people blowing something – or someone – up to make a point, political, religious or just fanatical.

In that regard, history has not changed at all.

And, you are still torturing people, are you not?

Guy Fawkes

Chapter One

The man lying in the darkness of the lonely cell could not decide what was most difficult to endure, the pain which consumed him or the bitter cold which burned him. For the first time in his life he began to believe that Hell was not a place of endless heat, flames and vile demons, but the empty lonely coldness of a dungeon when the body, which was of necessity lying on the ice cold floor, had been racked beyond endurance. He clung to life for no reason that he could rationalise in his pain-swamped mind. Why not let go, deprive them of their show piece execution, of their taunting and their smug satisfaction that another traitor had been dealt with? Why not give himself into the hands of the great God who surely awaited him in Heaven? Ah, he thought, groaning as another wave of intense pain swept him from head to foot, ah, if only it were possible to still the heart by a thought! If it were, he would do it in an instant but no matter how hard he tried, he remained alive – just.

Was it still night or was it already day? Would they come for him soon, to carry him to the traitor's death that he knew awaited him? He had lost all sense of time for the Tower was a dark place of endless torment and suffering. All he knew was that he hurt and that it would soon all be over.

He heard footsteps on the cold stone, a jangle of ice as chains rattled and keys knocked against one another. He heard a curse as the lock refused to give under the hand of the person trying to gain access.

Then the door opened and a light shone into his eyes. He painfully raised an arm to shield himself from the beam.

"It lives." Someone spat into the dungeon. "We will be back for you tomorrow, scum. Be ready to meet thy Maker!"

The door slammed, the mechanism protested but finally moved, locking him in, as if they believed the broken man could get up, open the heavy door and walk out. Fools, he thought with intense bitterness. Fools! I could no more raise a hand to them than I could fly through these walls and disappear forever.

But I can disappear for a while, came another thought. I can escape the pain. I can go back.

The darkness closed in on him like a thick, suffocating blanket. He allowed his mind to go blank and then to go back, back, back...

***

"Guy! Come downstairs, please! It's time for your meal."

Mother's voice carried that 'do not argue with me' tone which had to be obeyed. Guy reluctantly scrambled from his bed where he had been lying perfectly still, creating pictures by using the fine cracks in the ceiling. It was something he liked to do and hated being interrupted, but he knew well his mother would not tolerate any delay. He hastily straightened the quilted coverlet, tugged the pillow back into its place and left the room.

The wooden stairs, which sometimes felt as if they went on forever, creaked as he hurried down, through the hall and into the parlour where the table had been set for him and his sisters. Anne and Elizabeth were already in their seats, heads bowed, demure and quiet, their curls tied up with ribbons, for all the world as if they were waiting for Grace to be said. Guy suspected they had been talking about him and had stopped when he came in the room but he had no way of proving it. He loved his sisters but had no illusions about them. He knew well that they were prepared to join forces and gang up on him if necessary, if it was something they wanted or

12

something they wanted to get out of. Both these things happened with great regularity.

The parlour was immaculate as always, the plates, cups and cutlery precisely aligned on the gleaming white cloth which covered the scrubbed table. The fire had been made up so that it glowed with a friendliness that permeated the room, the cushions on the settle were precisely set against one another. He breathed in the smell of fresh bread, sharp cheese, wood ash and that indefinable scent of mother: soap, lavender and comfort.

"There you are!" She was standing by the door waiting for him and impatiently pushed him toward his chair. "Come now, quickly! Say Grace, all of you, and then eat. You know your father is said to be home early today."

The prayer of gratitude was murmured into the cloth by the three children in discordant harmony and then, before either of his sisters did so, Guy reached for the crusty loaf in the centre of the table. He paused as a ray of sunshine seemed to fall across the room, making a beam of light which illuminated the bread and the silver dish on which it stood.

"Look!" he said out loud but no one looked. His sisters were chattering again, his mother was indifferent to everything inside the house because she was listening to the sounds from outside. Guy knew she was awaiting hearing his father's footsteps on the pathway. I wonder if I will ever be the centre of someone's life, he mused even as he became irritated that no one else saw the sunbeam for what it was, a miracle, at least to him. A cloud covered the sun for a moment, the sunshine disappeared and the bread resumed its dull life as a loaf on a silver platter. But the moment, the memory, burned itself into Guy's mind. It was surely a gift from God, that sunshine, that food, that moment, a gift which he treasured. It had come so close after their saying Grace, saying thank you for the food, it could be nothing else.

He startled himself with the thought and knew he had to ponder it later, when he was alone.

Mother sat by the fireside, mending a shirt for Father while they ate. She was watching their table manners and listening to the two girls talking about lace and ribbons, someone's cat having a litter of kittens and their desire to have one or more of them, what someone had said about them … conversations which were of no interest to Guy. He ate mechanically: bread, cheese, meat, it all tasted the same to him because his mind was elsewhere. He was desperately trying to work out if there was a way of approaching Father to ask for help with the spinning toy that had mysteriously broken earlier that day. He doubted it, Father had no patience with broken toys and Guy consistently had a parade of them. He seemed to be cursed with clumsiness; things were damaged or fractured if he so much as touched them. His toys were invariably broken in a very short time but he could never work out how it had happened.

Although he ate without much thought of what he was eating, he did appreciate the spring water, drawn from their well, in the plain pewter tankard reserved for him. The water was cold and fresh - and needed. He had not realised he was so thirsty. The afternoon had somehow drifted away from him as he made pictures in his mind. He had been transporting his very young self to a place where there was no clumsiness, where all toys remained in one piece, where his sisters took him into their games and into their lives, where Mother considered him before Father, where he was not an outsider.

Mother's chair creaked as she moved to tend to the sewing. Elizabeth and Anne murmured together. Somewhere, possibly in their garden, a bird called endlessly as if it knew no other sound to make whilst other bird cries made a background sound that was part of life. Carriage wheels rumbled over the cobblestones of Stonegate, hooves clattered on the road, harness creaked, dogs barked, voices of both children and adults filled the small room where the Fawkes family sat. The whole thing became one pleasant sound and Guy absorbed it all, taking it in and holding it as a memory he thought he would cherish for a long time. Added to the miracle of the sunbeam lighting the bread, he thought the day was a special one, outstanding in a series of days which were very much like one another with only Sundays being the exception to the mundane routine.

Father was coming home early. That meant the moment they were through eating, Mother would rush around and clear the table, then, with the maid's help, begin the preparations for his father's tea which would be more elaborate than theirs. Father would have ale to drink from a fine tankard which Guy greatly admired but dared not touch. It had elaborate engraving all around it, a weaving endless pattern he longed to trace with a fingertip, but knew even that would be likely to bring disaster to the tankard and it was Father's, so that would never do. Mother would also ensure he and his sisters were in the house, no going out to play with the likelihood of getting grubby before Father arrived. This was so that he could greet his family and then take his place by the fireside. He would have the papers he carried home with him in a large satchel made of fine leather which was as soft as wool from years of use and polish. Papers that Father would study after he had taken his meal, papers that absorbed his every thought so that even if Guy stood by his side with the broken toy in his hands, Father would not know he was there.

It meant that they had to be quieter than usual, too, for Father was 'working' when reading the papers and he did not want the sound of boisterous children to disturb him. Guy knew the words even if he did not fully understand what they meant. Mother said them every time Father was due home, whether he was early or not.

Soon the food was gone and permission was given for them to leave the table. Guy knew his sisters were planning on collecting wild flowers which they would put in a vase to please Father. He wondered again how they could do that and not break anything. His experience of putting water into something on the table had resulted in a small flood which had earned him a stiff reprimand he still remembered. Well, they could go and get their flowers, something they seemed capable of doing without getting dirty. To be on the safe side, it was better if he stayed indoors, despite the fine weather which tempted him to go outside and play. Mother would not be best pleased if he did for he was bound to get dirt on himself somehow.

The stairs seemed like a mountain but he climbed them steadily, carefully, clinging to the banister with one small hand, pulling himself up. He wanted to return to the sanctuary of his room, with its feeling of security created by the rich panelling, the thick drapes around his bed, the rugs his mother had made for the pegged floor and the years of familiarity. He had known no other place to sleep. He loved the pictures he could see in the ceiling, the cabinet for his hose and boots, the shelves for his toys, the soft bed which cradled him, the casement window which looked out into the busy, bustling, ever changing street below. It was like nowhere else. It was his world.

He knelt on the large chest that contained his clothes, unaware of the hardness of the wood. The world outside was constantly moving, ever interesting. From that height he could watch people without them knowing he was there. He could see the carriages making their way through the throng. There were street vendors who carried trays or bags of wares, business men in smart clothes like Father's, ladies in their beautiful coloured gowns, shawls, bonnets and cloaks. He watched for an age, losing himself in the busy life of York, unaware of the passing of time. From this perspective he was not a part of the scene, but above it, an onlooker, not a participant.   There was a hint of loneliness in the realisation but one he ignored. It was good to watch and not be seen. You could learn a lot from that.

A larger than usual crow flew by the window, close enough that Guy could see the extended flight feathers. I wish I could fly, he thought suddenly. I wish I could fly out of here, swoop over the city, roost in a tree, go where I want and see what I want! And fly back when I had seen it all and I could then think about it.

The thought was interrupted by the sound of the front door with its distinctive thump. Father was home. Guy snatched up the broken toy which he had left by the side of the chest and walked out onto the landing, not wanting to rush and perhaps fall. His instinct was to run down the stairs but this was important. If Father was in a good mood, if the day's work at the great Minster had gone well, he might even be sympathetic to the request to mend it.

As he reached the top of the stairs, a sudden thought gripped his mind. He turned round and went back into his room to think about it before it escaped.

The ray of sunshine. It was a gift from God. Yes, that I already knew. But why me? Why did no one else see it? Or if they did, why didn't they say? Why was it there at that moment?

His parents had impressed on him that God was an all-seeing, all-powerful figure. The priest at church and various aunts and uncles had added to this, they invariably asked if he said his prayers before bed and asked for strength to be good. God was not a gift giving sort of person. He gave rules instead.

But He gave me that ray of sunshine! I know he did!

Guy tried to make sense of the conundrum, but he was too young to rationalise his thoughts.   He sighed, shrugged and went back to the door. If God was able to offer him a ray of sunshine then God was able to offer him some kind of reason for it all. If he waited long enough it might happen. One of his mother's favourite expressions was 'wait and see'. He would wait and see.

Another thought struck him. If that was God speaking to me, would He arrange for Father to be kind about my broken toy? If He could, then he would know the message was for him.

"God," he whispered into the quiet afternoon air, "if that sunshine was for me, give me a sign. Let Father be kind about my broken toy. This I know You can do." He felt a little scared for a moment: who was he to try and do some kind of deal with God? What if God decided to teach him a lesson? But then again, if God was trying to speak to him, he needed a sign. The priest talked of signs, of burning bushes, of manna from Heaven. Surely even a boy as young as he could ask for a sign?

With a fast beating heart he went downstairs.

Father was in his usual place by the hearth, ensconced in his favourite chair. It was solidly built, like the man who sat in it. He was a tall dignified man with curling brown hair, a small, neatly clipped beard, soft hands with trimmed nails, a gentle voice that could turn harsh in a moment and deep brown eyes that seemed to bore into a boy's very centre and reveal his secrets. He often did.

"Guy." The voice was soft; the hand outstretched invited him to go to his father's side. "What have you been doing today?"

"Playing, Father. But my toy broke."

"Show me."

The soft hands took the toy and turned it over and over, examining it from all angles. Guy stared at the floor, at the carved arms of his father's chair, at the sooted hearth, aware he was all but holding his breath. He did not want to look at his father, afraid of disapproval flaring across the normally calm features. Surely the damage was his fault; it usually was.

"It was poorly made, Guy. It was nothing you did, for once. I will arrange for another to be bought for you, a better one."

"Thank you, Father!" There was a rush of relief; the broken toy was not his fault for once, quickly followed by the quiet glow that came from remembering his request to God.

"Have you helped your mother today?"

"Yes, Father! I carried water and ran some errands and dug some garden."

"Good. I am pleased to hear it. Now, go along with you, I have work to do."

"Of course, Father. Thank you!"

Guy left the room quietly, taking care not to bang the door after him. The long hallway, with its red black and white tiles, beckoned him toward the kitchen and the garden where the great tree waited, its branches thick and firm and fit for climbing. It would be good to do that. He had been in the house too long; it was time to go outside again.

The kitchen was redolent of soap and cooking, the lingering smell of fresh baked bread combined with the cleaning of bowls and dishes. Something bubbled and spat steam from the pot over the fire. His mother was busy at the table with ladle, knife and mixing bowl. She glanced at Guy as he lingered by the door, hoping he could escape to his refuge without further tasks being handed to him.

"Going outside?"

"Yes, Mother, if you don't mind."

"Try not to get too dirty, please."

"Yes, Mother."

He was free. Father was in a good mood, he would have another toy, his mother had no more tasks for him. Surely God had smiled on him this afternoon!

The garden seemed huge to him. Just outside the kitchen door was an area of grass dominated by a huge tree, further on was the vegetable garden with its neat rows of growing plants, by the side were the fruit bushes covered with netting to ward off the birds. It all had its own mystery and its own magic. The tree was the best of all; the tree held his secrets, his dreams and his desires. Sitting high up in the branches he could begin to believe he was able to fly wherever he wanted and to see what he wanted; to do just as he pleased. He resented the fact he appeared to be held to the ground by an invisible force that refused to let him take to the wind, as he longed to do.

The afternoon sun slanted through the heavy boughs, patterning the ground below. The branch, his favourite one, was wide enough to let him sit comfortably with his back against the trunk, the whispering leaves talking their secret language all around him. He held fast to the belief that if he listened long enough, he might be able to make sense of the murmuring. It was all a dream, of course. His logical mind told him that it was so, the part of him which longed to dream wished – and sometimes knew - otherwise.

With the ease of practice he climbed the branches, hand over hand, secure in his knowledge of the foot holes, until he reached the higher levels. There he settled down and quietened his breathing and his racing heart.

I did a deal with God.

I was bad enough to ask God for a favour and He gave it to me. So, perhaps I was not bad after all, or He would not have given it to me.

He did give me that ray of sunshine, just as He is giving me the sunshine I see now. See how it shines through the branches; see how it makes the shadows dance.

Where are these thoughts coming from? Why can't I think properly – like everyone else does?

Or do they? How do I know that? Why do I believe they don't think like me?

The quiet, dark haired slender boy sat in the tree, alone and lonely with his strange thoughts, watching his sisters who had returned with their wild flowers. How delicate they were, all bouncing curls, smiling faces, small hands and soft skin. They had no real staying power for anything involving strength. It was as if boys were made specifically to help girls do the hard things in life. Neither of his sisters could chop wood nor haul water. They would hurt themselves. They were too fragile. Almost as fragile as the flowers they carried in those small hands. Mother would give them a vase, they would fill it with water and put the flowers in it, they would carry it to the table and Father would smile his approval at their efforts. This he knew, he had seen it before, many times, and every time felt the same intense pang that he did not recognise as jealousy. All Guy knew was, he had nothing to offer his father. He would not be interested in birds' eggs, in captured insects or unusual spiders, in knowing where the best bull rushes grew or how to find the thickest clump of trees and bushes where you could hide and watch the wildlife coming and going, where you could see the squirrels play their mad wild games around the trees, watch the shrews and mice dart here and there, hear the rustle of leaves and wonder if something larger was approaching and shiver in delicious fear.

Father had a proper job; he worked for the Archbishop who was all but uncrowned monarch in York. Everyone knew that those who worked in the Minster were the elite of York. Guy, young as he was, knew that his father's employment made the family different from the neighbours. They were just businessmen.

Time passed, the light began to fade; owls were beginning their nightly swoop in search of the very mice and shrews Guy had thought of, ones he might have seen from his hiding place. The moon was appearing in the sky, as full and round as a cheese from the dairy down the road. He knew it was time to go in. He was getting cold and anyway, it was sensible to go before he was called, it would make a better impression. Still with his turmoil of thoughts, he reluctantly climbed down and went back into the house.

Chapter Two

The tormented tortured man groaned as another wave of pain brought him close to consciousness again, but the darkness reclaimed him. There was just so much a human body could stand and he had been taken past that point – several times. The men who had tortured him had known their business well. After all, they had no shortage of bodies on which to practice their foul black arts. He could not hate them, they only did their work as ordered. But what kind of man would do that work? Men without hearts and compassion. Men without souls. Men destined for the blackest most horrendous part of Hell. Men who would find out how it felt to be tortured to the point of death and then not allowed that release. Men spawned of the devil himself.

***

"Fawkes, are you listening to me?"

The schoolmaster stared at his class over the top of little round spectacles, a frown furrowing the forehead that appeared to go on forever, as there was no hair to create a horizon for it.

"Sir!" Guy sat up straight behind his small wooden desk, pulling himself back sharply from the daydream in which he had been lost whilst the teacher had droned on about mathematics and something called algebra.

"Concentrate, Fawkes! You were daydreaming! There are cures for daydreamers. I have one right here if you need it."

Guy did not need reminding that there was an ever-present switch by the schoolmaster's desk. He had already felt it a few times and did not wish to repeat the experience. The problem was he had just seen a face in the clouds which were drifting across the otherwise clear sky. A beautiful face. He wanted to study it, not listen to someone going on about mathematics. He could add up and subtract, what else did anyone need in their life?

The schoolmaster turned his attention away from Guy and surveyed his class, the serried rows of small desks occupied by small boys who were reluctant to be there. He looked around as if wondering who to pick on and persuade to answer a few questions. Guy stole a sideways look at his friend Thomas sitting at the next desk, receiving a sympathetic grimace in return. Guy knew Thomas hated maths as much as he did.

He looked out of the window again. Outside was sunshine, green fields, freedom. Days of sun were rare and to be welcomed. The snowstorms of February had seemed to last a lifetime, shutting everyone off from the outside world. The whole winter had been one of unremitting cold and snow falling endlessly from lead grey skies. Animals had frozen to death, and a few people too, the homeless, the unwary, the poor. Father had been busy with committees organising relief for the frozen sufferers in York. He had been fractious and tired and they had tiptoed around him as best they could. The work had seemed unrelenting and had taken its toll on them all.

Spring had come late and reluctantly crept over the land, but now it had arrived there was a restlessness in him, a desperate longing to be able to roam in the warmth and the sunshine. That freedom was sadly not available to him until it was the right time to escape - for a while.

Outside was warmth, fecundity, grass, flowers, growing things, leaves sprouting on everything, his tree coming alive again after a winter of hibernation; inside was coolness, dust, chalk, droning voices and rigid rules. Did the massive blocks of stone which formed the building have any idea how many boys they trapped, holding them prisoner at their desks, compounding the school's efforts to hammer Latin, literature, grammar, maths and history into their stubborn minds? Did the blocks of stone actually care? Guy stopped his random thoughts and forced himself to think about his lesson. If he was not careful he would be in trouble and was in danger of being beaten again by the sadistic teacher who took such delight in punishing his pupils. He probably didn't realise or appreciate he wore a look of pure glee when he found an unfortunate boy to belabour but it was there and the entire class knew it.

Learning came easy to him, apart from maths. English grammar and literature were subjects he liked and absorbed without difficulty. Latin, being based on what he perceived as logic, came easy to him as well. He knew that maths should also come easy to him, as that too was based on logic but somehow the numbers seemed to want to go their own way and he was consistently bad with his lessons. It was as if they were a strange language not known to anyone, they jumbled in his mind, they ran riot over the page, they refused to follow one another in sequence or indeed any kind of logical order and the answers he gave to set questions were often so wildly wrong as to be ridiculous. The teachers could not understand it. Nor could Guy.

Eventually it was time for a break, a time to run and shout and breathe air not filled with dust and age. The cloud bearing the beautiful face had drifted away, much to Guy's disappointment. Thomas punched him on the arm.

"What was all that about?"

"What?"

"All that looking out of the window and getting yourself noticed by Sir!"

"Oh that. Seeing things in the clouds, shapes and stuff."

"Daydreaming, like he said. Come on, Oswald's got something to show us. Forget all that rubbish!" Thomas raced away, a whirlwind of energy and boyish frustrations.

'It's not rubbish!' Guy longed to say it aloud but instead ran after his friend, just another boy enjoying just another break from lessons.

But not inside. There lay the seeds of unhappiness, the need to connect with something bigger than himself, something to hold on to, something to –

There the thoughts stopped, for there were friends to talk with and tussle with and act as if he had not a single care in this world.

For a while he didn't.

Later that evening, ensconced in his favourite place high in the tree, in the coolness of the evening air, Guy pulled back the thoughts he had been considering earlier in the day. He relived the memory of the face in the cloud and asked himself what was missing from his life. He had been considering the question for some days without coming to any kind of conclusion, nothing that satisfied him, anyway.

He saw the arc of the sky, the movement of clouds, the seemingly perverse and yet purposeful flight of flocks of birds, saw the animal world for what it was, an intricately interlocked hierarchy of 'eat or be eaten' or even 'eat and be eaten.' The tiniest animals were food for the slightly bigger ones who in turn were food for larger ones and they in turn were food for night hunting owls. So it went on, a complex and totally fascinating world which began with insects and ended with man himself.

The question was: how had it happened, how had it come about? Who ordained the movement of the clouds, of the stars, for surely they moved, or seemed to, across the night sky? Who arranged for the smallest to be eaten by the next and so on and who ordained that man would and could be the ultimate creature on this earth?

Even as he thought about it, a shaft of late evening sunlight slanted through the branches and touched his heart. He remained perfectly still, hardly breathing, yet aware of the breath entering and leaving his body, aware of his hands gripping the bark of the branch, feeling the heat of the sun's ray as it touched him. Then, as quickly as it came, it was gone, leaving him in shadow but filled with the most intense fervour he could ever remember experiencing.

The unexpected ray of sunshine equated with the miracle of the ray which lit up the bread which he then ate. Then God had given him his answer. He had been given a new toy.

It was obvious. God had spoken again. God wanted him, Guy Fawkes, for something momentous, something earth shattering, something which would demand much - if not everything - of him.

The moment the thought took shape he threw it away. He wasn't ready for that kind of commitment: he had family, his mother, father, his sisters, his grandparents, his aunts, uncles and cousins.

The next thought was: why should I think God would take me away from them? What if this task is *with* them, not away from them?

And then the next thought, did this in any way match with the face of the beautiful woman I saw in the clouds?

"I need to talk to someone!" he told the quivering leaves and listened as they rustled in reply. They seemed to say 'wait – wait – wait' and he let all the tension drain from his body, tension he had not realised was there until he let it go. The sunshine had appeared to pierce him, to fasten him to the branch, to make sure he did not move. It also appeared to link him to God. That was too big a thought to share with anyone at that moment. The leaves were right. He had to wait and grow both in body and mind. The concepts he was struggling with were huge and very adult. He had no way of knowing that mystics from time immemorial had struggled with the same thoughts he was having but the truth is, had he known it would not have made his struggle any easier to cope with. He felt as if he walked alone in a world of insensitive people who would not see God's hand if He reached out for them. It was an intensely lonely feeling.

Life went from casual, easy-going schooldays and the calm security of a loving family to heartbreak, grief and uncertainty in the time it took for one man to cry out, grab at his arm and tumble face first from his chair by the hearth to the unwelcoming floor. Guy was walking into the room when it happened and stood, rigid with shock, in the doorway. His sisters scrambled from the table and ran to their father's side, desperately trying to comfort him, but it was too late. Guy knew his father was dead, knew it as surely as he knew his name. He realised his mother knew it too for she had not moved from her frozen position, interrupted in the process of pouring ale. Guy looked at her for guidance, even as he felt himself shaking with the shock.

Slowly her lips parted as if with a supreme effort. "Go and fetch the doctor, Guy!" It came out in what was almost a whisper.

He turned and raced out of the room, clawed at the huge front door, fighting the lock. Then he was free of the house and running as fast as he could down High Petergate to the doctor's house which he knew well. He darted around groups of people who stared at his white face and obvious distress, slipped on some ordure and regained his balance with a supreme effort, racing against time which was already lost. It was just that he had to do something, anything, for the man he had left slumped on the floor, already going cold. He knew it but he had to go through with it.

He hammered on the heavy plain door of the white stone house, using the large pewter knocker as hard as he felt his heart was hammering in his chest. The servant who opened the door after an eternity initially looked straight over his head and then looked down, suddenly realising it was a child who had knocked.

"The doctor's out." The man was brusque to the point of rudeness and Guy felt that he was being dismissed almost out of hand. He had to do something - fast.

"Tell him … tell him Mr Fawkes is taken bad this minute and needs the doctor!"

"Ah, Mr Fawkes, is it? I'll inform the doctor the moment he comes back."

Guy didn't stop to offer his thanks; manners were forgotten at a time like this. He heard the door slam as he turned and ran back home, almost sobbing as the breath caught in his throat. His lungs were burning. He had never run so fast, not even when playing chase. He had never felt such intense emotions, even when in his tree eyrie. His heart hurt so much it seemed as if it was determined to knock itself lifeless against his ribs. He thrust open the front door, ran in and slammed it after him. He hurried into the parlour. Not much had changed whilst he had been gone: his sisters were weeping, curled up on the floor at Father's side. His mother still stood by the table, although she had put down the jug of ale. His father was still on the floor, even though he had cherished the remote but forlorn hope that by the time he got back, his father would have got up and resumed his place in his chair, laughing over the small incident which had sent him tumbling to the rug.

"Mother, the doctor's out, the man said he'll be along as soon as he returns!" The words were gasped round his need to draw breath properly.

"Thank you, Guy. Not that the doctor can do anything. Your father is dead."

There was no doubting it. The body slumped on the floor in front of the fire was totally bereft of life. It was as if his proud dignified father had become nothing but a stuffed effigy, the hair falling around and hiding the face, one hand still clutching the papers he had been studying before his heart had stopped suddenly and violently.

Guy stared at him, unable to look away. He had seen plenty of dead animals, rabbits, pigeons, even a fox one time, stiff and pathetic under a bush, but not a person. The stillness seemed greater, more significant than in the animals. His sisters were sobbing, heartbroken; his mother seemed incapable of saying anything but "hush!" She was dry-eyed, her face white, her mouth set in a firm almost bitter line across her face. The usually soft woman people went to for comfort had turned into a cold sharp widow in the moments it took her husband to die.

They stayed in their tableau of shock and hurt, awaiting the doctor for what felt like an age before there was a loud bang on the door, then it was thrust open and the doctor rushed in, snatching a wide brimmed hat from his mostly bald head. "I am sorry, I was called out to a fatality. I-"

Guy noticed, almost inconsequentially, that the doctor's narrow shoulders seemed to be bowed as if carrying the weight of all his patients. He saw him look at the body and then at the grief-stricken family. He turned to make a small bow to Guy's mother, "I came as soon as I could, Mrs. Fawkes." He knelt and looked closely at the suffused face of the corpse. "Heart," he announced. He stood up, took Mother's hand and held it for a moment. "My deepest sympathies. He was a fine man. You know how long I have known him. I feel I have lost a good friend, but that is nothing compared with your great loss."

Anne and Elizabeth had moved at last and were at their mother's side. She put her arms around them, a hen sheltering her chicks. Her face still appeared frozen. "Could I prevail upon your kindness to arrange… disposal of the body, Doctor?"

"Of course." The doctor turned to Guy who was still trying to quieten his trip hammer heart. Tears burned the back of his eyes but he refused to let them fall. "I will have to leave your mother and sisters in your care, young man, until you can arrange for relatives to come and help."

Guy nodded and then remembered his manners. "Thank you for coming so soon, Doctor."

"For Mr Fawkes, it was not soon enough, I am sorry to say."

"In truth, Doctor, I doubt you could have done anything for my husband." Edith Fawkes stood up, grasping her daughters' hands. "It happened so fast and was so sudden – and complete-"

"With the heart it often is, Mrs. Fawkes. A quick and I believe a relatively painless death. I will attend to the undertakers on your behalf. Sadly, it will be my second visit to them this day."

He put his hat on, looked round at each of them and sighed. "I am so sorry. I liked Edward Fawkes very much. I will do what I can for you. Send your son to the house with a message if you need anything."

"Thank you, Doctor."

Guy escorted the doctor to the front door, solemnly shaking hands with him before he left. It was a very adult thing for him to do; he felt as if he had just made a large step into manhood. He was nine years old and was the only male in the house until an uncle or someone arrived to take over responsibility for the shattered family. It was a heavy mantle to assume.

He went back to the lounge and stood by the door, staring at the corpse untidily tumbled on the floor. Everything seemed very quiet, as if the world had stopped. No carriages rumbled by, no voices were heard outside, no dogs barked, no birds sang. The family was in shock, wearing tear streaked faces, shocked expressions and no one able to look away from the once living, all powerful, revered head of the family, now nothing more than a bundle of clothes which still contained a body. Guy remembered something he had seen. He went to the cupboard in the hall and returned carrying his father's cloak. With great reverence he covered the body, so it became nothing more than an inanimate mound on the floor. It seemed to release them from their shock. At last they could move, speak, cry more freely. His mother said nothing but her eyes expressed her gratitude to her son for his thoughtfulness.

The time between the doctor leaving and the undertakers arriving was a dark and sorrowful eternity of silence, shock, grief and determination. The men were quietly deferential to the widow and gently removed the body of Edward Fawkes. Only then did Guy feel he could leave the room. His limbs flared with pins and needles where he had been standing rigid, terrified of doing or saying the wrong thing and starting everyone crying, including himself. Once he had covered the body, he had taken up a position by the window, waiting for the men to arrive, trying to act like the man he was supposed to be, the one he would grow into, he hoped.

He went up the stairs, recalling a time not so long back when he had felt they were his personal mountain to climb, heading for the sanctuary of his room. Only then could he truly give way to all that was bursting out of his overwhelmed heart.

Chapter Three

A rat crept from the mire in the corner, whiskers twitching, keen to investigate the possible source of food which had been thrown into its lair. Sharp cutting teeth began to test the meat. The wounded man flung out an arm to dislodge the creature. The movement caused such intense pain that the dungeon echoed with fearful screams. The rat fled.

***

"Fawkes, I wanted to – would you kindly accept my condolences on the death of your father?" Guy looked up at John Pulleyn, the Headmaster, with something approaching fear. He was an imposing figure, standing head and shoulders above most men with a breadth of body to carry it, too. His long white hair was perpetually swept back from his high forehead, giving him the look of an aesthetic. No one knew his real feelings about anything: his religion, what he taught, the state of the economy in York, for he simply never said. Such reservation created an air of mystery which added to his awesome presence for the boys at the school.

"Thank you, sir." Guy stood stiff, shoulders back, ill at ease. He had wondered why the Headmaster had asked to see him, hoping it was not something he had done wrong or some lesson in which he had failed miserably.

"Your father was a respected member of the community. I am sure the Archbishop and his staff will miss him a great deal."

"I believe so, sir." What else was there to say? That Father regularly brought home masses of papers to work on, that he had made the position of Proctor at the Minster his life's mission, that the shadow of the work had fallen over the household more times than he cared to remember? The condolences which had flooded in since his father's death had been revealing to the young Guy, he had not truly appreciated the high regard in which his father had been held. He had no knowledge of the business and financial world of York or its society, that was something he had assumed he would discover in time through his father's connections.

"Well, I wanted to say that and I have. Please convey them to your mother for me, too. Now, I trust you are capable of working at your lessons?"

"Of course, sir."

"Go along then, your class awaits you."

Guy bowed and hurried from the room. He was glad to be free from the Headmaster's presence and the unwelcome attention the summons had brought him. His classmates had been quick to ask what he had done when the message had arrived for him to visit the Headmaster, putting all manner of thoughts into his head, fears of dire punishment or expulsion. Instead he had been met with courtesy and sympathy. It was hard to reconcile in his mind. He bowed to his teacher and as quietly as he could, slid behind his desk and picked up the sheet of paper he had left there. He began to study it. The figures danced in front of his eyes, refusing to stay in neat columns. He realised, with a sense of shame, that it was due to the blurring caused by tears filling his eyes. Sympathy was hard to handle when grief was raw. He rubbed them away and tried again to concentrate.

The sun was streaming through the classroom window, illuminating the paper, Guy and the desk. Guy looked around to see that his friends Kit and Jack were also in the sunshine, joined to him by the brightness. He looked down and the paper itself seemed to glow. In that moment everything on it made perfect sense. A block had been removed, the figures settled into columns that were logical and sensible. He picked up a quill and began to work, delighting in the accomplishment of making sense of something that had eluded him since he started school.

Sunshine and illumination of the mind. The two things had come together; they were clearly linked. Guy stored the thoughts for later, to consider when he was alone. He needed to pursue it on his own terms, in his own sanctuary, the tree. There it seemed nature spoke to him, God spoke to him, in a place and in a way he could understand.

During the break in the lessons, his friends crowded around, demanding to know why he had been called to the Headmaster. He had nothing to offer their eager minds but the Head's condolences. They seemed disappointed, convinced that there was something more meaningful to it than that.

He realised there was a knowledge gap between himself and those he associated with. His friends still had their fathers in their lives. The concept of bereavement, of being without a father, was beyond their comprehension. They tried to sympathise with Guy but could not do it properly, not as an adult could, those who had been through the process of losing someone several, if not many, times. Guy did not blame his friends, he knew he would be the same if it were the other way round.

Jack hung around, shoulders hunched, fiddling with a piece of stone, waiting until some of the boys drifted away. Then he moved closer. "Come on, give, what was it really about?"

"Told you. He wanted to offer his condolences."

"Really? That was it?"

"Look, I know you all want to make more of it, but Father-" Guy all but choked on the word, "was a big person in the Minster and in York. Lots of people have been saying the same things to us, especially to Mother."

"I suppose that was it, then."   Jack seemed disappointed and in some ways Guy could understand that. There was little excitement in their lives, one of their classmates being summoned to the Headmaster was An Occasion and they hoped for something dramatic to come out of it. Instead all he had to report was something they could all utter but none could truly appreciate.   Until they lived through their own bereavement, they would not understand his sense of loss.

It was as if a central pillar had been removed from his life. Everything had revolved around Father, his coming home and his going out, his mealtimes, his working periods, the need to be quiet, the constant injunctions not to bother him when he was reading the papers he had brought home or was just resting. None of that was there any more. Mother had nothing with which to fill her days, which had been spent hustling and bustling, preparing his meals separately from the children and her own, clearing their plates away and making the table right for Father to come home, keeping the house immaculate for him and the unannounced visitors who sometimes accompanied him. She had lost the centre of her life and it showed. For the first time in his life Guy saw his mother seemingly uncaring of the state of the house and her appearance, although she made sure he and his sisters were clean and tidy before they went out to school.

"Did you see…" Guy stopped the words before they went any further, suddenly realising he did not want to share the thoughts about the ray of sunshine, afraid that his friend would laugh at him and spoil the images he was constructing in his mind. He knew he had to squash the desire to share anything like that in the future. Look how Thomas had reacted to his 'face in the cloud'.

"Did I see what?" Jack asked but he was not really listening. A squabble had started between two fairly new boys and, without waiting for Guy's answer, he raced over to the group, pushing his way in. Jack was ever one for a fight, Guy mused, as he wandered away to be by himself. What was it that drove someone to want to fight all the time? Both Jack and his brother Kit were like that, constantly getting into trouble for fighting both in and out of school. It was as if they needed the aggression to keep them going.

What do I need to keep me going? He asked himself the question, knowing he could not find the answer. It was out there, in the big world, the one outside school, home, even outside York. He was not old enough or wise enough to be able to go and find it.

But I will be, he told himself fiercely. As soon as I can, I will go and find out all that I need to know.

Before then, there are questions I want answered. I wonder if…

It was time to return to lessons. Time to watch closely and listen closely and choose his teacher wisely, the one of whom he would ask the questions that might possibly shape his future.

Chapter Four

A light in the corner, a light in the bitter darkness that was the dungeon. The doomed man stared, knowing in truth there could be no light in his darkness, so it had to be from another source. He smiled, the first smile since the moment of discovery, the moment the men walked in and found him with the gunpowder, the moment he realised they had been betrayed. His heart lifted for a moment as the light floated closer to him before it winked out and returned him to the darkness of his memories. They at least held a degree of comfort and now he had the additional reassurance of the unreal light too. Someone was watching over him. He would, eventually, be all right. Eventually, he would be free of pain, forever. Eventually. Before then, he had a lot of enduring to do. That he knew, that he sorrowed over. That he would have avoided if it were possible. But his heart refused to stop beating and his body refused to stop hurting. The nightmare went on.

***

Guy and his sisters were sitting at the table, eating as quietly as they could. It was routine, an essential part of life. At set times they sat down to eat, at a later time they got up and went about their lives, his sisters to their collection of ribbons, lace and dolls, he to his books, his tree or his nature studies. Mother was busy with household duties and he did what he had to do to help out but she asked little of him these days.

There had been virtually no conversation in the house since the funeral. The grief which hung over them like a pall stifled the words they would normally have exchanged. The funeral, two weeks earlier, had been a solemn and respectful affair, with half the dignitaries of York attending, or so it seemed to the Fawkes' family.

Guy had not realised how many people had known his father, or appreciated how many had held him in high regard. The non-stop flow of condolences had been surprising; the actual attendance at the funeral was amazing to him. The local church had been full of solemn people, all offering sincere words to him and his mother. There had been a constant stream of callers for a few days but then it slowly and quietly stopped, leaving them alone with an empty chair by the hearth and an empty space in their hearts, minds and lives. Sometimes it felt as if they still expected Father to walk in at any moment to take his rightful place by the side of the hearth, where he would work on his many papers and they would tiptoe around him. Then Guy would remember and once again see the lifeless body slumped on the floor, remember how empty that body seemed once the spirit had left it for places unknown. What his sisters were thinking, he had no idea but his life had been tipped upside down and he had a dreadful premonition that it was about to get worse.

Suddenly his mother spoke. "I need to get away from York." It was said in a normal everyday tone but the implications were shocking and far reaching. "There's too many memories here. I can't go on like this. I'm sorry. I'm making arrangements for us to move to Scotton."

"But-" There were a hundred things to say and in that moment he could not think of any of them. His mother stared at him. Her eyes were no longer hard and cold as they had been at times, when she had been immersed in her sorrow. She was softer now; there was a gentleness in her look which had been missing. She understood his consternation.

"God has not been good to me whilst we have been here, Guy. He sent his Dark Angel and took away your sister, the one who arrived before you did. I had her with me for just seven weeks and then she was gone.

Now He has done it again. He has taken your father from me. I want to go somewhere else. I want to start again in a new place. Maybe He will look kindly on me and those I love if I start again somewhere else, somewhere away from this accursed city. I have little money to live on and this large house cannot be paid for with such a little amount of money. We would end up starving."

Guy hardly heard her words. He was overwhelmed by the knowledge of a sister who came before him. If she had lived, there would have been four children in the house. What would she have been like, he asked himself? Would she have been one to run and tumble and climb trees and explore the plants and wild life with him, or would she have been another one to whom ribbons, curls and lace were more important than where the badger had his sett or where the woodland creatures lived and moved and died?

Those thoughts diverted him for a few moments from the statement made by his mother but he had to consider the words and what they meant to his life. A move. An upheaval. A new place, new people, new friends, new everything. No. Could not be. A move would take them away from Father's grave as well as from the memories which would haunt them, no matter where they went.

He understood memories, he had his own fair share of them to lose and in some ways he would be glad to lose them, but he dreaded the thought of a new home, new friends, another school to get used to and most of all, of not having his beloved tree where he had spent so many hours working out intricate problems and from where he had observed so much. He consoled himself with the thought that there must be another tree to climb, another convenient branch where he could sit and contemplate the world, inside and out. Surely that was so. Surely Mother would find a house with a big tree in the garden where he could be alone. Friends could be made, surely; perhaps it wouldn't be too bad. Scotton? Where was that?

His thoughts were tumbling in all directions; none of them were making much sense. He had to stop going round in circles and start pushing his thoughts in one direction – the future.

He also realised his sisters had not spoken a word. They were both sitting perfectly still, holding a piece of bread in their hands, as shocked as they were the day Father had fallen down dead. He registered the fact that he had been able to think that without the usual prickling at the back of his eyes. Was he growing up at last? If so, it was time to act like someone who was growing up and take the initiative.

"Do you know anyone in Scotton, Mother?" he asked tentatively. She had been fragile since Father had died, he was almost scared of touching her in case she fell to pieces. He wasn't sure how he knew this: like so many things, he just did.

She was silent for a while as if thinking; then she put her hands flat on the table and looked directly at Guy.

"There is family in the area, Guy, but not in Scotton. The reason I want to go there is – I want to be in a place where there are Catholics. I think God is punishing me for moving away from the true faith."

'No!' His mind screamed in response. 'God does not do that! God is good! God sends sunshine and pins my body to the branch and blesses the bread I eat and speaks to me beneath the Protestant speech of teachers who are surely not Protestant in their hearts.' What could he say that did not sound stupid to someone older and wiser than himself? He was only a boy in physical terms, although he knew that at times his reasoning was at a level of someone much older.

He watched as his mother turned her gaze onto the two girls, sitting as if petrified of something. "What do you think?" she asked gently, "Anne? Elizabeth? Come on, so far only your brother has spoken and he hasn't asked the questions I expected."

Elizabeth seemed to jolt herself back to life, her dark curls moved as she turned her head from side to side as if releasing a stiff neck. "What – what is Scott - Scotton?" The words finally emerged and Guy sat back in his chair, relieved that someone else had asked the question that he had wanted to but instead had taken a different approach and then had been shocked by the answer.

"Scotton is a village. Small and a bit isolated, but there are good roads and regular carriages back to York if we want anything. There are – contacts there and, if all goes well, I can start a new life in the true faith."

"But Mother, the true faith is-" he broke in, needing to voice the heretical thought.

"I know, Guy." There was a determination in her voice that he had never known before. She was a different person; she was still his mother on the outside but a stranger on the inside. A person who thought the Dark Angel was punishing her for not worshipping in the old ways. "I know full well what is legal and what is not. Henry VIII, may God rest his soul and restore him to the truth of what he did, destroyed much of what we had and changed the way we conducted our religion for his own ends, not for the good of the people. The true Church needs to be restored to England for England to become great again."

The words were outrageous, spoken in a home which had relied heavily on the Protestant church for its very being, but deep inside Guy knew that what his mother said made sense. He knew too that his mother's family had never fully agreed or been content with the Protestant marriage she had made.

"Well, as the responsibility for this family is now mine to shoulder, I have decided we will go and live in Scotton and leave York to its Protestant ways."

The words and their tone brooked no disagreement. Guy knew part of his childhood had ended when his father died so suddenly, but this was an even bigger thing. Somehow he had believed they would go on living in the same house, that he would go to the same school and have the same friends, just that he would have to live without his father there. In a moment of frankness and honesty with her children, his mother had changed all that. It was like throwing a pack of playing cards into the air and watching where they fell. Everything would be different. Whether it would be better was anyone's guess. That in itself was a frightening thought.

Mother had spoken and none of them argued with her. Instead they were given tasks, endless tasks, more work to do than he ever imagined. They had to choose what to take and what to leave, discarding old worn out things that were being kept 'just in case' but being told there would be no room for that in their new much smaller home. Guy kept trying to image how much smaller the house would be. He had grown up in the large rambling property in York with its many rooms, spacious stairs and hall and its large garden. The amount of staff they were retaining was to be reduced; it would mean more work for them all. Change permeated every part of his day and he hated it. He stole as much time as he could from the clearing out and packing to climb 'his' tree and listen to the leaves, knowing there were not many days left he could do that. Surely they had a message for him, one he could take to his new home. If they did, they never spoke of it. Night after night he returned to his room disappointed that nothing had been said.

One day, he told himself, one day I will understand the language of the leaves.

The dreaded day arrived, the day when they were to leave. Everything that could be packed had been attended to, clothes, possessions, china, pots and pans and such furniture as they were permitted to take from the house. Much of it, Guy was told, had to remain in the house, as it did not belong to them. This had never occurred to him, he had believed his family had owned everything, including the house. It was a child's way of viewing the world, he realised. His mother had patiently explained to him that they had rented the house as part of his father's employment. It was another reason they had to move. Properties in York were far more expensive than out in the country.

The carter and his helper loaded the cart in total silence. They had obviously worked together many times, for they did not seem to need instructions or suggestions from one another. Furniture was manhandled, secured with rope, then more items went on with rugs and other soft things being packed between them to prevent damage. Guy watched with intense interest as the two men toiled together in perfect harmony. It almost distracted him from the thought of what was actually happening, the fact his home was being dismantled and conveyed somewhere else. To his surprise everything his mother had ready to transport fitted on the cart and it was all done in a very short time. Then the door was closed and they got on the cart. He saw his mother dash away a few tears which had escaped her reddened eyes but his sisters openly cried as they made their way down High Petergate and out of York. Guy felt as if a huge stone had lodged somewhere in his chest. He was worried about a lot of things, what it would be like, how he would cope without his friends, the fact he would have to start over again with his wildlife studies, but the biggest worry of all was the change in his mother. She had been quiet for some days but in a different way from her manner during the awful time following Father's death. She seemed – determined. It was the only word which fitted.

Determined to make the move, against everyone's advice, even to the point of being abrupt with his Headmaster when he called to suggest, gently, that it would be good for Guy if they were to stay in York, as he was doing so well at school these days. She had told him she had personal reasons for leaving and that she was sure Guy would do well, no matter which school he attended. She was polite enough to offer sincere thanks for his interest but it was made very clear to everyone Mrs Fawkes had made up her mind and nothing but nothing was going to change it.

Determined to make a fresh start somewhere else, away from York.

Determined to break the ties with the Protestant church - and that bit worried Guy more than anything. What if she refused to go to church? What if... the thoughts stopped right there. The 'what ifs' could cause him a lot of sleepless nights if he let them. They might not happen. He had to hold on to that thought with all his strength.

The journey to Scotton seemed endless. It was hot and they had nothing to cover them from the relentless sun. The cart jolted over the ruts in the hard baked road, making it a very uncomfortable ride. Everyone was silent, lost in their thoughts. They had the sound of the wheels, the creaking of the cart, the jingle of harness and clop of hooves as their accompaniment and in a very short time they became so familiar they might as well not have been there. The surly carter and his helper had nothing to say to the family uprooting itself after a major bereavement which they surely knew of, for everyone knew Father, didn't they? For the first time it entered Guy's mind that no, not everyone knew Father and perhaps they weren't as important as he believed they were. It was a sobering thought. It was as if the silence was contagious, none of the Fawkes family spoke to one another, either.

The outskirts of York slowly melted away; they were out in open countryside, bleak and empty under the summer sun. They grew hotter and Mother fanned herself with her bonnet before putting it firmly back on her head and sitting up straight, looking for all the world as if a move was part of her every day existence. The horse did not seem to want to go faster than its gentle trot, no matter how many times the reins were flicked at its back. It had its pace and it was determined to go no faster. Determined. Guy was confronted with that word again. He decided God was trying to tell him something.

He had to be determined, strong, to be sure of himself, to be man of the house. Surely Mother would not find herself another man … he stopped himself before pursuing that thought any further. That was another pathway he could not pursue.

The helper pulled a leather bottle from under the seat and he and the carter shared a drink. They munched on fresh bread and ham, but nothing was offered to the family sitting in the back. It was obviously not part of the deal. Guy realised they should have brought something with them. If there had been any food left in the house, Mother would have packed it away safely for the journey.

After what felt like hours and hours of being jolted around and baked by the sun, of feeling empty and hollow from lack of food and drink, a cluster of houses appeared before them, almost like a mirage.

They grew larger, came closer and then the seemingly impossible happened. They stopped. All movement ceased. After the jolting and swaying, it felt strange to be still.

"Here you be, Missus." They were in front of a small house in the middle of nowhere. Guy looked around. The village was a single street lined with small houses.

He could see the outline of a tiny church and guessed there would be an inn. It was so different from what he had been used to that York might as well have been the other side of the known world. He stared at the house and stared at the village and wondered how this would ever feel like home. Where were the usual sounds, the carriages, the street vendors' cries, the people's voices? Here the only sounds he was aware of were endless bird calls. It seemed – empty.

The door of the small house was opened, the furniture and possessions swiftly deposited inside. The men were paid off and the cart bounced back along the road, heading for York, for light, for life, for colour and – his past. Guy watched it go with a deepening sense of sadness that refused to lift, despite the tickle of anticipation at having a new home. For the moment the memories of the old one clung to his heart and mind, colouring everything with sadness.

His sisters were excited, rushing from room to room, not doing much to help put things away. He explored quickly, checking everything as he thought he should. It was all right, he thought, but lacked the space and the convenience of their York home. The real disaster, though, was the garden. It was no more than a small plot of land where they could grow a few plants and perhaps some vegetables but – no tree. He sighed and wondered how long it would take him to find a new sanctuary, somewhere God could seek him out and speak to him as He had done in the past.

Chapter Five

Pain was a tidal wave, it allowed for nothing in its way. It swept through him, taking all but his most treasured memories with it. He cried out, softly, clinging to the thoughts which had seen him through the empty hours, for they were a lifeline. Without them he would surely be insane by the time the men came for him. Was he already insane? Going back hurt almost as much as being in the present but there was no alternative. Somewhere there had to be an escape from the relentless agony and the biting cold. Somewhere there had to be a portal to a world that contained sunshine, even if it was in his mind.

***

If anyone had asked Guy how he knew certain things in advance, such as the fact his mother was going to get married again, he would have laughed and said 'I don't know anything!" It was a secret, this foreknowledge, one he did not plan on sharing with anyone. The new friends he had made in Scotton or the old ones he saw from time to time when they returned to York for special occasions connected with the Minster or to buy essential items for the house or themselves, would have laughed in scorn if they had known of his belief that he had a direct contact with God.

But he did. He spent hours in the fields around his home or watching from his narrow bedroom window as the owls hunted and the small animals screeched their last under the claws and beaks of the scavenging birds, as the stars slowly made their progression across the night sky and the moon went through its phases. All the time he was asking questions: how does it work, what holds the moon there, what makes the stars move, who said which animals preyed on which and why? And the

48

big question, why did Father die so soon? Some questions were answered, some remained unanswered and he believed he had to resolve the biggest question which was plaguing him before he could resolve the unanswered ones.

The biggest question of all was a complex yet simple one: which was the true Faith?

At school they talked of Henry VIII's break with Rome and the Reformation and then it talked of Queen Mary re-introducing Catholicism and then Queen Elizabeth removing it again. Where then was the true heart of England's religion? What should people believe? Should they be told to believe a certain way?

"It should be for each person to decide," he told the silent sleeping night as he leaned on the window frame and breathed in the freshness of the autumn air. The tinge of cold was almost comforting, despite it being the harbinger of the bitter winter ahead. The long summer days had been good but Guy preferred the colder times, the colours of Autumn, the sense of everything dying back to be renewed again come Spring, after the long winter sleep.

It had taken a time, more years than he cared to remember, to become part of Scotton, years when he had grown taller and, according to his sisters, quieter. They teased him about that, trying to provoke discussions or even answers to their questions, running off, pouting when he would not answer them. He had too much to dwell on to be bothered with girl-talk, as he thought of it. He had no answer to whether Tom from the inn thought either of them was pretty or whether James from the farm close by was as nice a person as they thought. They were fast becoming interested in the opposite sex and he had no way of empathising with that, as he had already dismissed all girls as having light heads, empty minds, incessant giggling fits and so, taken overall, they were not worth the effort of his trying to understand them.

Scotton had - almost - become home. There was a quietness about the place which pleased him, there was less bustle and hurry and more time to be himself, to think his thoughts and, more importantly than that, to pray his many prayers and listen to God who spoke to him in the dark hours. It was in those times that the 'predictions' came to him in the form of visions or a voice, a quiet authoritative voice, which spoke as clearly as the schoolmaster did when intoning Latin or preaching the rules of English Literature and grammar.

It was in this way he knew, without a single doubt crossing his mind, that his mother was going to marry Dennis Bainbridge, a local landowner and known Catholic. The question was, how did he feel about it?

His sisters had their lives to lead; they were growing up, interested in boys, lace, satin and fripperies like that. They played with kittens and complained when they were scratched. They argued and cried and protested to anyone who would listen that they hated one another. It was untrue, it was girl nonsense and he dismissed it. They did their chores like grown up women and then went back to being silly girls again. They did not seem to miss York and all that it had to offer, nor did they seem to worry unduly about the considerable of attention Dennis Bainbridge was paying to Mother. He seemed to be at the house more times than was strictly necessary and no one said anything about it.

Mother seemed happier, more confident than she had for a very long time, as if Father had kept her in the shadows and now she had come out into the sunshine. Guy didn't know why he felt that way but that was the image he had and it helped him reconcile himself to the forthcoming marriage.

When his mother announced her intentions, about a month after Guy knew it would happen, he smiled and nodded, as if giving his consent without saying anything. Not that it had been asked for. Mother had decided and she would go her own way regardless of his opinion. He knew that.

Elizabeth and Anne squealed with excitement and began a frenzied dance around their mother, demanding to know when and where and would they have to move – the answers came immediately. When was within the month, where was the local church with a blessing from a priest to come later and yes, they would move for their new stepfather had a bigger home than the one they were living in at that time.

Change. Always change, thought Guy, listening to the heated chatter and smiling indulgently at the women in his life. Then it occurred to him that he would no longer be head of the household, that Dennis, someone he quite liked and looked up to, would take on that responsibility. He asked himself how he felt about that and decided he was relieved. He had enough to think about. It was good that someone else was taking on the worries of his family.

For a long time he had known that his father had left him a small legacy, land and some income, and that his mother had been using it to live on. What he did not anticipate was Dennis Bainbridge, or his new stepfather, if he chose to think of him that way, would also use it. Dennis did not seem to work, but was perpetually at Wheatley Hall, the family home, a place much in need of finance.

It didn't matter. The important thing was the Catholic influence Dennis was bringing to the family. More and more Guy had felt himself drawn to the Catholic faith, despite it being illegal, despite the dangers it attracted, the very real risk of being imprisoned. None of them went to church and could be arrested for being recusants literally at any moment. He did not doubt for a moment that his mother would welcome that kind of martyrdom, her faith was everything to her. It was an essential part of her relationship with Dennis.

Mother told him, when the girls had gone to their room, that there was a chapel set up in the cellar at Wheatley Hall and that a priest would come and hold Mass there when it was safe to do so. She spoke of the Pulleyns, local influential Catholics and he gasped, realising that his 'old' headmaster had been a Pulleyn, which explained the almost subversive Catholic influence at the school in York, something he had only realised after he had left and was able to compare that teaching with the local village school.

It was something else to think about, to examine in the long, often lonely, hours he spent in his room or under one of the great trees in the area.

Another move but this one more welcome, in many ways. Wheatley Hall was a magnificent, if slightly rundown, home for the family. There were plenty of rooms to choose from and his sisters were each able to have space for themselves for the first time in their lives. Guy had a room at the back of the house, one with an uninterrupted view across the countryside. From there he could gaze at the moon, stars and endless sky as much as he wanted. Even better, there were trees, although he thought he might be getting a little too old and certainly too big to climb them these days. That left the soft mosses beneath the trees to sit on and a solid trunk to lean against, though. A fair exchange, all things considered. Trees continued to speak to him, to whisper their secret language into his ear and he tried just as hard to break the code and understand their message, still without success.

People came and went all the time, the house was abuzz with visitors which made a change from the quiet life they had led before. Pulleyns and others came, all

Catholics, his mother told him, anxious to bring the family into the true faith, into the fold, to follow the right teachings, to draw her back to her core beliefs and erase the pain of the deaths she had endured. Guy said little to all this, not wanting her to question his beliefs, which although they did not run counter to hers, certainly differed a little. He felt she was wrong in blaming God for taking his sister and father home. He really believed that God wanted them home, that their time had come and they had to go back to Heaven. It did not mean anyone was being punished. There were plenty of Protestants around who had not suffered bereavements and surely God wanted them in the True Faith as much as he wanted Edith Fawkes, now Edith Bainbridge, in the True Faith.

Thoughts to ponder, things to consider, even as the secret preparations went on for the visit of a priest and the illegal holding of a Mass right there in Wheatley Hall. It would be Guy's first ever opportunity to attend Mass. It almost overcame all other thoughts for a while.

"I am not giving you an ultimatum, son," Dennis told Guy as they walked in the garden. It was a beautiful late autumn afternoon, the sun was low in the sky, sending deep shadows across the overgrown lawns of Wheatley Hall. Guy looked at the untidy grass and wondered why no one had thought to cut it. He swiftly amended his thought; the grass was studded with wild flowers which would be killed if the grass was cut. Even as he listened to his stepfather he was aware of the glory of the day, the colours, the touch of the afternoon sun, the cool breeze which chilled just enough to make it feel good. "No orders, nothing like that. I would not ask you to do something that was against your conscience. I have to say I have never known a boy so young to have so much spiritual knowledge and understanding."

Guy blushed. His stepfather rarely said anything that complimentary to him. A sudden thought flashed through his mind, how did Dennis know of his spiritual knowledge? They had held brief discussions on various points of philosophy but that was about it. Unless … he had given away the depth of his thinking in those discussions. That had to be it, he had never, at any time, told anyone of his experiences, his visions and his hearing the voice of God.

He was also surprised to be taken notice of at all. He often felt as if he was baggage that had happened to arrive with Dennis' new wife. He was kind, he had welcomed the children into his home and his life, but mostly there was a degree of indifference. They were just – there. Well, the girls were but perhaps Dennis couldn't associate with them very well. They were certainly wrapped up in each other's lives to the exclusion of everyone else most of the time.

Logically, Guy knew everything came with a price; his mother's happiness and his new home had been bought with the use of his small inheritance. His stepfather simply did not work, as he had surmised before they went there. He did not question his stepfather's lack of employment of any kind, it was not his place to do so, he decided, although everyone else he knew had some kind of employment, a business to run or paid work. Dennis Bainbridge spent all his time at home, where he seemed to have constant meetings with people whose purpose for coming was concealed from the children. They were just 'visitors' and Guy and his sisters were instructed to be polite, greet them and then keep out of their way.

For Guy, it was enough that he had a home, schooling and religious education of the kind that was important to him. Everything else was for others to think about, those who were more capable of understanding what was going on. All that mattered to him was that he lived in an area and knew people who were of what he continued to think of as the True Faith and that his mother was happy. Not that she said anything to reveal the way she felt. It was there in the gentle way she spoke to his sisters, her endless patience with him, the way she looked up with a smile and a light in her eyes when her husband walked into the room. All this and more he noted and stored. He shared his thoughts with no one, not friends or family. No one, that is, on this side of life, as he thought of it. The occasional glimpse of something unearthly kept his mind firmly turned toward Heaven, toward God, toward the great unseen Force that controlled the earth, the moon, the stars and planets, the seasons and the life giving sun. It had been a long time since a ray of sunlight had pierced him but his memory of those times was vivid enough to see him through the conflict caused by his stepfather's gentle insistence, without actually saying it, on Guy becoming part of the True Faith. It had been there for some time, hanging over every conversation he had with his stepfather, fleetingly referred to and then dismissed, tempting him, drawing him in.

"We were thinking," Dennis seemed almost reluctant to say the words out loud. "We were thinking … it was about time for you to consider becoming a Catholic. What do you say, Guy?"

At last it had been brought out into the open. He had thought about it, prayed about it, reasoned it out with himself many times. He knew without a shadow of doubt it was what he wanted. But he also knew he wanted to make the decision in his own time and in his own way, not under duress from the family. No matter how much his stepfather insisted it was not so, that was how it felt to him.

He ducked the question, instead speaking about what he would do when school finished, when he was able to go out into the world and earn a living, not be a burden to the Bainbridge side of the family. The subject was quietly dropped. Dennis could obviously take a hint.

"The law may say we are to be Protestant, but we do not have to give our hearts to the law, do we?" One of the Pulleyn family, Guy didn't know which one, there were several of them, was holding forth at a social evening, knowing he was speaking to the truly committed and as such there was no danger of informants. "We can pay lip service to the so-called lawful church and still retain our faith in our hearts. What difference does it make to attend a Protestant service if our hearts are firmly with our God in our own faith?"

"No, sir, that is not right." Dennis was on his favourite subject, denial of the law. "If God had wished us to be Protestant, there would be no Catholic Church. My heart, my mind, my soul, remains committed to the True Faith and if that means being a recusant, so be it!"

"You place yourself and your family in danger, Mr. Bainbridge, if I might say so. It is wiser to pretend and avoid drawing attention to yourself."

"Who notices who attends church and who does not? There are enough people attending the services to fill the place and fill the coffers without the Bainbridges going as well." The man all but glared at Dennis, red faced and bloated with his own importance.

"I say again, you are risking your family, sir. There are those who are very aware of what goes on. I would reconsider, if I were you. York Castle is stocked with recusants and will continue to be so." The Pulleyn, whoever he was, stalked off to talk to someone else, someone more amenable to his way of thinking. Guy watched people move from group to group, exchanging gossip and – more? Were serious matters discussed at these gatherings? Occasionally people stopped to smile at the tall serious quiet young man standing apart from everyone, perhaps wondering where he stood on the subject but not wanting to engage him in conversation for some reason. Guy didn't mind. He was happier listening than talking, for then his thoughts could go where they wanted, without his having to chase them before he put words together that made sense. They always did in his head, but rarely when they were spoken aloud. Am I doing the right thing, he asked the wise counsellor who stood at the back of his mind, the one who seemed to have the answers whenever he wanted them. Am I doing the right thing by holding back for the moment? Father, this father, wants me to come in. I don't feel I am ready. What am I waiting for?

The answer came: *You are waiting on another sign. Just as you had the sunshine, now you await another sign.*

He sighed. Yes, he was waiting; he was anticipating divine intervention to show him which way to go. He was not prepared to take a human being's word that what he was doing was right. He had relied on divine guidance so long that it was the only way he could decide anything.

The Catholic community had its own 'underground' system of communication to spread news to each other. It worked well. Guy was fully aware of the names of the Catholics who shared their strong belief in the restoration of the True Faith. The name of Margaret Clitherow was known to him, she was a leading supporter who he knew was very active. It was said she had been deeply impressed by the death of Earl Thomas, someone who refused to give way to the authorities and died a martyr to the cause, at least in the eyes of everyone who supported him. Would I go that far, Guy mused, would I be able to walk proudly to my execution for my faith?

Yes, whispered the inner voice, the one that supported him through his bad times. He did not argue with the voice, it had been right too many times.

"She takes too many chances," his mother muttered one day, when she heard of yet another close call for Margaret. The authorities had closed in again on the Clitherow house but the priest made his escape through the network set up for such an event. Margaret served her time in York Castle for being a recusant but nothing made her change her mind.

When the news came of her arrest for harbouring a priest, the family huddled together in the cellar of Wheatley Hall, discussing the implications of this for them and other Catholic families. This time she did not face a period of imprisonment but execution. There was no escape from the law on this 'crime'.

Guy could not fully comprehend why having a priest in your home would mean a trial and death sentence, why the innocent children of Margaret Clitherow should be caught up in the unholy mess and how it had come to that in England anyway. He knew that she had been before the court several times, knew that the authorities had been watching and waiting their chance to seize her but it seemed an extreme penalty.

"She's a good Catholic," his stepfather mourned. "Been a good friend to the Catholic community." His mother agreed, with sadness for the family, for the authorities were cracking down even more harshly on the dissidents, as they saw them.

Margaret Clitherow was dragged before the Assize where she was formally accused of harbouring a priest. She refused to testify and, to everyone's disbelief, she was sentenced to death by crushing.

Guy spent hours praying; seeking a reprieve for the principled woman, but it was not to be. They waited for news of her death, waited with increasing sadness and even despair that the authorities could and had done such a thing.

"She was brave beyond belief." The family risked arrest and imprisonment themselves by accepting the cleric into their home but they needed news and that was hard to come by without openly declaring why they wanted to know. As far as the authorities were concerned, the letter of the law had been followed. A criminal had refused to testify; a criminal had been executed. It was Good Friday, a sacred day, was it a good day to die?

"She was brave beyond belief," the man repeated, obviously distraught, shocked by what had happened. Guy stood back, watching as his mother and stepfather absorbed the news.

"What happened?" Dennis asked eventually. He plied the man with wine; he seemed to need it.

"They crushed her." There were tears but he dashed them away. "Ah, but they changed the sentence, for which God be praised. They were going to deny her sustenance for three days, they were going to strip her naked to kill her, but they changed that. She sewed herself a linen gown and she put that on to cover her nakedness. They put a large stone under her spine so it would break; they put a door on her. They hired two beggars to pile the heavy stones on. They could not bear to do it themselves. Cowards. They can sentence a woman to death but cannot carry it out themselves. God grant mercy to the men who did the terrible deed, for their sins are heavy now."

There was a long pause for wine and time to gather his thoughts. "They put the stones on her. Heavy great stones, hard to lift. It was quick. She was dead in fifteen minutes." He shuddered. "I can still hear her. Oh beloved God, the scream, the sobs! When her back broke the sound and her scream could be heard in Heaven, I am sure of it, and she sobbed all through until her breath went…"

"The children…" Edith began.

"The children were saved from torture. They were removed to a safe house. They will live on. What law is it that threatens to torture children if the mother stands trial? The neighbours are safe, those who had the tunnel to get away. She saved them all by giving up her life."

At that point the man collapsed completely, tears pouring down his face, uncontrollable shudders racking his body. The goblet rolled across the floor, spilling blood red wine, just as Guy envisioned Margaret Clitherow's blood to have been spilled, even if it was metaphorically so. Dennis led the man away to a quiet room where he could rest and say his prayers.

Guy stood as if rooted to the spot. It was as if a huge light had come on somewhere above his head and was filling him with intense joy and radiance, almost unearthly in its glory. He knew what he had to do.

When Dennis Bainbridge returned to the room, Guy turned to him and held out his hand.

"Father, I am ready to become a part of the church of the True Faith."

Chapter Six

Pain came in waves of heat, head to foot, foot to head. It prevented sleep; it prevented escape into the darkness of oblivion. Every tendon, every joint screamed its own cacophony of anguish. Move on, his mind demanded, move on! There is much to cover, to remember, to relive, to escape this torment! Move on, I say! If not the time will go and I will not reach the end of the story before I reach the end of my life!

    As if it mattered...

***

Schooldays were over - at long last. It had seemed he would never be a man, able to go out to work, to earn a living and contribute to the household. School desks, school friends, lessons, they were a part of life and were locked forever in his mind. But at last he was free to walk his own pathway. For a while it felt odd, almost unreal. It took some adjustment in his thinking to accept he had shaken off the restraints of school and could go where he wished, even if it was to the other end of the country.

Guy had developed into a tall young man, slim, dark, good looking, someone who attracted the attention of the young girls in the village. If he had told them he had long since decided marriage and women were not for him they would not have believed it. They thought most men could be turned by a pretty face, a full bosom, a charming manner and dancing curls. Unfortunately Guy meant it. He had one love, the blessed Virgin Mary. No other was allowed to enter his heart and mind. From the moment he converted to the True Faith, women were not part of his future. He knew it, getting others to accept it was another matter. He knew he would be looked at strangely, as if his preference was for men instead but he hoped by being steadfast to his vow of chastity that eventually people would believe he had no interest in either sex nor in the act of sex itself. It had no appeal for him.

It was time for him to go out in the bigger world and actually work for a living. Where he would go, whom he would work for, what home he would end up in, he left to his mother and stepfather. They seemed to have it all in hand, judging by the comments, letters which were chasing back and forth and sometimes whispered consultations. In the meantime he could enjoy freedom, total freedom, to walk, think and be alone. When the arrangements were finalised and he was told of them, he was pleased. They had managed to obtain for him the position of footman in Viscount Montague's home in the south of England. The position of footman was a good one which had been arranged for him through the network and he was grateful for the opportunity. He just wished it wasn't so far from home, but then again, it was time he learned to stand on his own feet. The mere thought of leaving his home and family sent cold shudders through him but he knew he had to be strong, to face up to the actuality of life. There was employment, a prestigious position awaited him and he had to go there and take it up. Otherwise all the arranging and helpfulness of the network would be wasted.

Sussex was a thousand miles from Yorkshire. It felt like a thousand miles, even if it was only from one end of the country to the other, to Guy, anyway. He had new breeches, shirt and jacket, highly polished boots only worn by one other person, a smart new hat and a new bag containing a change of clothes and his letter of introduction, along with mementoes from home which his mother had impressed upon him. This all combined to make it a tremendous experience for him. The crowded coach travelled relatively fast but not fast enough for someone who was anxious and excited about being away from home, about to start making his own decisions, beginning a new life of independence and freedom, most of all no longer bound by his mother's restrictions.

All the passengers were men, some prosperous looking, some not so well dressed and with very small amounts of baggage. Including himself, there were six people on the coach, pushed up against one another. Guy sat, quivering with suppressed excitement, trying to look as if he travelled every day of the week and it was not of any importance. He wanted to look as casual as the other men, who were showing different phases of boredom, ranging from half closed eyes to those who appeared to fall asleep the moment the coach set off. The sound of the wheels, the jingle of the harness, the creak of the coach itself, combined to make a cacophony that Guy thought he would never get used to, if they travelled non-stop for a week. As the coach rattled along, his anticipation and excitement changed to a form of sickness, in part due to the motion of the coach itself, in part the winding down of the surge of emotion which had gone through him as they set off. It also began to be extremely uncomfortable very quickly. The seats were not very well padded and this, combined with the motion of the coach, mentor that he very quickly lost any comfort he was feeling. But the novelty of being in a coach, leaving York for a new destination, made up for it to some degree for a while.

He was aware that the passengers in the coach were eyeing each other surreptitiously. It was as if they wished to speak but no one quite knew how to break the ice. Guy was far too self-conscious to begin a conversation with someone, instead he watched the endless landscape through which they were travelling, rugged, studded with stones, and stunted trees. Although it was spring, there were few signs of new life on the vegetation, as if winter was reluctant to release its hold. There was little in the vista to keep his thoughts occupied and the novelty of being in the coach began to wear off. He thought it was likely to be a very long journey indeed and then one of the men, a young looking man with a well-to-do air about him, pulled a small bottle from his pocket and held it up.

"I don't have much to share, this bottle of being quite small, but all of you are welcome to a draught. I'm travelling to London to be married and wish to share my good fortune with you all."

He handed it to Guy who looked at the man in astonishment. "Sir, thank you." He took a small drink from the bottle, almost choking on the strong spirit and handed it back. "My very best wishes to you for your future happiness."

"Thank you, young man." The bottle was handed around, congratulations were offered and the atmosphere in the coach became friendlier. One of the other men, an elderly person with a hook nose and thinning hair, leaned forward and spoke to Guy.

"Forgive my presumption, sir, but you look as if your clothes are new. Is this your first trip to London?"

"It is, sir. I hoped it would not show so much!" Guy was a little embarrassed, not sure how the other passenger would take such an admission.

"Seasoned travellers will know the new ones every time but it is not a bad thing. The whole of the country awaits you! New experiences, new discoveries, ah the joys of being young! Where are you going, might I ask?"

"I am bound for Sussex. I have a position there." Guy said it with obvious pride and the man smiled, revealing brown teeth which Guy found slightly off-putting.

"Sussex!" A passenger on Guy's side of the coach looked round. "Fine county, sir, fine county. Green and fresh and pleasant. You will like it there. Where are you to work?"

"Cowdray House."

"Ah, I know of it. Not been there myself but know of it. Supposed to be a fine house."

Conversation began to flow between men who had been pushed together in a coach which was rattling down the main road from Yorkshire on its long journey to London. The talk was of business, of the best way to invest money to gain the maximum return, of the vagaries of customers, and even more the vagaries of suppliers. This was talk Guy could not contribute to, he having no experience of business in this way. He knew his stepfather had some investments, but he had no idea where the money had been placed or what sort of return it gave. It did not seem to be a lot otherwise the home would have been better maintained.

He spent his time looking out of the window. The countryside, familiar to Guy, gave him a sense of security for a while, but it slowly began to change as one county border blended into another. Granite grey homes rooted firmly into the landscape began to change to those which seemed to stand more proudly, not having such dreadful weather to contend with. Sheep were scattered over the fields like puffs of dandelion seed, cows looked up as they passed and went back to grazing again, a coach to London was not of significance in their life, no matter the importance of those who were being conveyed at such speed to such a large and important destination.

Before he knew what was happening they were in Leeds, where they were able to leave the coach for a short time whilst the horses were changed at a bustling wayside inn. Guy took the opportunity to relieve an aching bladder, and was back on board the coach just before the call for all the passengers to take their place once more. Everyone sat in the same place, as if it was theirs by right. Guy was pleased that he had a window seat, being a new to travel of this distance he wanted to watch the changing landscape.

One of the other passengers, a man of considerable girth, looked over at Guy and smiled. "Next stop Sheffield," he said with a sigh. "It is a longer journey than that which we have just endured, and thanks be to God I will leave the coach there. It is time they found a way of making these seats comfortable!"

A ripple of laughter went around the other passengers. Guy shifted in his seat. "I know what you mean," he smiled ruefully. "There is just so long one can sit on these hard boards."

There was a general grunt of assent, and then they all fell silent. Guy leaned back against the board behind his head and through half closed eyes watched the landscape grow much less rugged, the trees less stunted, and the hedgerows alive and alight with masses of early wild flowers. He fought to keep himself awake by naming them, but in truth he was too tired and his eyes kept closing. But just as he was about to fall off to sleep, the coach would hit a rut of some kind or a stone and he would be jolted back into consciousness again.

It was certainly was a longer journey than the first phase of the day, and by the time the outskirts of Sheffield came into view, the horses were visibly tiring and he was aware of a ravenous hunger. The coach stopped at a large rambling inn, and they all dismounted with obvious pleasure. The man who was terminating his journey there and shook hands with all the other passengers, coming to Guy last.

"I wish you success in your new life young man," he said with what seemed like genuine emotion. "It is a long time since I was setting out on a new pathway. I almost envy you."

Guy flushed a little, not quite knowing what to say. "My grateful thanks, sir," he finally managed. "This first day has been quite an experience."

The man turned to walk away. "I am sorry to say you have three more days of travelling, young man. I wish you well." And then he was gone.

Guy went into the inn with the other passengers, who were already calling for food and ale. The landlord must have anticipated the arrival of the coach, for the bar was lined already with tankards of ale and the smell of fresh meat and pastry was emanating from a back room.

"Who needs a bed tonight?" The man shouted over the crowd in the bar. Guy eased his way to the counter. He picked up a tankard and drank deeply before asking, "you have a cheap room?"

"Is this your first venture out into the world, young man?"

Guy wondered if the word 'innocent' was written across his forehead. Surely after some seven hours of travelling his clothes did not look as new as when he had set out. Then he looked at the others, whose clothes were obviously worn, and realised that, yes, he still did look like a raw recruit. He hastily put some coins on the counter to pay for the ale and looked longingly towards the room where the food was being prepared. The landlord saw his look.

"The food won't be long, young man." He smiled at Guy. "I don't have 'a room' but I have a cheap bed, it is clean enough, there are no bugs."

"Thank you, sir."

That night, full of good fresh food, and two tankards of ale, Guy stretched his aching limbs out on the narrow but clean bed, covered over with a blanket and resting his head on a thin pillow. It might as well have been the finest down mattress in England at that time and the blanket made of the purest spun wool. Despite the fact he was sharing a room with six other people, he was asleep before he could even close his eyes properly.

It seemed a mere moment before the call came for breakfast and by passengers to get back on the coach. Guy struggled to get himself ready quickly, snatched a breakfast, and was back on the coach shortly after the rather portly gentleman, the anxious bridegroom, the gentleman with the hook nose, and a new passenger, someone who looked like a cleric, where already in their places.   He wondered why everyone went and sat precisely where they were before, as if each of them had laid claim to that particular spot before they left the coach. It was something he puzzled on for a little while, and then thought it was something territorial; he had no other explanation for it. It was a strange quirk of human nature.

Within a very short time the other passengers were on board and the coach was ready to move on.

The bridegroom, who Guy understood to be a man called Shelby, was impatient and seemingly anxious. He kept looking out of the window as if by doing so he would make the coach go faster. "I have to be in London very soon," he said, looking round at everyone. "My bride will be waiting for me."

"This coach can go no faster," said the hook nosed man, a Mr Thomas. "If the horses are pushed any harder with the load they are pulling, they will collapse and we will be considerably delayed."

"Not to mention the chance of the coach overturning," said the 'cleric'. He had not volunteered a name. "There is a very good chance of an accident, if the wheel should hit a stone or a deep rut or if the driver is careless on a sharp bend."

Guy looked anxiously at the man. He said nothing, but it had not occurred to him that there could be an accident. Then he realised this was a foolish thought because human nature dictated that there are always accidents. The last thing he wanted was to be injured on his way to his first post. What would his family say if he was incapacitated? How would they explain that to Viscount Montague? He began to develop pictures in his mind of an overturned coach, of screaming horses, the shouting agonised passengers who might be trapped and injured in the wreckage. 'Lord God protect me,' he thought,' and give me one of your signs if it be thy will.'

He stared out of the window, watching the landscape unreal as it passed by and then saw a cluster of rain clouds stark against the blue sky. A single wide ray of sunshine came down from the clouds to strike the land, or so it seemed to his eyes. He sent out a silent prayer of thanks. Around him in the coach a murmur of conversation was going on but he heard nothing of it, it did not seem to be directed at him, and it was obvious that no one had seen that ray of sunshine. Of course not it was entirely by him. He knew then that the journey would be conducted in safety and he had nothing to fear. With that thought in his mind he leaned back against the seat and prepared himself for the long tiring journey to Nottingham.

After a short time all conversation ceased, as each man tried to accustom himself to the discomfort of the coach, its motion and the unpadded seats.

There was one short break, to change horses and for them to stretch cramped legs and relieve themselves, to buy food from the inn and then they were up and away again, heading toward the rain clouds and the darkening sky.

All too soon the rain began to fall and the road quickly became very muddy. The pace slowed considerably, much to the obvious annoyance of the passengers. There was much muttering, most of it incoherent, but Guy ignored it. There seemed little point in becoming annoyed with the weather, as none of them could do anything about it. Although the horses were moving much slower, they were still travelling. The time to complain would be if they came to a complete stop.

As long as they were moving, Nottingham would be getting nearer.

In fact the rain stopped, although it had left the road somewhat wet, it had not slowed them down very much. Everyone retreated into silence again, leaving just the creaking of the coach, the noise of the harness, and the occasional crack of the whip to assail their ears. The sound of the hooves had disappeared.

After what seemed like an interminable period of time they reached Nottingham.

More stretching of tired, cramped limbs and rubbing of aching backsides, of attending to the need for relief, food and ale in about that order, a bed, another night of sleep cut short by the call to breakfast and back on board again. Each time he got into the coach, Guy thought he would never stand another hour of the travelling and each time he got through it by simply losing himself in thoughts.

He wondered for the thousandth time if he was doing the right thing in leaving all he knew and loved for people he had never communicated with, not even so much as a letter, for a position he knew nothing about. He knew it was a high ranking place and he would have to use all his natural ingenuity and good manners to make a success of it, that didn't worry him as much as the fact they were Southerners and might not like a Northerner in their midst. A tinge of worry sat somewhere deep in his mind and he could not dismiss it. Silent prayers did nothing to ease the concern. He put it down to being away from home and heading for an unknown destination but still it refused to move.

Nottingham to Northamptonshire, quieter countryside, it was the only way Guy could describe it, that it was quieter. As were the passengers, apart from the occasional muttered apology if the coach swung round too hard and tipped one person onto another, they remained quiet. It was more of an endurance test than a journey by this time. Every muscle ached, every ounce of fat seemed compressed between the weight of the bones and the hardness of the seat. It was difficult to ration food and water, sheer boredom pressured him to eat and drink just to alleviate that boredom for as long as it took to consume it, but if he did that, the endless hours became even more endless when stretched out before him, with nothing to break the monotony but the occasional stop at a shabby inn, there to drink watered ale and stamp around for a few minutes, to get the feeling back into his legs and then they were on board and away once more.

Northampton, a cluster of houses, an inn, a bed, a few hours of total oblivion before the journey to Oxford began the next morning.

It was fast becoming a nightmare of unreeling landscape, sullen silent passengers, endless cacophony of harness and coach, hooves and shouts.

And threading its way through it, still, was the thought 'should I have done this, am I a fool to leave Yorkshire for places unknown, for people unknown, for work unknown' and the answer was – wait and see. But it was a long way to travel to find out it was not right for him. After a while the journey stopped being an experience and was just a hell to crawl through.

Oxford – elegant stone buildings and beautiful scenery held them for a meal and a drink. Then the coachman announced to the gathered passengers that they could press on to London and try and get there by nightfall, or they could stay overnight in Oxford and leave first thing in the morning.

The prospective bridegroom was all for going on, so were the majority of the other passengers. A couple said they could not face any more travelling and would take the coach next morning instead. Guy opted to go on, what was the point of delaying any longer?

No one else boarded, for the first time there was room to actually spread out, to move arms and legs without hitting someone and for a while it made the journey acceptable. Then the same boredom overcame everyone, coupled with a desperate longing for the small breaks to change horses.

But eventually the sprawling empty counties that lie between York and the capital city were finally traversed and London was upon him. There were clusters of buildings, busy streets, lamps glittering behind windows, lamps carried by those about their business, even at that late hour. Gratefully they all got out of the coach, into the inn and straight to the beds allocated to them by the Landlord. A few hours of oblivion were ahead and they all, every last one of them, needed that.

Next morning he woke with the thought in his head 'this is London!' He got up to stare out of the window. Soaring above the roofs of the houses were the spires and towers of London churches, the sound of bells could be heard which, after the sound of the coach which had become so familiar after the endless journey he hardly noticed it any more, was a relief and a change to his ears.

His fellow passengers had gathered in the tap room, busy with their goodbyes. For all the lack of conversation, they had become a close group and now they were to go off to their individual destinations. He stood there among them, feeling that it had been an age and yet he was there, in London, a raw young Yorkshireman away from home for the first time, with everything feeling and sounding strange, no one to tell him what to do or where to go. He bid goodbye to his fellow travellers, wishing the man to be married yet more good fortune. He briefly wondered what it would be like to be bound to a woman and then dismissed it. That was not for him.

Being in London felt good and yet frightening at the same time. He was hungry but he could not bring himself to eat right then, he wanted to go out, he wanted to see everything. He had his bag with him, he was ready to walk, to explore the Capital City, as he thought of it. And it was out there, the other side of the wall, waiting for him.

He paid his bill and walked outside. There was a pie seller on the other side of the street, he bought a hot pie and walked on, eating it as he went, looking at everything with wide open eyes, forgetting about trying to look as if he did it all the time. Everyone seemed to be in a hurry, hustling their way along the roads, shouting across to others, conversations mingling with the vendors shouting their wares, the wheels of passing carriages and coaches combined with the clatter of hooves, dogs which persisted in barking even when he had passed them by, children screaming as they shouted and ran aimlessly in and around the carriages and coaches, risking their lives, it seemed to him. The hustle and bustle was terrifying and he realised he had got out of the habit of city living. Sleepy isolated Scotton had truly become home. To add to his consternation, London was larger, busier and more intimidating than York had ever been.

The streets were awash with recent rain, mud, droppings and the general detritus of everyday life. His boots were splattered immediately but his interest in the buildings, the fine church he saw, the many people, some with different coloured skin which intrigued him, made him overlook such small things as dirty boots. Everything was a source of interest. People's clothes were different; he felt as if he stood out, as if he was the epitome of a north countryman newly arrived from the middle of nowhere. It added to his sense of isolation and displacement. He had the oddest longing; he wished to be part of it, not outside observing it.

He walked for most of the day, exploring side roads and main roads, wondering how so many people could

live in such small buildings, so tightly packed together.
Where did they find space to breathe, to see the
sunshine, the trees, the grass, the wild flowers? And yet
there was a tremendous feeling of energy, everyone there
was busy making a living, no matter how they did it.
Another pie, a half tankard of ale in an inn, and he was
ready to walk on, getting the ache out of his flesh and
bones and relishing the exercise.

A church bell tolled and he recalled suddenly he
needed a place to stay. Time was slipping away fast, it
was growing dark, lanterns were being lit in the
buildings he passed by. Disappointment set in: he
wanted to walk a lot more, to see, to listen, to
experience, but he could not tarry too long. He felt as if
a lifetime would not be long enough to explore the great
city and its many layers, for he realised there were
several classes of people, from the extreme rich to the
extreme poor. That had revealed itself in the very short
time he had walked the streets.

Guy was passing an inn at that moment that looked as
if it might be respectable. He stepped in to find a fresh
sanded floor and a clean counter. The landlord was a
lean, serious looking individual who appeared to be
cultivating a fancy beard, judging by the shape. It was
not entirely successful. The drinkers looked round but
he had to get used to the fact that everyone looked up
when someone walked in, whether they were strangers
or regulars.

He approached the counter and tried a smile. It
almost worked.

"I need a room for the night. Do you have space?"

The man nodded. "Sir, I have a spare room. Let me
get the boy to show it to you." A bellow brought a half-
starved cowed boy into the bar. "Show the gentleman
the room at the back first floor."

"Thank you." Guy nodded to the Landlord, turned
and followed the waif up the stairs, noting the patched

ragged clothes and pathetic sharp bones showing through the skin. The inn looked reasonably prosperous, why was this child so starved?

"Here it is, sir." The boy indicated a doorway. Guy walked into the clean room, saw the bed was covered with a white coverlet and knew it would be all right. A room for himself, not to be woken by others coughing, spluttering, turning over in their restless sleep, making the beds creak. It was a luxury.

"Thank you. Would you tell the landlord I will take it for the night? I'll be down shortly to order a meal." There was an overwhelming need to use the facilities; the ale he had consumed earlier had gone straight through him. The boy nodded and went to leave but Guy stopped him with a gentle hand on the stick thin shoulder. "Here. Buy yourself a pie or something." He put a coin in the boy's hand and whispered: "Tell no one! That is for you!"

The boy's eyes widened and his mouth opened to say something. Then he turned and ran out of the room, his face tight with emotion, unable to speak.

Guy stood for a moment, wondering where that impulse had come from. Something in the boy had touched his inner heart, the one that had flowered under the touch of God through sunshine and shaped clouds. He was glad he had done it because he felt truly at ease in his mind for the first time since he had left Yorkshire. Nothing had changed; he could still feel the touch of God in his heart. Foolish though he knew it to be, he had feared that distance and strange places would block the communication with Heaven. Now he knew it didn't; he could move on and go to his new position with increased confidence.

He stowed his bag under the bed then went downstairs to the crowded bar to buy a drink and order a meal, every bit the assured man out in the world. No one need ever know it was his first time in the city.

After a breakfast of bread, cheese and ale, Guy paid for passage on a coach which was less crowded than the one he had travelled in from Yorkshire. This one was going to take him to Sussex, to his new home at Cowdray House and his new employer, Viscount Montague. His confidence had grown after making that momentous journey to London. He sat in a corner seat in the coach, assessing his possessions and his future. He had with him two changes of clothes, a letter giving his credentials, a few coins and his new-found – newly confirmed - devout faith. He had been assured that the Montagues were Catholic and that he would have no problems practising his faith there. It was another thing that encouraged him to be confident in his new position in life, a working man rather than one reliant on family. He did not see the boy from the inn when he went down for breakfast, but the memory of that small action lingered and warmed him.

The journey seemed overly long, yet he knew it was no more or less than some of the stages from Yorkshire to London. Perhaps it was because he was impatient to arrive although he noted with interest how the countryside changed as they went. It flattened out, became greener and a good deal softer than the landscape he was used to. Spring had already arrived in these more southern counties, everything was budding or in leaf and there were masses of wild flowers along the sides of the road and in the fields.

At last they arrived in a small thriving town which the coach driver announced was Midhurst. They had stopped in front of a white-washed inn. Guy swung his bag down and put it on the ground at his feet whilst he looked around. From where he stood he could see at least two inns and quite a few shops. There were carriages, men on horseback and a goodly amount of people walking about. It wasn't anywhere near as busy or as colourful as London but it had its own appeal. He thought about asking if there was a conveyance to Cowdray House but then decided he wanted to walk, to breathe in the air of this strange and new part of the country. He decided he had endured enough coach travel, at least for the time being, and it was good to walk.

It was late afternoon; the sun was just beginning to lose its place in the clear sky. He asked the coach driver for directions and, following the gestures made with the whip, collected his bag and began the trek toward his new home.

Sussex was milder and fresher than Yorkshire, the people he overheard spoke with softer voices. There were no fells or great rushing rivers that he was aware of. It was altogether a very different land and it was hard for him to believe he was still in England, the country he loved. He had the same sovereign, Queen Elizabeth, he had the same language, just, but he still felt as out of place as if he had been dropped into some foreign land where he could not understand a word anyone said. He saw himself as being more out of place in the countryside than he had in cosmopolitan London where it seemed anything and anyone could be accepted. Again he wished he could have stayed there longer, but work was work. He had no excuse for arriving several days later than arranged.

The afternoon was fading fast, the light changing as he walked, making the green less intense, easier on the eyes. The road was reasonable and, with his long legs, he made good progress. A mile was nothing to him; he was used to walking.

He passed fields of new crops, the plants just showing above the rich fertile looking soil. The hedgerows were full of wild-life which rustled and scampered away as he walked past. He listened to the birds, identifying each call. At least they were the same as home.

Just when he was beginning to think he would never get there, the great house seemed to rear up out of the landscape, its imposing towers reaching to the sky, as if challenging all who viewed it to deny its right to exist. Dark clouds were building up behind it and Guy, ever looking for symbols and signs, wondered if that was an omen. If it was, the sooner he confronted it, the better.

As he neared the gates a sudden wave of homesickness overwhelmed him, taking him completely by surprise. A longing for the wilder Yorkshire landscape, for the comforts of home, for his mother's smile, all rocked him to the core for a moment. Then he realised was hungry, thirsty and most of all tired from absorbing too many impressions all at once. The dark cloud seemed more lowering, more threatening. If it held rain, the sooner he was under cover the better. He muttered a quick muttered prayer to the Virgin Mary and banged on the gatehouse door.

It seemed an age before anyone opened it and then a hunched old man appeared, looking at Guy as if he were a murderer or arsonist or something, such was the level of suspicion in his eyes.

"Well?"

"Fawkes, come to be footman to Lord Montague."

"Oh. Right. Yes, I recall something about a new footman. Been waiting on you, we have. You're late, they said."

"I had to travel down from Yorkshire." Guy wondered why he was apologising. He had not stated the time or the day when he would arrive.

"Yorkshire? That far off place? No wonder you're late. Come in."

Guy walked in, wondering still why they should think he was late. He also wondered if that would be held against him. It was not an auspicious way to start a new position.

Oddly, there was a sense of protection, of security, inside the great walls. As the gate slammed shut behind him, he looked around with interest. The stone structure was solidly built, the walls were thick and built as if for defence, the gate imposing in its grandeur. The house itself was magnificent, viewed from across the courtyard, a fine building with elegant windows and huge carved portal over the entrance. The old man shuffled toward Guy and gestured that he should follow him to the house.

The front door was massive, even bigger and stronger than the one at the gate. Guy wondered what the Montagues were trying to keep out – or in – with such defences. The door was opened by a young man who just about managed to utter a welcome. Was it his imagination, or was the young man looked down at him? Guy ignored it, walked in and waited for someone to tell him what to do next. It was better that way. He did not want to seem presumptuous.

"Girl coming," the young man muttered, almost under his breath. She was indeed coming, a young girl in a maid's outfit who simpered and glanced at Guy from under fluttering lashes, unaware, as they all were, that he found her empty headed and of no merit. She was pretty, in a bland sort of way. Guy had the distinct impression that she thought she was more attractive than she actually was.

"You for the new footman position, then?"

"Yes."

"Best come and see His Lordship then."

"Thank you."

He is in difference to her must have shown. She frowned when she realised he was not reacting to her and looked down as she led him along corridors lined with panelled walls and intricate carvings. There seemed to be many doors. She knocked twice on one door which had nothing on it to indicated what it was, entered and gestured to Guy to follow her.

An aged, white haired shrunken man had his feet propped up on a stool in front of a blazing fire in a huge marbled hearth. This had to be Lord Montague. His Lordship was close to the heat despite the relative warmth of the pleasant spring evening. He appeared to lack flesh on his bones and no doubt felt the cold. Guy looked around, seeing yet more fine panelling, heavy portraits, rich tapestries and drapes, silver glinting on the table and mantel. The place spoke of money in a most unsubtle way.

"The new footman, sire." The girl curtsied, even though she had not been acknowledged and left Guy standing on a thick rug in the centre of the room.

He stood, uncertain, turning his hat in his hands, waiting to be spoken to, hoping he had kicked off sufficient mud and dust from his boots before walking into the luxurious room. He wondered if the rest of the house was the same and thought that was a foolish notion. Of course it was.

After an eternity Lord Montague turned, saw him and gave a half smile. It did little to reassure Guy for the smile only rearranged the wrinkled flesh without displaying any warmth or feeling.

"Fawkes, isn't it?" The words were abruptly spoken, as if speaking was an effort.

"It is, sir."

"Brought a letter with you?"

Guy fumbled for the letter, approached Lord Montague and handed it over; hoping it was not creased from being in his pouch. His nerves were on the point of breaking.

His Lordship had trouble opening the letter as his hands were shaking quite badly. He studied for some time before the head was raised and a direct gaze was turned on Guy once again. The look made him uncomfortable, as if His Lordship was probing the depths of his heart.

"Catholic, I take it?" The words were as sharp as before.

"Indeed, sir."

"Married?"

"No, sir."

"Going to be?"

"No, sir."

"No woman in your life?"

"Just one, sir, the blessed Virgin."

"Ah. I see. All right. You'll do for now."

Lord Montague roused himself from his chair and walked, a little unsteadily as if he had been too long at the wine, to the door. He opened it and shouted for someone called Spencer to be brought to him. Guy didn't hear anyone respond to the command, but assumed someone had heard and would do something about it. The elderly man stumbled back to his chair and sank into it with a sigh. Guy belatedly wondered if he should have helped him but then thought it might have been viewed as a presumption on his part. He did not yet know with a surety that he had the position and if he did, what duties it entailed. There was a long uncomfortable silence in the room as the occupants waited for his arrival. Guy's nerves were being drawn tighter and tighter. He didn't know whether to speak, to make himself amenable to his employer, or simply stand, a mass of uncertainty, until Spencer, whoever he was, arrived.

The door opened and a stocky man with a mop of reddish-brown hair came in. He was well dressed and carried an air of authority. "Sir." It was not a question. Then he turned and flashed a warm smile at Guy.

"Spencer, this is Fawkes, the new footman." Lord Montague waved a hand in Guy's general direction. "He seems all right. Got the right recommendation anyway from a family up north. Over to you." He picked up a cup and totally ignored them both.

Spencer shrugged without his employer seeing him, held out his hand to Guy and said; "Welcome to Cowdray House. Come, I'll show you to your room and tell you your duties."

He led the way out of the study and through the hall to the stairs. They went up to a second floor and along another corridor. Guy was in shock. The majestic house, almost a castle really, was overwhelming in its grandeur and elegance. It was the way Wheatley Hall should have been but wasn't, he concluded, as he walked along what seemed like endless halls and passed what felt like hundreds of doors until they reached one where Spencer stopped. He opened the door and stood back to allow Guy to walk in. Then he came in and closed the door after him.

"This is yours. Hope you like it. Stow your gear and come down to the kitchen, then we can talk." He lowered his voice, even though no one had appeared to be in the corridor. "Take no notice if I act as if I don't know you or your family, it's safer that way. Go with it."

"You..."

"I was approached by the Bainbridges to get this place for you but it's best not to say so. Others will be thinking you're being shown favouritism. It's the worst way to start a new position. You'll be fine, I do believe. Just do your work and keep quiet. Best way."

"How do I find the kitchen..."

"You'll find it. Follow your nose, it's the best way to learn your way around."

It appeared that 'the best way' was Spencer's most used expression.

He winked and left the room. Guy took a deep breath, turned slowly and surveyed his new home.

It was a small room, with large windows opened wide to the spring evening. He could see the walls of the grounds but better than that, he could see over the walls to the gently rolling countryside beyond. As he stood there an owl took off from the turret of the tower at the gate and swooped across a field, silent, deadly, perfectly designed.

The view was enchanting which was a bonus for him. The room contained a narrow bed with a clean patchwork coverlet, a table, some shelves on which he found a bible and a few religious books and there was a sort of cupboard where he could stow his clothes. He hung his cloak on a hook behind the door. He turned back to look at his room again and saw a small, delicately carved crucifix on the wall above his bed. His heart turned over in surprise and intense pleasure.

"I will be happy here," he told himself. "One way or another, I will make this a good position for myself, with God's help." He contemplated a quick prayer but decided prayer and thanks had to wait for now. Spencer, who seemed to be in charge of the household, was waiting for him in the kitchen, wherever that was. He paused, wondering why he had to tell himself he would be happy there, why he had not just accepted he would be. A touch of coldness in his heart said not all was as good as it looked. He sighed, decided he had to make the best of it and left the room to find his way to the kitchen.

In fact, the kitchen proved easy to find. Guy followed servants who were carrying trays and ewers, or armfuls of linen. It was a large spacious place, with plenty of windows open to the soft evening air. There were pans and bowls hanging on one wall and herbs drying in bunches hung on beams running across the ceiling. The large table in the centre was a jumble of chopped vegetables, pieces of meat, chunks of bread, plates, cups, tankards, bottles … maids and men rushed back and forth, taking trays out or bringing some back, putting items in the big sink to be washed up, thrusting dirty linen into a huge basket in one corner, no doubt destined for the laundry room at the end of the day.

A large lady with a red face and deft hands appeared to be in overall charge, everyone deferred to her; she was issuing orders as fast as she was working, mixing and seasoning almost by touch.

Guy stood by the door, watching the activity, wondering whether he could just walk in. Every now and then his nerve seemed to fail and his confidence would flag. He saw Spencer ensconced by the hearth with a mug of ale and a hefty amount of what looked like fresh baked bread and a hunk of cheese. Guy's stomach rumbled loudly, it had been some time since he had eaten.

Spencer saw him and gestured to the large lady. "Madam Poulter, this is Mr Fawkes, come to be the footman here."

She turned her flushed face toward Guy and nodded. "Mr Fawkes, I be glad to meet you."

He nodded and mumbled a greeting, a bit overwhelmed by the whole situation.

"Do Mr Fawkes the goodness of providing him with some food, Madam Poulter. He is half starved, having made his way here from the dark and dismal North of England."

The cook had not stopped her preparations, she worked on even as she watched every person coming and going in and out of the kitchen and assessed Guy at the same time.

"When was the last time you ate?"

Guy thought for a moment. "When I was in London, before the coach journey here."

She tutted. "Too long without food. Hold on there a moment and I'll find something for you."

"Thank you." Guy wondered about sitting down without being given permission but that decision was taken away when Spencer gestured to him to come closer and pushed a stool toward him.

"Come, rest while you can. This household is busy from dawn to dusk and sometimes later or even earlier, depending on His Lordship's whims. Have you been employed before?"

"No, sir. This is my first position."

Spencer's eyebrows rose in astonishment. "First position and you are nominated as footman? Methinks someone has a high opinion of your capabilities. I trust you will live up to it. Where are you from?"

"Wheatley Hall, Scotton in Yorkshire. Some miles from York."

A platter of bread and cheese was put into Guy's hand; a tankard of ale was placed on the table by his side.

"Eat that," Mrs Poulter urged him. "Tis the finest bread in the area, even if I do say so myself."

"The cheese is good too, Mrs. Poulter, when made under your direction."

"Be gone with you, Spencer, you and your compliments!" But it was obvious the cook was pleased, there was a gleam in her eye and the hint of a smile touching her mouth.

As Guy began to eat, he began to observe the comings and goings. Everyone obviously had some part to play in keeping Cowdray House running smoothly. There were few words spoken, just a good deal of work. It was something he noted and knew he would have no difficulty in following through. It suited him, not being one for gossip or idle talk of any kind.

"Wheatley Hall, is that the Bainbridge home?" Spencer enquired, when some of the bread and cheese had been consumed.

"It is, sir. My mother married Dionysus Bainbridge a few years ago."

"I thought I heard tell of the Bainbridges in that area. Pulleyns as well live around there, I do believe?"

"Yes, sir." It was as if Spencer was laying out his credentials for Guy's information. He knew the area, he knew the Catholics who lived there.

"And you are Catholic by faith, Fawkes?"

"I am, sir, and proud of it."

"You'll do well here. I'll arrange for your uniform to be provided as soon as I can. Before then, here are your duties."

Guy listened in silence as Spencer reeled off the many and varied tasks he would be called on to do during the course of a working day, starting with cleaning boots first thing in the morning and ending at night with collecting boots to clean the next morning. During the day he would be doing everything from emptying chamber pots to clearing tables, opening doors, assisting people with their carriage or horses. It seemed to him that he would be doing just about every task there was and then a few more which doubtless someone would find for him. A few moments to himself would be rare and precious and he knew he would welcome the time spent in prayer, just to be able to be calm. But it was a position and a well-paid one, too. He was obviously of some standing as a footman and that also counted for a lot. He knew his mother would be pleased when he wrote to tell her of his new life.

That sudden thought brought another burst of homesickness and he was glad when Spencer said he would give him a conducted tour of the great house, so he would know where everywhere was and not have to ask or hesitate or delay in carrying out any orders His Lordship issued. It was good to divert his thoughts from home for a time. He knew the dreadful longing for his family would return when he had a moment of quiet.

The house was as grand as he had thought from his first impressions. The tour took an hour and at the end of it, his mind was overwhelmed with directions and instructions. He wondered if he would ever remember it all. Spencer was a kindly person and answered all questions patiently and calmly, even when stopping to direct one of the other servants in a task. It seemed the entire smooth running of the House was in his hands, whilst Mrs Poulter laboured all day every day to keep everyone fed and watered, whilst watching over the laundresses and their chores, too. Between them, Lord Montague had nothing to worry about.

At one point, when Guy mentioned how busy everyone seemed, Spencer laughed and said: "this is day to day living, Fawkes. Wait until His Lordship decides to host a banquet or a ball. Then we really know what work is!" Guy thought it was impossible for any of them to be working harder than they already were but obviously Spencer had handled that kind of event a few times or he would not have mentioned it.

He was grateful to get back to his room and start to absorb the mass of information he had been given. He crossed over to the window and looked out, seeing the silver washed fields and trees. It was a very different landscape but one that he hoped he could identify with. He stood very still, listening to the sounds of a large house settling down for the night within a countryside alive with wildlife. The moon shone as large and clear as it did back in Yorkshire and the stars looked the same, something to hold on to in a world which was as far from his home as anyone could believe it to be.

'This will take a good deal of getting used to,' he thought as he breathed in the soft, scent-laden breeze, 'I just hope I'm good enough for this position.'

He undressed quickly and collapsed into his bed. Before a prayer of gratitude for his safe arrival and new position could be said, he was asleep.

The next evening Guy wrote to his mother.

> From Cowdray House,
> Home of Anthony Browne, 1st Viscount Montague,
> Midhurst, Sussex.
>
> March 17. Year of Our Lord 1589
>
> Mother,
>
> I wish to let you know I arrived safely, after an arduous but most interesting journey south. London is a great place of bustle and people and I would have liked to explore it further but time did not permit me to do so. Midhurst, where this great house is situated, is a green and pleasant place with soft-spoken people and little of the harshness and rugged scenery I am used to.
> The house is very large and there are many rooms. I have much to do in the way of duties and there will be little time in which to do nothing. I hope to be happy here and make a success of this position which you and Father arranged for me.
> Your grateful respectful loving son,
> Guy.

Guy discovered, from muttered, almost clandestine conversations, that Spencer was a relative by marriage and had been instrumental in getting him the position at Cowdray House. The Network had its uses, it seemed. Guy looked up to the older man and sought to emulate him in all he did. Spencer was the consummate diplomat when it came to staff problems, or soothing irritations on the part of those who employed them. Somehow he kept everything running smoothly so no one could see the oil he applied to the works to keep it going so. A word here, a smile there, a helping hand where needed, a hint of advice or encouragement and the whole house ran like clockwork.

There were many things for Guy to do during the day, he was kept on his feet for hours, going from floor to floor, from room to room, from kitchen to dining room, running errands, attending to clothes, footwear and just about anything anyone did not want to do for themselves. The work was not demanding in itself but it needed careful attention. Should any part of the boots not be cleaned properly, there would be complaints, if his service at table was not impeccable, it would be noted, if he tarried when carrying out an errand or task, it would be recorded against him. At least, that is how it felt and he strove to be as conscientious as he could all the time.

He was aware that the maids and even the older women in the house were giving him flirtatious looks from time to time. He studied his features in the scrap of glass as he shaved, wondering what it was that attracted them. In his eyes he was no better or worse than any other man, but it seemed he was a source of great interest to them. Unfortunately for them, he was able to ignore every comment and glance, the fact they contrived to brush against his arm as they passed him whilst bustling around the kitchen, or the way they sometimes tried to stop him leaving a room when they were entering. He simply side-stepped them as if they were not there and carried on with his tasks. It was a sort of game and he was determined to win. Sooner or later they would see he had no interest in them and they would leave him alone. He hoped so, anyway.

"No interest in women, Fawkes?" Spencer said casually one morning as he watched Guy labour over sponging mud from the hem of a cloak. Guy knew that at least one of the maids had been trying very hard to get him to take notice of her and he had consistently managed to look the other way.

"No." He paused, considered the terseness of his answer and smiled slightly. "I have no interest in any woman but the Blessed Virgin, sir."

"Hmm." It was almost a grunt and almost a word. Guy looked up, suddenly cautious. His senses had been alerted by the tone Spencer had used.

"Is that likely to become a problem, sir?"

"His Lordship tends to think so. I would be careful if I were you."

"Why…"

"He thinks that men who do not favour or welcome the advances of a woman would welcome the advances of a man instead."

The words seem to hang in the air between them. In that moment Guy knew his position at Cowdray House was in danger, simply because he had no interest in either men or women, but he knew too that Lord Montague would not believe that. He doubted that His Lordship ever listened to anyone but himself. It was a flash of intuition he felt was right.

He looked down at the cloak and sighed. The one thing he did not want or need was a problem like that. "I have no intention or desire to accept the advances of men, either, sir."

"Asexual." The word came in a sort of quiet exhalation. "You'll have trouble getting people to believe that, someone of your age with your looks."

Guy stared at the steward for a moment and then asked, diffidently, "Sir, what do you mean by my looks? I think I am no better favoured than the next man."

"You are a handsome man, Fawkes, sturdy of body and strong of limb. You have good features which would attract any woman – as it has here, judging by the way the females are falling over themselves to get you to even glance in their direction – and altogether, combined with your quietness which drives them mad wondering what you are thinking, you are a desirable person."

Guy flushed bright red and Spencer laughed. "That blush tells me you never gave it a thought!"

"No, Sir, I didn't. I truly thought I looked much like everyone else."

"Well, you don't. I will try and explain this to His Lordship, if the occasion arises. I should warn you, though, he has a hatred of the man-man thing."

"There is nothing I can do about the way I am, Sir!" Guy protested. The colour had left his face and he looked pale and sickly.

Spencer smiled. "No, of course there isn't. I wouldn't expect it. I'm just warning you, that's all. I expected a robust woman-chasing individual, not one who is silent, thoughtful and not interested in anyone. It has really set them going, I can tell you!"

Guy stood silent, considering the situation from all angles. It seemed as if he could not win: if he had shown interest in any of the maids, the others would have been jealous, if he had shown interest in any of the men, he would have been scorned and called catamite. He did neither and found himself the centre of attention because of it. It was strange that getting involved with someone would bring problems, yet not wanting to get involved with anyone brought its own problems, too.

Finally he said quietly, "I try to do my work as best I can, Sir. I try to keep to myself as much as I can. There is little time in a day to do anything but work. I welcome the chance to attend prayers and seek only to do the Lord's will and that of his blessed lady, too."

"I know." Spencer got up, looked at the cloak and nodded. "You do a fine job here, Fawkes. I am well pleased with you. When the occasion arises, I will tell His Lordship that."

"Thank you, Sir." Guy looked down, hesitated and then got on with his task, wondering if the steward's words would be enough to keep him in employment. He became angry, wondering why his sexuality should be a problem to anyone; then, with a supreme effort, he put the anger to one side, knowing there was nothing he could do about it.

Days flew by in a flurry of work, snatched moments to eat or to pray and even sleep seemed to be truncated to minutes instead of hours. Guy found he was losing weight but feeling better for it. His uniform hung loosely on his body and he cinched the belt in a bit tighter to disguise the fact. The cook eyed him up and down and served him bigger portions but the work just kept on coming and the weight would not stay on his bones. For all that he felt a sense of satisfaction at being of service to people. He liked the house, the family and the staff and thought he had found his place in life.

The house was extravagantly furnished, with many fine tapestries, paintings, and carvings, especially around and over the fireplaces. Great chandeliers hung from the ceiling of the dining room and the banqueting hall. The plate from which the family ate gleamed as if newly minted every time it was used. The house seemed perpetually to be in a state of anxious activity, there was much coming and going on the visitors, all of whom seemed to be of high rank, who needed a good deal of attention. They in turn brought their own servants with them, whether they were making a short social visit or staying for a few days. Guy wondered regularly how the Cook managed to cope with this constant flux of visitors and family.

The Viscount's wife, Lady Magdalen, hardly glanced at him no matter what he was doing. It was as if he were invisible yet providing a service, opening doors, filling her glass with wine, serving food, and all the other myriad tasks allocated to him as footman. He knew it was foolish to resent this, but he did and it was hard to overcome. Lady Magdalen, hard faced with a tight prudish mouth and seemingly a personality to go with it, appeared to have a considerable wardrobe of clothes, and employed a whole range of maids to take care of them. The silks and brocades were highly colourful and although Guy felt it was not his place to criticise, which indeed it was not, he did think at times she rather overdid the colours, not worrying too much whether they blended or clashed. Lord Montague wore the same velvet smoking jacket most of the time, whether out of laziness or because it was his favourite Guy did not know.

The two children of the marriage, Elizabeth and Henry, had their own servants and their own rooms. There seemed to be no end to the money and luxury of Cowdray House.   One thing that struck him quite considerably, though, was that there was very little attention given to religion. There were token family prayers from time to time, there was a Bible in the lounge, but aside from these happenings, there was very little that differentiated the Montagues from any Protestant family. They did not even offer Grace before meals. He asked himself whether this was to ensure the family did not create difficulties for itself, it was illegal under English law at that time to hold any kind of Catholic service, to welcome or harbour a priest, in fact to do anything which was against the Protestant religion could result in arrest and imprisonment. Those who did not attend the Protestant church services were fined heavily or imprisoned. There were many executions of both women and men, all in the name of their faith.

It quickly became clear that this family made only token acknowledgements of their Roman Catholicism but it was not clear how they evaded the law on attending the church. For Guy this was a great disappointment.   He had hoped to find a Catholic sanctuary where he could practice his faith in the security of the great walls. Instead he felt as if he would be doing something illegal if he attended a Mass more than once a week, when a surreptitious service was held.

Word went round that the Viscount's daughter Mary, would be coming with his friends one evening. That meant a full-scale banquet, and he realised for the first time what Spencer meant when he said: "Wait until His Lordship decides to host a banquet or a ball. Then we really know what work is!" She had apparently included nephew Anthony in the invitation, someone Guy had served several times and not thought anything of it.

Every part of the dining room was cleaned. Maids brushed at the carpet, other servants cleaned down the walls, and Guy and Spencer spent a good deal of time cleaning silver which was already mirror bright. The great chandelier was lowered, cleaned, set with candles, and left in that position to be raised up again once the candles had been lit. Guy was not allowed to touch the chandelier, in fact Spencer did practically all of that work himself, with only the merest hint of assistance from a man called William who had been there for many, many years and knew how to handle the delicate piece of equipment.

Once the cleaning had been done, the table had to be set, just so. This took the best part of the morning, and then the great sideboard was laden with tureens and serving dishes, which he was told would be taken to the kitchen nearer the time for the cook to fill with the vegetables and meats which would be on offer. Wine was put on the sideboard ready to be served. Flowers ornamented the table and all in all a guy thought he had never seen such an ostentatious display of wealth in his life. He looked at it at first in awe, and then remembered the stick thin boy in the inn, remembered the disbelieving yet average look he got when he gave the boy a coin. And here was wealth spread out for no other reason than to entertain a daughter and some friends. It was hard to accept that people could use their money in this way, whilst others were starving. He knew well that this was a generalisation. He knew from his short time in London that there were layers of wealth, extensive at the top, working its way down to those who had nothing. He asked himself why he could not accept this, why it seemed unfair. Surely the poor have always been with us, he thought, but surely somebody as rich as Viscount Montague could do something toward the local people who were so poor. Not at any time had he heard of any benevolence being shown to those outside the walls of this great house.

In truth, there was little benevolence shown to those inside either. It was one endless round of work, no consideration given to anyone who might be weary, sick, hungry or thirsty. The demands of the family came first. This, added to the lack of obvious faith, made him restless and unhappy with the position. But with all that, he knew it was a good position and he had to work at it at least for a while. But he longed for some quiet time to walk outside, in the coolness and beauty of the countryside around the great house, to observe the wildlife as he had back in Yorkshire, to hear first-hand sound of the birds, to study the wild flowers, to be on his own without someone demanding that he do this or that or something else often all at the same time, something that was physically impossible for him to do. He needed to time to commune with his God, to make his devotions to the Virgin Mary, to sense the presence of the Almighty in his life instead of snatched prayers before falling into an exhausted sleep. He may not physically have been damaged by this lack of time, but his heart, mind and soul definitely did. Since the illuminating moment on the journey from Yorkshire when the sun had lit up the ground, there had been nothing in the way of visions and that's bothered him a good deal. He was used to time to be himself and to speak with God. Here, in Cowdray House, that time was stolen by the need for constant attention demanded by the family.

The imperious Lady Magdalen was the most impatient of all. Where Lord Montagu would give someone time to fulfil an errand, his wife would not. Accordingly, most of her demands were met by people who were virtually running from one end of the house to the other, depending on what she had asked for at that time. Guy was not sure whether she disliked him, or actually liked him, because her expression did not vary from one moment to the next to tell him either way. All he knew was that she constantly picked on him to attend to her, to deal with some service or other that she needed. He was very aware that he had to keep on the right side of her ladyship, as she had considerable influence with the Viscount. But it was extremely difficult to fulfil all her demands all the time and keep a bland face turned to her. He wanted to say 'give me time, for goodness sake!' But he did not do it. The only consolation he had was that she treated her maids even worse then she treated him. He had heard tales of her throwing a hair brush or some other item across the room to hit a poor unfortunate female, who had not moved quickly enough or done the right thing in that instant that she had asked for it. It seems so wrong to him.

One night, lying awake, listening to the owls and other night life, he tried to pin down why life in Cowdray House was so different. Apart from the very obvious, wealth, the amount of servants, there was something else, something that set this place apart from his own home. In that moment he realised two things. The first was that he was overwhelmingly homesick, not only for Wheatley Hall but for Yorkshire itself. The second was that it was very clear to him there was no affection whatsoever between the Viscount and his lady wife. It had obviously been a political marriage, and he had no doubt that the first marriage of the Viscount was the same. There was no tenderness in the way they spoke to one another, looked at one another, and he had noticed they never ever touched in any way, not even a hand to hand. He wondered how they had managed to produce two children. He also knew that the children were as cold and as imperious and as demanding as the parents. Because of course they knew nothing else. Where was any kind of affection? Surely people needed that to be married. He thought of his mother with Dennis, how she would put a hand on his arm or he would reach out to her and maybe touch her face or hair and Guy realised that the two of them were deeply in love. There was no love in Cowdray House. There was no feeling for the Virgin Mary, for Jesus Christ, for any of the Saints, and this coldness filtered down to the staff as well. If Spencer had not been part of his family, Guy wondered whether he would ever have been spoken to him at all. Some days he would have breakfast, lunch, and dinner, without anyone saying a word in the kitchen. He knew they were all tired, from the daily demands of the family, but there is always time to exchange a word of encouragement with a fellow worker. He wished he had the gift of such easy polite talk, but he did not. He was by nature a solitary and silent person. That only added to his sense of isolation.

On the night of the banquet Guy was literally rushed off his feet, so many people to serve whilst others were calling for more wine, water, a dish, anything. But he did observe the younger Anthony Browne watching him very closely. At first Guy thought it was to ensure that he did nothing wrong but then something happened which could have been his imagination or again not. He leaned over to serve meat to Anthony and he felt a touch on his inner thigh. He backed off immediately and as he had finished serving, he went to the next person. He felt unclean, contaminated in some way, he wanted to go and wash but he couldn't leave the room. Instead he managed to avoid going anywhere near the man for the remainder of the evening, by busily attending to everyone slightly longer than he need, which meant someone else answered the man's imperious summons. It seemed all aristocrats had that demanding manner with subordinates. It was not necessarily inherited, he decided.

Later that night, in his room which had become so familiar as to be soulless, he thought about the incident and knew that in many ways his days at Cowdray House were numbered. There were things he could not tolerate. He shared the Viscount's hatred of what Spencer called 'the man-man thing' and there it was, in evidence from his own son. Either way, whether he left of his own accord because of it or whether his Lordship decided he had to go, he would be returning to Yorkshire ere long. Somehow the thought was not displeasing to him.

The days, weeks and months flew by, nothing else happened and he began to think it was all forgotten, but the quiet time came to a sudden grinding halt when Lord Montague called to him from his usual place by the fire as he went to leave the room after delivering a message.

"You … Fawkes, isn't it?"

Guy returned to stand by His Lordship's chair. "It is, sir."

"I don't think I want you here anymore, Fawkes. Best pack up your things and get back to wherever you came from. I'll get your money made up."

Guy felt rooted to the spot by shock. "Have I displeased you, sir?"

"No. There's no fault in your work, but – you bother me. You aren't – right, are you?"

"In what way, sir?"

"Don't like women."

"I explained that when I arrived here, sir. I worship the Blessed Virgin and no other."

"Yes, yes, I recall all that, but…"

Guy turned to leave but Montague stopped him with a shout. "You can't just walk out on me like that!"

"Sir, I do not think there is anything I can say."

"You can admit which way you are."

"I am no particular 'way', as you put it, sir. I have no interest in either men or women."

"They all say that." This time the tone was definite dismissal. Guy bowed and left the room, determined to search out Spencer and find out if there was a way he could stay. Oddly, although he knew it was coming, he did not want to be dismissed so easily. He felt he wanted to fight back, for a while at least. He wondered at his contrary thoughts and then decided it was not worth worrying about. He would try for a bit more money, if he could.

Spencer was sympathetic. He heard him out in silence and then sighed.

"I knew this was going to happen, he's been hinting at it for a few days. Leave it with me. Have you got anything to do right now?"

"No, sir."

"Go on up to your room. I have an idea. I'll be along later." Guy left the kitchen and went up to his room, where he stood looking out of the window, wondering if his dream of being gainfully employed had vanished because of his inability to associate with women. He had hoped that perhaps one day he would be steward, a secret he had kept close to his heart ever since he arrived at Cowdray House and saw the work Spencer did. He saw Lord Montague's words as a weak and foolish reason to dismiss him and thought that he could have come up with a better excuse to get rid of him than that if he really wanted him to go.

He went and sat on the edge of his bed, sending up prayers, heartfelt prayers, for the security of his position for just a bit longer, at least until he came into his inheritance and had money of his own, rather than working for it. It was not exactly what he wanted, the need to serve was paramount, to be useful rather than live off an inheritance, but if it was all he could do, then he would do it.

Spencer knocked and walked in without waiting for the summons. He was smiling.

"His Lordship's grandson has offered to pay your wages and employ you to wait at table, Fawkes. That's less work and possibly less money but I'll see about that. He's talked to His Lordship and told him not to be so pernickety, someone not interested in anyone else can't be bad, it means less trouble all round."

"Thank you, sir!"

"I'll see to it that you get a chance to give your thanks to Mr Anthony-Maria yourself. Meantime, get back downstairs, there's work to do!"

Relieved not to be writing home that he was unemployed just yet, Guy hurried out of the door after Spencer, hardly believing his luck. Then he stopped and offered up a prayer of thankfulness. His plea to stay had been heard.

Then he stopped as a thought crossed his mind, an unwelcome one. At what price? Would that man who was not entirely a man demand some recompense? He had a reason to pay for Guy's continuing employment, everything came with a price. He shrugged and started to go back downstairs to his work. If it meant another few months of paid employment, it would do, but the moment the man began his unnatural touches again, he would walk out. No hesitation. Nothing. But before then, there was money to earn, to take back to Yorkshire with him. Now he was more sure than ever that is where he would be going ere long.

Chapter Seven

The darkness no longer held terrors for the tortured man. Within the darkness now he could see images, his past life coming to him, showing him the good moments, the bad moments, the illuminated moments when he felt God Himself had spoken to him through His many wonders. The life he had led could not be taken from him, no matter what they did on the morrow. He would take the memories with him to his Heavenly home, where surely he would be welcomed back with open arms, as someone who fought for the True Faith. In the darkness he found comfort for his mind, if not for his body.

***

It ended, as most things do, quietly, with the minimum of fuss and difficulty. Anthony-Maria seemingly lost interest in Guy not long after employing him. Spencer brought the bad news one evening, when Guy was particularly weary from a long day of standing, which was more tiring than walking, he had found. It had been long expected and he had no more than a flicker of regret when Spencer spoke to him. He did wonder how much pressure his grandfather had put on Anthony-Maria to ensure Guy no longer worked at Cowdray House and how much his deliberate evasion of any degree of closeness to the man was part of it. Once he had made it clear he was not 'available' he knew the position was no longer his.

Spencer had some compensation for him; if he wanted to use it, he had an introduction to an army unit through the Catholic network. That was far more detailed and widespread than Guy ever imagined. His position at Cowdray House had been arranged through the network and there he was, leaving that position with yet another recommendation for yet another place arranged through the same 'organisation'. It was something to think about, how much more could the network do for Catholics in England, given the right leadership and the right time?

For all that, there was a sadness in packing up his few possessions, taking his uniform off for the last time and folding it neatly to put on the bed. He realised how much weight he had lost when he put his own clothes on. He had to cinch the belt tightly to make the tunic look less like it was hanging on some kind of skeleton and more like the fact it was covering the body of a living person. He shouldered his bag and went down to the kitchen to bid goodbye to the cook and the other servants who happened to be there. The cook impulsively kissed his cheek.

"Go with God, Fawkes. I feel you will be better out of this place."

"I cannot entirely agree," Guy said, blushing at her attentions, "but I will remember you with great affection." He did not mean all of it but it seemed the right thing to say.

Cook wiped away a small tear and smiled as Guy turned to leave. "A true gentleman," she murmured as he got to the door. He paused, turned back to smile and then walked out.

Spencer was in the hall, waiting for him. He handed over the wages that were due and shook his hand. "I am truly sorry it didn't work out but you have the letter, yes?"

"I do, and I thank you for that."

"A new career, one might be better for you. Think on it. Before then, give my remembrances to all who know me back in Yorkshire. I see the grey mists of the moors in your eyes at times, Fawkes. It is hard for you to be here in this soft South. Go with God."

Guy had no words, just shook Spencer's hand again and walked out of Cowdray House for the last time. He was not blind to the beauty of the south but kept superimposing the rugged north over the gentle downlands and sweeping vistas around the House and knew he would be glad to go home for a while, until he worked out what to do next.

The walk to Midhurst from Cowdray House seemed to be shorter than the walk from Midhurst to Cowdray House. Perhaps the thought of returning to Yorkshire had helped him to walk a bit faster. Whatever the reason, the early spring air was good to breathe and the fact he was going home more than compensated for the fact his first position had lasted no more than a year. There were a few regrets, a few pangs, but the letter in his pouch and his sudden sense of freedom offset that. He hadn't appreciated just how confining the work had been. He had not seen the outside world or spoken with anyone who did not work at the House the whole time he had been there. It was almost a closed community. With so much to do and so many people demanding his attention from dawn to dusk, he had not been able to visit Midhurst or any other place. Sundays were taken up with religious devotions; all the other days were nothing but toil.

Midhurst was as busy as he remembered, the streets were a crush of horses, carriages, vendors and people afoot, all trying to make their way to one destination or another and creating a sort of chaos as they did it. Guy looked around, thought about staying for a while but then noticed the coachman and ostler hitching up a fresh team.

"Are you London bound, sir?" he asked the coachman cautiously, not wanting to appear too much of an ignoramus.

"I am that. One place left if you want it."

Guy handed over the fare, hoisted his bag into the coach and climbed in. The other passengers, all men as it had been on his journey south, nodded politely but did not speak. They shuffled up to make room and he settled himself in the corner by the door, sending up a silent prayer for a safe journey, no accidents or disasters, as he did so.

The coach began to move, the horses' hooves raising dust as it did so. A few passers-by waved and he quelled the instinct to wave back. What was the use? He would never see them, or Midhurst, again. That brought its own pang, for he would have liked to have wandered for a while to absorb the atmosphere of the place. As the countryside unrolled beyond the window of the coach, Guy made up his mind to spend some of his money on a few days in London before returning to Yorkshire. It would probably be his only chance to see the place before he found work which would keep him firmly anchored back in the North. This time, he vowed silently, he really would see the great city that dominated England. It was fortuitous that the coach for London was about to leave just as he got there, it was obviously meant for him to move away immediately. It was too late to have second thoughts about wandering around Sussex. London would be much more exciting.

***

It was raining heavily when the coach arrived in the City and stopped outside a ramshackle inn whose sign was all but obliterated by weathering. Guy and his fellow passengers wearily got down from the coach, reaching for their luggage, stretching cramped limbs and breathing in the London miasma, glad to be out of the confines of the coach, even it was to stand in the rain. After a year in the clean fresh air of Sussex, it was a shock for Guy to smell the many odours, everything from sewage to what was suspiciously like rotting meat and fish. Even worse was the noise created by so much humanity crammed into a small space, jostling for room, trying to grab every opportunity to make a living somehow, anyhow. Vendors and merchants, urchins and beggars, respectable women and those who obviously were not, elbowing their way through the crowds to get to wherever they were going. If it meant pushing someone into a pile of fresh manure to do it, they did it. Guy stood with his bag in his hand, his back to the wall of the inn, the heavy rain falling on him, surveying what seemed like utter chaos. He had thought Midhurst crowded but it was nothing like this and he was surprised how quickly his memories of London had faded. This was the city he had seen when he first arrived from Yorkshire, the busy bustling frenetic place, full of every type of person he could imagine and some who came as a surprise to him. A year in the confines of a great home and the fleeting memories of the small town of Midhurst had somehow overlaid his impressions and the reality came as a fresh shock to the senses. People shouted, muttered, complained, carried on loud conversations over the noise of the wheels of carriages and the clop of hooves even as they walked through and round the groups of bystanders who were congregating for no apparent reason. There was the cacophony of trades being carried on and dogs barking and snapping at anyone who came near them. Above everyone's head scavenger birds hovered, seeking their chance at food and water, pigeons, crows, even seagulls screeching their raucous cry and adding to the mayhem that was London.

Too many people, thought Guy, far too many people in one space. He was getting very wet but seemed incapable of looking away from the sights, of shutting his ears to the sounds, of closing his nostrils to the variety of smells, pleasant and not so pleasant, the whole assaulting his conscious mind, threatening to send his thoughts into overload.

The inn where he was standing was shabby and rundown. It was likely to be cheap, though, and with his money being limited and he having no idea whether he would gain employment when he got back home, he thought he had best make the most of it.

With an effort he moved away from the wall and entered the building.

The fat sly-looking landlord seemed to assess Guy in one sweeping glance, putting a price on his clothes, his ability and his standing in the fraction of time it took to look him over. Then he stood up straight, his considerable gut preventing him from getting too close to the rather grubby counter.

"Sir?"

"I may be staying in London for several nights. Would you have space for me?"

"I do, sir. Never short of room for a gentleman, sir."

Guy noted the compliment and smiled shyly. "Thank you. Right now I would like a tankard of your best ale, please." He placed a coin on the counter which disappeared as if by magic into the pouch hanging on the man's ruinous apron. The ale was poured and Guy stood with the tankard in one hand, trying not to look as if he was staring at everyone.

The drinkers were, for the most part, busy with their ale and their talk and seemed to be ignoring him although he knew, from the surreptitious looks he intercepted, that he was a source of great interest. Yet surely, with the coach stopping outside, visitors were normal to this place?

"You be from up North, then, sir." It was not a question.

"Yes. I'm going back to Yorkshire after a short stay here."

"Thought as much. Tis in the voice, sir, can't get rid of it, that North sounding way of saying words." The man looked smugly at his customers, as if he were the fount of all wisdom. Guy was somewhat irritated by his attitude but let it go. The ale was weak but at least quenched his thirst.

"Would you like to see the room, sir?"

"Yes. Please."

The Landlord walked ponderously around the counter and headed toward the stairs without looking to see if Guy was following him. Guy snatched up his bag and hurried after him. The man's breeches were old and tired; his weight was putting a considerable strain on the seams. He tried not to look in case anything happened on the seemingly endless walk up the long flight of stairs, although later he realised there were no more or less of them than in any other place he had been.

The room was shabby, as he expected, but reasonably clean. The window looked out into the street so there would be noise but was compensated for by the fact he could observe the comings and goings of London people. The rate was reasonable and he handed over the coins, watching in amazement how fast they disappeared into the pouch.

"Would you be requiring a meal, sir?"

"No, thank you. I want to walk for a while, see something of the city whilst I have the chance."

"Right, sir, leave you here then. Thank you, sir."

The room seemed larger once the corpulent landlord left. Guy put his bag under the bed, looked out of the window, saw the rain had eased off and decided to go out immediately. There would be vendors out there offering a variety of foods. He would walk and eat, try to see as much as he could before he felt he had to go home.

London, even soaked from the rain, or perhaps because of it, held an enchantment for Guy. Buildings shone in the late afternoon sun, puddles threw back flashes of light and every tree seemed freshly washed just for him. He was impressed by the many shops and offices, the busy streets, the overwhelming grandeur of the churches, even if they were Protestant. He was not tempted into them, he merely stopped to admire the elaborate buildings from the outside, standing with pie or small loaf in his hand, sometimes forgotten as he walked and looked. The well-dressed people who sauntered here and there, held conversations, shopped or sat in inns and meeting houses, had rich fur trimmings on their clothes which were beautifully made and often ornamented with what looked like gems. Their footwear looked strong enough to keep out the water and mud and they often had servants or guards to protect them. The carriages they rode in glittered with polished fittings, the horses were well groomed and gleamed in the sunshine. Ostentatious wealth.

There was poverty too. The extremes were very extreme; such as the ragged starving children who eyed his food with hunger writ clear on their faces to the point when he felt like handing it over to them. But if he fed one, what about the one next to the starving child… he walked on, trying to ignore their pleading looks. Men ragged and thin, women trying to sell their blowsy bodies for a few pence, cats which were no more than skin and bone; surely they had their fill of the vermin which he saw darting around the piles of rubbish and even daring to run under the hooves of passing horses, too, dogs whose ribs showed clear through their skin, who snarled and snapped and then ran from his boot.

The contrasts bothered him. There seemed little middle ground, no place where the poor could make their way up to a higher level and have some kind of standard of living. He wondered where the church stood on this vast divide, whether they should not be doing more. But then, he asked himself, what could they do? There were so many poor and if all the wealth were spread about London, would it feed and clothe every last one and give them a better life?

He finally turned back and made his way to the inn. It was time to rest and allow the impressions to sink in. There was always tomorrow.

The new day dawned clear and bright, all trace of rain burned away by the sun and the passage of people who somehow never seemed to sleep in this city. There had not been a moment in the night when Guy had woken and heard nothing but the night birds. Here there were no birds to call to one another, only the sound of passing feet and rumble of wheels as yet another carriage made its way through the winding streets. Once he was shocked awake by the sound of a fight, but it had broken up and the combatants gone away before he reached the window. He thought it would take some getting used to after the quiet life he had known.

"Be sure to visit the Parliament place, won't you, sir?" the landlord commented as he brought Guy his fresh baked bread and ham next morning. "Worth a look, I would say. Won't see naught like that in the North."

"That's…"

"North from here, sir, if you follow my meaning. But anyone'll tell you where it is, if you don't want a carriage, that is."

"No, no, I like to walk. You see more if you walk around."

"Suppose you do." But the look the man gave said he did not approve of walking. He seemed to study Guy's lean build and then moved away, slowly, as if he was proud of his weight and his inability to walk far or fast.

Guy had the inn to himself for a while. He was able to sit and watch the London world go by, observing yet again the tremendous contrast between the rich and the poor. He wondered where he fitted in; he was far from being a rich man although he had an inheritance of land and a home in Yorkshire to return to. He could not be said to be poor and yet his money would not go far. He could not afford a home in London with all that entailed in the way of financial outgoings. He did not seem to fit – but then he asked himself, when had it ever been different? He had not fitted in at school, or at home. He was constantly at odds with the world, wanting to see it as a clean, perfect place when in fact it was evil, dirty, overcrowded and, for the most part, unpleasant in its violence and its uncaring attitude.

In that moment he decided to take a look at the Parliament building, walk around just a little more, then return, collect his bag and take the very next coach to Yorkshire and the clean air of the dales. It really was time he went home.

He said nothing of this to the Landlord, just finished eating and then went out into the street, narrowly avoiding being run down by a carriage that was hurtling its way through the press of people and animals as if racing from or to a fire or some other dire emergency. No one seemed to take offence at having to step back out of the way; they just walked on when it had passed. It all helped to reinforce Guy's decision to leave. He felt it was too much of a dog-eat-dog place and he wanted to be out of it.

The Parliament building was huge, impressive, awe-inspiring and – in his eyes – totally hateful. Somehow it epitomised all that he had been feeling during his stay in London, the opulence, the wealth, the grandiose buildings and the ostentatious wealth contrasting with the poor, the downtrodden and most of all, those who were oppressed because they dared to believe differently from that which those who governed them said they had to believe.

He wanted to stand in the grand entrance and shout "I AM A CATHOLIC AND PROUD OF IT!" but it would have been counter-productive, he knew that. It would also have been stupid; he knew that, too. So he wandered around where he could, saw what he could, stored the information to take back to Yorkshire, knowing he would not be able to describe the grandeur of it or convey to anyone the overwhelming feeling of hatred he had conceived for it, no matter how hard he tried. He stood in the grounds and looked up at the soaring roof reaching to Heaven. An abomination, he told himself. It should be razed to the ground.

Guy turned his back on what was to him the centre of Protestantism and all that was wrong in England. Turned his back and, without so much as a single glance toward the building, set off in the direction of the inn. He planned to retrieve his bag, settle his bill and catch the next available coach to Yorkshire – and home.

Chapter Eight

Why, he asked himself, did I think I could destroy the building and all within it and not be found out? Why did I think it would work? What evil seed crept into me that I would consider such a thing? And why now do I see the error of the ways? Too late! If Satan had a part to play in it, then He has had his fun. I have suffered. I continue to suffer and no amount of Purgatory can be worse than that which I have endured. Man against man. Man cruel to man. Man indifferent to man. Great God, I should not have thought of taking life, any life! It is against Your will, Your commandments. Have I suffered enough? Is there forgiveness for me in the moment of death which approaches – I know not when for I have no way of telling the hours. This is hell. This place is hell personified. If hell be worse than this then I – no, nothing is worse than this. Nothing.

***

He packed his bag, paid the surly Landlord – earning a disapproving distrusting look as he did so – and walked outside. As had happened in Midhurst, a coach was loading right across the road from the inn and as happened in Midhurst, there was one place left. He paid the man, got in and put his bag on his lap. The top of the coach was already loaded and there was no space for his luggage. Again his fellow passengers were all men, each of whom looked at him but no one spoke. It was as well there was silence, for his mind was in torment and he needed a time of quiet solitude, even if it was within his head, to rationalise his thoughts.

The first day of the journey home seemed endless, the unreeling landscape passing slowly by where on the outward journey it had appeared to race past the window. He faced long torturous days of coach

112

weariness, of sullen uncommunicative passengers, of the relief of the short breaks for food ale and easement, the entire journey unreeling itself in reverse, without the expectation of a good job and a fresh start awaiting him at the end of it and it was dragging him down. His thoughts were going in all directions, none of them pleasant.

For a long time Guy could not shake from his mind the look the Landlord gave him when he said he was leaving, as if the decision to go was a reflection on the state of the inn. It wasn't, it was a reflection of Guy's state of mind but he could not explain that to a stranger. He doubted he could explain it to anyone, in truth. He was unsure of his own motives; he was going by instinct more than logic. Home called and he obeyed the summons.

London attracted him by its very cosmopolitan air, variety of buildings and open spaces. London repelled him by its extremes of wealth and poverty. He wanted to buy every starving child something to eat but, as he had rationalised earlier, what good would it do, for he had insufficient money to feed them again tomorrow or the next day or the day after. Something needed to be done about the poor. They needed assistance from those who had more than enough for their needs. Where was the Protestant church when its help was so obviously needed? Such enormously elaborate buildings, such grandeur, such splendour, with such poverty on its doorstep. The next logical question was, would the Catholic Church be any more giving, caring or providing? Maybe not but the problem was, they were not being given a chance to show whether they could or not by being banned.

From thought to prayer was a simple step for Guy. He prayed fervently that the Blessed Virgin or the great God Himself would show him the way he had to go, how he could go about putting right the wrongs he could see in the great capital city of England. He left it in God's hands and drowsed for the rest of the journey, waking only occasionally to see fine rain on the windows and mist covering the landscape. The regular stops for change of horses were an indication of how far they had come and how far they had to go. It seemed endless. As with most things in life, when you want it – in this case to get home and rest – it seemed to take forever.

It turned out to be an arduous trip, there was a breakdown and lengthy delay when a wheel came off, a problem with a cantankerous passenger who demanded a return of his fare because of the delay caused by the problem, with tempers being roused through the sheer ennui of a long distance coach journey, a none too comfortable coach at that.

At last the landscape became more rugged, the peaks more pronounced and he knew he wasn't far from home. It almost felt different, but he told himself he was being over-sensitive. For all that he offered up heartfelt prayers that the journey would eventually end, that he would be set down near enough to Scotton that he could walk the rest of the way and re-acquaint himself with his environment.

Soon the outskirts of York were sighted; he could rouse himself and begin to think about how his family would react to his sudden homecoming. With a shock he realised he had not written to tell them he had lost the position and was coming home. He had taken it for granted they would welcome him back, despite the lack of news. All he had been concerned with was packing his belongings and leaving, to shake the dust of Cowdray House from his shoes as soon as possible, the house and all that was contained within it in the way of cynical exploitation, covert sexuality, the 'controlling the lower classes' attitude of the family, all of it had become abhorrent to him in the end. He only realised it whilst sitting in a rocking, bone-jarring coach bearing him far away from the softness of the southern counties back to the solidity and security of the North.

He left the coach late in the evening with a sense of gratitude that they had made it without further incidents. The soft mist laden air and the Yorkshire countryside had worked its balm on his troubled thoughts: I have been dismissed from a fine position, what if I can't find another one, what if the Army will not take me, what if I find the family do not want me back, what if – and so the thoughts had gone around and around in his head throughout the journey in some kind of atunement with the wheels of the coach and, like the wheel on the coach, had come off and almost landed him in a ditch. The blackness of his thoughts had threatened to overwhelm him but the walk through familiar countryside eased his mind and gave him a different perspective to consider. God would take care of him. God had work for him, that was obvious. It was God's will he had been released from what he now saw as virtual imprisonment. With God's help he would take the next step in his life, whatever it was.

His bag weighed very little, his limbs delighted in the freedom from the cramped confines of the coach, he took long strides and rejoiced in the ability to walk at his own pace, to look at everything as he went, to see the burgeoning signs of spring in hedgerows and fields. It helped, like a balm on troubled skin, it helped. All that remained was to discover whether he was welcomed back at Wheatley Hall once more and whether he could explain to his family's satisfaction just what had happened at Cowdray House. It would not be easy.

He could see the Hall, shabby as ever, dominating the landscape as it had done for so long. He could not see any signs of life, though. He hesitated at the end of the drive, wondering if he was doing the right thing, then took a deep breath and began the final walk to the front door. Oddly, that seemed longer than the walk from the coach to Scotton had ever been.

It seemed he had hardly touched the knocker on a door whose wood was weather-beaten and worn, when his mother was in his arms, shouting "Guy!" and clinging to him so hard he could scarcely breathe. Her tears were wetting his jerkin but there was little he could do to stop them. Over her head he saw his sisters, changed out of all recognition. They seemed quite different people in the glow of the lantern which one of them held up. They were young women, both of them, blushing and smiling and awaiting their turn for a hug. His stepfather stood smiling, waiting in the doorway, saying nothing. It was not exactly the reception he had visualised. He had expected smiles and greetings, not this clinging semi-hysterical woman. Where was the strong person he had left a year earlier?

"Mother." He gently tried to break her embrace but it was obvious she was not about to let him go. He allowed his bag to fall to the ground and held her, feeling her bones through the flesh and wondering why. She had always been what he thought of as a substantial woman, now she was a mere shadow of her former self.

"Are you back for good?" she managed to ask, through floods of tears and tremulous smiles.

"I don't know. I have a letter of introduction to the Army but I would like to spend some time here… oh for goodness' sake, we can talk of this later. Can I not come in?"

His mother ignored his comments, hanging on to his arm as if he would take flight and disappear in a moment. She talked on, non-stop, hardly taking a moment to think of what she was saying. Motherly concern was wrapped around with motherly happiness that her son had returned. The result was chaos.

"What, why, weren't you happy, I only had the one letter, I wondered…"

"Let the boy come in!" Dennis moved forward, gently tugging at her arm. "Come, Edith, let the boy come in! Goodness, he's just arrived and here you are, making his clothes wet and not letting him into the house! Not to mention demanding to know his future plans! Guy, come in, do!" He took the lantern from Elizabeth.

Reluctantly Edith let go and Anne and Elizabeth rushed forward, both wanting a share of the hugging. Guy held them both, one in each arm, marvelling at their blossoming figures and grown up faces.

Then he was able to stand up and hold out his hand to Dennis.

"It's good to be back, Father."

"It's good to see you back, my son. Come on in, everyone will want all the news. What's it like down South? Is it as soft as they say it is? How was the house where you worked? Listen to me, I'm every bit as bad as your mother! Come on in. Your room's just as you left it." Everyone was talking too much, covering their uncertainty and shock at the reunion, no doubt wondering what had gone wrong, why he had so suddenly come back home. The tension was so obvious Guy thought he could actually see the crackling of it in the air. After their hugs, his sisters had stood back, looking at him as if he were a stranger who had just arrived.

His mother continued to cling to his arm as he picked up his bag with his free hand and walked in. She really was acting as if she was afraid he would escape, that he would go and catch the next cart or coach to York and be gone again. He smiled down at her, seeing a fresh lot of tears about to spill and then the heavy door closed after them, shutting out the world.

The house felt smaller after the grandeur of Cowdray House but it closed in around him with familiar security and comfort. The hall was a little dusty but smelled of polish and spoke of home. There were 'kitchen' noises from the back of the house where food was being prepared. The noises distracted his mother for a moment. Almost reluctantly she let go his arm and said, "I have to arrange some food for you. I won't be a moment."

Guy stood, holding his bag, wondering if it would be impolite to go straight to his room or whether he should wait for his mother to return. Dennis seemed to read his thoughts.

"Go on up, Guy. Candle's there as it always was. Put your bag down in your own room, then come down. Edith should be done with her instructions by then. Sorry about the emotional greeting, by the way, you rather took her by surprise."

"I hadn't realised how much she'd missed me."

Dennis grimaced. "You've been the topic of conversation every day since you left. Not that I minded, but the lack of news did worry her as time went on."

"I realise I should have written more often but..."

"The job was demanding. Yes, those positions are, no time for yourself. Go on up to your room. As I said, it's as you left it except it got dusted and swept a few times. I'm right glad you're back, Guy, for my sake as well as Edith's."

"Thank you."

He climbed the familiar stairs, carrying a candle and walked into his room. His room, not one granted to him by some Lord or his overseer. Dennis was right. Nothing had changed. Guy put his bag down, set the candle on the shelf, crossed to the window and opened it. He looked out across the countryside, smelling the richness of the new growth, sensing more than seeing the unfolding leaves on the trees, the thrusting shoots of wheat in the fields, wondering why he ever thought he could be happy in the south. It just wasn't his kind of countryside at all. With a big sigh of contentment he looked around, feeling the comfort of familiarity flow through him like a breath of fresh welcome air. It was good to be back.

He sat on his bed just as the door to his room opened and Elizabeth came in with a wriggling bundle of bright eyes and golden brown fur in her arms. "Guy, meet Pip. He's new, well, new since you were here last."

Guy took the puppy and admired it, petting the smooth head and tugging at the ears before handing it back to his sister. "He's lovely. How old is he?"

"Six months. I had to wait until he was old enough to leave his mother before I could have him. I thought the time would never come!" She clutched the puppy in her arms, holding it despite its desperate attempts to get free and play. She looked at Guy and said thoughtfully, "I thought you were never coming back."

"It was just a job, that's all. I would have had time off to visit if I had stayed any longer."

She sat on the bed next to him, looking alternately at his face and then out of the window. "We didn't hear from you, so we didn't know if you were happy or not."

Pip finally struggled out of his mistress's arms, leapt on the floor and went to investigate Guy's bag. Guy took Elizabeth's hand in his, marvelling at how slender and soft it was. "I wrote to Mother when I arrived, did she not get that letter?"

"Oh yes, but we didn't hear from you again."

"That's because of the job. I was up at dawn and in bed by sundown if I was lucky. I was just busy, all day, every day. Sundays were the busiest, with work to do even though it was a rest day and services to attend as well. I never seemed to have a moment to myself."

"What went wrong? I know this isn't a visit, or you would have said when you came home. Did you walk out?" Her face was trusting, full of affection for her big brother and his heart melted under the impact of her love.

"No. They told me to go. I didn't – fit in with the family very well."

"Because you're a northern man and they're southern people?"

"Yes, that's about it."

"Then they're stupid." Elizabeth got up, scooped up the puppy and started to walk to the door. "I don't care, though, I'm just glad you're back." She hurried over, planted a kiss on his cheek and then left the room in a swirl of skirts and petticoats.

Guy sat for a moment, wondering at the half lie and also wondering whether he could sustain that story. Then he decided against it. His mother and stepfather would want the truth and he could not, in all conscience, live with a lie. But as far as his innocent sisters were concerned, that story would do well enough. It wasn't that far from the truth. There had been a distinct Northern bias at times among the staff at Cowdray House but it was far from being the sole reason he had left.

He put his few belongings away in cupboards that had remained all but empty since he had left, just over a year earlier. He discovered a jerkin he had left behind, a shirt that seemed too old to be of use but which might be all right to wear around the house and boots that had gone stiff with neglect. I could get these polished up and wear them again, he thought, realising as he did so he was putting off the moment he had to go downstairs and talk to his mother about his reasons for coming home.

He walked across the floor with the intention of replacing the boots in the cupboard when a ray of moonlight pinned him to the floor. It wasn't shining through the open window, but the sheet of glass next to it. He stared. It seemed to go through his right foot and hold him in place. He knew there was a message for him in its brightness but it took a few moments to filter through the impressions and jumbled thoughts. Truth. He had to go and tell his mother the truth, lay out for her the reasons for what looked like a disgrace. Truth was everything; truth cut through everything just as this moonbeam was cutting through the glass and shining into his room.

As he thought it, a cloud covered the moon for a moment and the ray disappeared. It was enough. He knew what he had to do. He looked around his familiar/strange room and thought how good it would be to lie in his bed once again, listening to the sounds of the countryside, the wildlife, the coursing wind blowing through trees and crops, the noises that had been a lullaby for him as long as he could remember. There were no people here demanding attention all the time, no ringing of bells, no raised voices and hasty feet rushing to and fro on the other side of his door. Here was peace and that was just what he needed. He glanced at himself in the small mirror, noticing that his face was more sunken than it had been before he left and wondered if anyone would notice. Then he straightened his jerkin and walked to the door. He could not put off the moment any longer.

He noticed the stairs were slightly dusty, knowing well that would not have been tolerated at Cowdray House. Everything there was swept and polished every day. Here and there were small paw marks where the puppy had scampered up or down with his young mistress. It was a comforting homely touch; something he had missed in the precisely run and immaculately kept house. Being clean was good; being clean to the detriment of making it a home was something entirely different.

There was ale and meats; fresh baked bread and a pot of butter waiting for him on the parlour table. He went and sat down, realising he really was hungry and put a good deal of it away whilst his mother sat and patiently waited to speak, smiling at him from time to time. She reached out and patted his hand, then withdrew her arm quickly as if she had done something wrong. When he was through eating, he took her hand across the table and held it tightly for a few moments.

"I'm sorry I didn't write." He looked into her eyes so she would know this was not a half apology. "So many times I wanted to but the work of the house never seemed to end. Up at dawn, bed at sundown only if I was lucky. Cleaning boots first thing, serving meals, rushing here and there, opening doors, closing doors, helping people into and out of carriages, pressing clothes, cleaning clothes, serving at table…"

She smiled at him. "You learned a lot, my son."

"Yes, I did. I learned among other things that you cannot be chaste and be accepted."

The smile vanished. "I don't understand."

"Nor do I," he said with the first trace of bitterness he had allowed himself since he had left Sussex. "Lord Montague could not accept I did not desire women. He thought that meant I desired men instead, which he deplored and abhorred. He could not accept I did not desire men either. I have laid with no person, Mother, and that is the truth."

"And for that you lost your position?" She looked incredulous.

"It…" he broke off as Dennis walked into the room. "Father, I have just been explaining to Mother why I did not write again after the first letter. The work was very demanding."

Dennis sat down in the big chair by the hearth and nodded.

"Footmen work all hours, my son, I know that. I told her that, too, didn't I, Edith?"

Somehow it had been easier to talk to Mother on her own, with Dennis there it became embarrassing but Guy gathered up his courage, took a deep breath and carried on.

"I was just explaining to Mother that Lord Montague could not accept the fact I was chaste. When I arrived, His Lordship asked if I had a wife or a woman in my life. I said no one but the Virgin Mary. He said that was all right. Later he asked me again if I had a woman and I said no. He told Spencer I had to go as he didn't want 'my kind' around the place. He assumed 'no woman' meant I preferred men. He could not and would not understand … I desire no other person, no matter who they are."

He stopped, drank some ale, stared into their set silent faces and continued.

"His grandson, Lord Montague's grandson, that is, kept me on to wait at tables but he soon forgot about that and eventually I was told to go. Even Spencer could not find a way to keep me there."

"You have had – no woman anywhere, any time?" Dennis asked with obvious embarrassment.

Guy looked at him, concerned and irritated at the same time. He was not used to his word being questioned. "Why do you ask? No, never! I remain virgin and I serve the Virgin." He blushed bright red and looked away. It was not something he had ever believed he would need to discuss with anyone, let alone his closest family. Then he stopped to wonder why they were asking.

Edith looked at her husband. "I told you the claim was false, Dennis."

"You did. But it seemed logical and…"

"Tell me what you're on about!" Guy was getting more irritated as they spoke. It was clear something had happened whilst he had been away, something related to everything he had just said.

Dennis came over to the table, poured ale, picked up the cup and looked at Guy over the rim. He looked embarrassed.

"Do you know a Mary Pulleyne, Guy?"

"No. Who? There were Pulleynes at the last gathering I attended, as I recall, but I know none of their names."

"A member of the Pulleyne family came here not long after you left, saying you had secretly married Mary Pulleyne and she was with child. She has since had the child and called it Thomas. She swears it is yours."

"She lies!" Guy looked at his parents with an open, frank face that spoke the truth of his words. "Let me speak plain to you. I have known no woman, nor man, in my entire life. I have no need of that kind of release. I do not know this woman, nor do I know of any child. It is a way of trying to get money from the Bainbridges or a part of my inheritance, perhaps, if any Pulleyne knows of it. She lies and that is the end of the matter."

"It is for me, too." Dennis reached out and shook Guy's hand. "I had to ask, you realise that."

"Yes, I do." But it was a lie. Guy was upset but did not want to show it. He did not want to spoil his homecoming, so he rambled on, trying to cover his distress. "Men take advantage of women all the time, especially young ones. You were not to know it was not my child, my hasty marriage. But you should have known, if you had thought about it, that I would not bring dishonour to the family in that way. Father, if you must know, I took a vow of chastity when I was a young boy. I thought to tell no one as it was between God and myself."

"It still is, Guy, it still is!" His mother reached out and gripped his arm tightly. "I should have guessed. You always were the devout one of the family. Everything you said makes sense."

Dennis looked abashed and stared down at the table. "I had to ask," he muttered again, as if in apology. There was a difficult silence for a few minutes as they all fought to find something to say and fill in the obvious gap. "I'm sorry the position didn't work out." Dennis was trying to make up for the embarrassment of the allegation he had brought into the open.

"I'm not," Guy said quietly. "It was like a prison. I saw nothing of the countryside, nothing of the town nearby, nothing of anything but the house and the endless work to keep it clean and the people in it contented with their lot. They said they were Catholic but they paid no more than lip service to their religion. They worshipped luxury and all the rest of us were there to provide that. Walking out of the house was like walking out of prison."

"And you are back for good?" The question was almost whispered, as if his mother was afraid of the answer.

"I don't know. I have a letter of introduction for the army, but think I will-"

"You said that when you arrived. Spend some time with us first, please!" That was an all-out appeal and he smiled.

"Of course. I've been away some time. I didn't know about Pip and – are there any other new arrivals, apart from the son I'm supposed to have, I should know about?"

Dennis laughed out loud. "You'll be all right, Guy! We'll fend off the Pulleynes if they come here with their claims. Yes, there's kittens out there somewhere, a few pigs, chickens ... your mother has ideas of being self-sufficient. It isn't working yet..."

The laughter was forced to some degree, but it broke the stiffness which had been present from the moment he arrived. His unscheduled return had obviously worried them, posing many questions: what had gone wrong, why had he left a good job, what was this about the marriage and the child? That one they had obviously lived with for some time and they had been left wondering whether it was true or not. Guy wanted to ask whether they had believed the story even for a moment but decided it was best left where it was. The words had been said, he had answered them, Dennis had said it was the end of the matter and so it had to be the end. To pursue it would bring out things he did not wish to discuss, the level of his piety, the strength of his devotion to the Virgin Mary, whether he would ever marry and present his mother with the grandchildren he knew well she wanted.

He could almost see the questions writ clear on the somewhat dusty walls and appreciated their concern and their consideration in not throwing it all at him in one go. It was strange, or was it? That the reason for his dismissal also answered the question of this claim of a child that was his. Whoever this Maria was, she had no doubt desired the supposedly good-looking young Guy and laid claim to him, not realising he had his own very good reason for denying it. He felt himself relax and only then appreciated how tense he had been from the moment he had arrived.

The talk turned to general things relating to Scotton and Wheatley Hall, to the kitten Anne was hoping to bring into the house, despite Mother insisting all cats be kept in the outhouses, to the puppy Elizabeth had acquired even though, again, Mother was insisting that animals be kept outside. It was obvious the girls had a way of getting round her restrictions and commands. Guy listened to the talk with a gentle smile curving his lips. He was home. It was all that mattered. Later he could decide where to go and what to do. He began to take more interest when his stepfather spoke of his at last taking charge of his inheritance.

"You could rent out the land, Guy. It would bring you some money, at least until you decide what to do with your life."

"That's a sensible thought, Father, thank you. I don't know yet what I want to do, apart from learning a trade and practising my faith freely."

"Two good aims, Guy, two very good aims. Give yourself time, though, it's been a while since you were able to think for yourself, by the sound of it. Those positions are very demanding, as you found out."

"They are." Guy looked around the room, as if seeing it for the first time. "It's so good to be home. I really thought I could be happy there but-"

"Consider everything, my dear son. Think it through. For now, just rest. You're home and for that I thank God and the Blessed Virgin." His mother's tears began again but they were of happiness for her face was beaming as she sat crying silently. Guy was moved beyond belief and had no words to express his feelings. The year he had been away might have been a lifetime, everything felt different and yet the same. It was a strange emotion to deal with and to have his mother so openly crying with happiness over his return made it feel even stranger.

"I'll get to my bed now if you don't mind," he said eventually. "I've had a long journey. It's four days to get to London."

"Four days!" Edith looked shocked beyond belief. "To think you've been that far, son!"

"And a further five hours travel after that to get to Midhurst!"

"Sleeping in inns where there were crawlies, no doubt." She looked affronted at the very thought.

"No, the beds were clean, Mother, truly they were. Now, let me get some sleep and we can talk again in the morning." He kissed her gently and then left the room, feeling infinitely sad for a reason he could not quite pin down.

His room was less strange to him the second time he went in. He stood at the window, listening to the night sounds as he had done so many times before, sensing the wildlife out there, the plant life busy growing, the whole world carrying on just as it had done for thousands of years and would go on doing for yet more thousands of years. His one year of exile, as he thought of it, was nothing in the great scheme of things, nor was he, but there had to be a way he could make his mark on the world, a way he could get people to remember that he once lived and died and contributed, possibly, to the society in which he lived.

"I'm going for a walk round," he said next morning, getting up and reaching out to put a hand on his mother's arm. "I want to see everything. I've got a lot to catch up on."

His mother smiled and nodded, looking at him with such overwhelming devotion Guy wondered how he had managed to leave in the first place and even more importantly, how he was going to leave in the future, if he could not find work.

He left the room and walked through the house, listening to the very different sounds of home. He could hear his sisters chattering madly somewhere, laughing and giggling over the noise of the puppy's feet on the floorboards. The servants nodded respectfully to him as he passed them but no one spoke. He went through the kitchen and out into the grounds, marvelling at how it all felt familiar and yet different.

The spring sunshine bathed him in quietness, the grounds, overgrown and comforting in their irregularity, were a joy to his eyes after the regimented garden at Cowdray House. The differences were amazing and could only be appreciated after a time away. He walked over to a low wall and sat down on sun warmed stone, resting his weary body. The journey had tired him but more than that, the tensions that his homecoming had generated had taken a toll far more than he appreciated. Even after a good sleep, he still hurt. Muscles held in check began to ache after a while. Out here, in the sunshine and the familiarity of the grounds, he could truly relax and only then appreciate how tired he really was. With luck he would sleep well again that night, knowing he did not have to rise and clean a load of dirty boots before waiting table on the indolent who had risen some considerable time after he had.

He had been gone only a year, but what a difference those twelve months had made. He had seen wealth, true wealth, in all its opulence and waste, had seen London twice, been made aware of the levels of poverty and riches, had been with people who professed to be part of the true faith but who were negligent and even indolent about their attendance at church and the daily offices. The contrasts bothered him. It was as if the whole rotten system needed to be rooted out and burned in some way, so equality could be brought in for all men. Why should some own more land than others, why should some have more money than others? Why should some children starve and freeze whilst others grew fat and lived in warmth? He wondered whether others had thought these thoughts and if they did, how he could find them and talk with them so he would know he was not alone in what he thought of as his strangeness.

The year away had done something else. Despite his mother's happiness at his return and his sisters' obvious joy at his being there, he did not feel welcome; he felt more of a stranger than he had anticipated. Somehow, during his time away, something had changed.

He stood, feeling the worries slowly drain out of him. It could wait; all of it could wait. He had one thing he wanted to do, something he had wanted to do from the moment he climbed in the coach at Midhurst.

The oak tree awaited him. Not the one he was used to, not his old friend with the special branch which had angled itself just right for his slender body, but a welcoming one for all that. With agile movements he swung himself up into the branches, found a comfortable one and leaned back against the ancient trunk. There he could sit and listen to the secret language of the leaves, just as he had done when he was a boy. Now he was older, he might even begin to understand what they were talking about.

Sunshine. Green growing things. In the darkness these things did not exist, in the darkness it was hard to remember that they really did exist somewhere outside the walls. To believe that out there were people who did not know what went on inside or if they did, they had no thought of what it really meant. Of the brutality of men to men. Of screaming agony in every part of his body. Of the madness it brought to the mind. Of the loneliness ... oh blessed Virgin, the loneliness!

Home was good – for a while. There was a strange novelty in experiencing the old as if it were new, re-acquainting himself with his mother's way of running a house, the different but same mealtimes, the different but same meals, the new/old garden and fields where he could walk for hours and let his thoughts tip-tumble round his mind, squirrel-like, leaping from item to item as the squirrel leaps from branch to branch. He spent time re-learning his wildlife skills, remaining still enough to watch the small animals go about their lives and the larger animals using them as a living food supply. Once again the mystery, the sheer majesty and perfection of the entire ecological system enthralled him and he wondered how he could have shut himself away in stone walls for so long without contacting the very essence of life, nature itself.

In this almost surreal half-life, not quite feeling he belonged and yet knowing he did, Guy tried to settle down. He took on a small tutoring job with a local land-owner, attempting to teach basic Latin and English grammar to two young boys. It brought in a little money to add to the rent being paid on the land he had inherited, enough to help him buy some decent clothes and have his own horse. He drifted through the days, doing his work, helping out around the Hall, putting some fields under crop so there was a harvest at the end of the summer to help with his family's finances, but there was a sense of disconnection that he could not overcome. His family had made him welcome but he did not feel he should be there. The constant restrictions on Catholics bothered him; he longed for freedom to express his faith in the way he wanted, not the way the church or the state wanted him to. Repression of Catholics was still going on, recusants were fined or imprisoned or both and this angered him, the more so because there was nothing he could do about it. Not by himself, not one man against the system. Nothing had changed. Queen Elizabeth's anti Catholic stance had been taken on by her chosen heir, King James, and the executions and the restrictions had not eased at all. He had refrained from attending church very often but wondered when the authorities would realise he was back and his lack of attendance noticed. It was not right to live in such fear when all he wanted to do was practice a faith slightly different from that dictated by the authorities.

There came times when the rebellion inside was too much for him to handle. Then he took long solitary walks or rides, looking for days when he could be alone, days when he could take the time to contemplate his place in the world, his connection with his God and the Blessed Virgin and to ask himself what service he could give to both her and her Son. Finally the conviction settled into his mind that he had to fight in some way for the true faith against those who opposed it. If only he could go back to the time of the Crusades, so he could join the brave ones who rode out against the infidel! They were long gone, though, and it was probably as well, they were dangerous times and he would have been at risk from the moment he left England. Not that it was guaranteed safe even now, but it was better than those savage times.

There had to be another way, another path he could take to fight for his God and all he believed in.

He thought of the letter of introduction he had which would take him into the army and perhaps teach him some skills he could make use of. He had very little in the way of knowledge and skill that he could use, he could impart formal teaching but he could not progress the cause of Catholicism through his own efforts.

He had no idea if this was his next pathway, whether it was right for him, but without trying it as a way of life, he could not find out. Something, a voice, an impression, an urging, was saying this was the way forward, that once again he had to leave the security of home and move out into the world, find out what was going on and where he fitted into God's scheme. It was on one of his solitary walks, when he was turning these thoughts over yet again, a sudden illumination flashed through his mind, almost a statement.

He had to find out where he fitted in God's scheme, even if it cost him his life.

That thought stopped him in his tracks by a small creek. He stood so still that small animals carried on their lives, rustling close by his feet. Was he prepared to give up his life for what he saw as the cause?

Sunshine sparkled on the surface of the creek, sending shards of light into his eyes. In them he seemed to see the answer he sought and he knew it well, in the depths of his heart he knew the answer.

Yes, he would. Where and how and when were in the hands of God and His angels. He just knew, somehow, he would have to give up his life in some way. How that would affect his mother and sisters he had no idea, but knew that he could not let family ties get in the way of what he had to do. He took a step forward and felt as if he had crossed his own personal Rubicon.

Decision taken. *'Lord God, I am yours. Use me as you will.'*

The words were not said out loud but they were said clearly in his mind. The answer came in a feeling of great peace, of being surrounded by angelic wings and sounds, lilting music, touches of feather-light beauty and incredible sensitivity, with fantastic colours flashing before his eyes. It lasted a fraction of a second but it endured for a lifetime. He knew he would never forget the feeling.

He spent the rest of the day sitting by the creek, allowing himself to slide into a fugue that was almost a meditation, simply letting his mind travel free of his earthly body. The sun was warm on his face and hands, comforting in its gentle rays. The small animals scampered around and over him as he sat, unmoving, watching, wondering. Only when the sun began to leave the sky did he rouse himself, with difficulty, and begin the walk home, stiff limbed and aching physically but calm and determined emotionally. Everything was clear. Everything was set out for him. All he had to do was walk the pathway the Lord God would lay out for him. A journey he would take one step at a time. A journey that would end where God dictated it would, not where he wanted it to end. A journey meant ridding himself of encumbrances, he wanted no ties – other than filial ones – to hold him in place. If God wanted to use him, he had to be free to go where God wanted him to go and do the work God wanted him to do. He would start by getting rid of the land. He had no need of it and the money would be useful. His family would not like that, he knew it, but he also knew he had to stand firm and do what he had decided was right for him, not for them.

One morning he took a coach to York, having decided to see how he felt being amongst a lot of people again. Planning and considering a new life whilst living and walking in comparative isolation was one thing, keeping a level head and the same thoughts when surrounded by the activity and bustle of city life was another, or so he reasoned. He told his mother he wanted to visit York and walk the familiar streets, saying nothing about his inner turmoil. She accepted that and gave him a few letters to deliver to old friends, an errand he was content to do for her.

York was bustling, full of life and colour. In many ways it resembled London in its crowded streets and air of general busyness and felt more frenetic than it had when he last visited. He thought there were more people, more carriages and coaches, more bustle and hurry and a greater sense of money-making going on. The great Minster towered over everything as it always had done, calm, serene and alien all at the same time. It cast a great shadow over the streets and houses around it. Guy paused at the doorway, glanced in at the coolness, wondered at the hidden depths of it and then turned away. It was not for him.

He walked down High Petergate and found that his old home had been neglected somewhat, the door could have done with a fresh coat of stain and the lock and knocker needed polishing. His mother would never have let it get like that, he mused. The windows were dirty and as for the doorstep... It was obvious others did not have her standards. When he stood back to look and realised some slates had slipped and one was missing near the ridge tiles, he turned and walked away with a determined step. That made two places he would not revisit and he had only been in the City for an hour. He delivered the letters and then found himself at a loose end, unsure, undecided about staying or leaving. Why can't I make up my mind? I am as indecisive here as I was in London, wanting to stay, wanting to go. Always there is something pulling me in another direction to the one I intended to follow. What's wrong with me?

He noticed some of the younger women he passed were giving him friendly smiles and he half smiled back, not wanting to appear off hand but not wanting to encourage them, either. He had enough on his mind.

The inn he was passing looked reasonably inviting, he decided to get a drink and allow some of his impressions to sink in before going out and seeing more. The place was crowded but he found a stool at the end of the bar where he could watch everyone without it being too obvious. There were a couple of women at the counter with their arms around the necks of men who were obviously drunk. One winked at Guy but he did not respond. She pulled a face at him and he ignored her. She looked reasonably young and pretty but she made no impression on him at all. She left the man she had been embracing and walked over to Guy. Up close he could see she was not as young as he had thought, but then, they never were. Her face was painted, that offended him but she was not to know that. Her perfume did little to cover up her body odour, which was even more offensive. Her eyes told of experience and avarice.

"Want a good time, handsome?"

"No thank you. I am waiting on an acquaintance, when he arrives I must of necessity be gone."

"Fair enough. Remember me if you come into York again, won't you? Not often we sees someone as good-looking as you. I'm always here if you want me."

She went back to the man who was calling her, much to Guy's relief. He wanted nothing to do with such women.

A group of men pushed their way in, laughing and fooling around, calling each other by silly names. The camaraderie was strong and for a moment Guy was stung by what he realised was jealousy. That kind of friendship was missing from his life. Not since schooldays had he been able to jostle and play-fight with others, use comic names and half insults, to become part of the group, not feel he was standing on the outside looking in. In a house mostly dominated by women, there was no opportunity for such a thing. His father, remembered fondly even after all these years, had been a distant figure. His word had been law, his presence something to tiptoe around. There never had been a sense that he could have indulged in any kind of light-hearted nonsense with him. Dennis was a softer person but even he seemed to keep his distance. There was little humour there, more acceptance than true affection which was a flimsy foundation for a relationship. Sometimes Guy felt as if Dennis was a stranger to him, despite their being both part of the one Faith and sharing common ideals as far as that was concerned.

Even at Cowdray House there had been no chance of friendships of that kind, because everyone seemed to keep their distance from each other, he had not felt like an outsider but equally, he had made no friends. They had been like strangers to one another, no matter how many years' service they had put in. Listening to the banter and laughter of these men, Guy thought that it had been a long time since he had laughed, truly laughed at something. His life had been far too serious in every way.

Where could he go? Seriously, what could he do? Yorkshire, although home, had little to offer in the way of worthwhile employment and there was still no chance to be free to practice his faith. Always there was the sense of being watched, noted, the authorities biding their time before they leapt on anyone not obeying the laws of the land. He did not want to be a recusant but he did not want to worship in a Protestant church, either. He went, under protest from his own conscience, just to keep the record straight as far as he was concerned. But he hated it, hated being made to do something that was so obviously – to him – wrong in every way.

One thought continued to bother him. Staying in Scotton meant a possible resurgence of the nonsensical Pulleyne claim that he had fathered a child and he had no way of disproving it. It was her word against his, whoever the girl was. How many times did people listen to the woman, not the man? He would be better off gone. He had a reputation to preserve and he would not allow anyone to sully it. A child? What did he want with a puling brat pulling at his heartstrings and purse? What sort of tie did that constitute? One that lasted a lifetime, either his or the child's. I would not have been a good father, he told himself as he thought over his mother's pleas to stay. He knew she longed for him to marry and give her a grandchild, but his sisters would be doing that soon enough, they were pretty in a flirty mass-of-curls way and had suitors calling at all times to take them 'for a walk'. It would not be long before they were wed and presenting newborns to the world. He did not feel the need to add to the population.

Would the Army give him the kind of friendship he had just seen, or was he doomed to spend his life always on the outside, looking in?

Whatever God wanted, he thought, draining his tankard. But even God needed a little help at times. Nothing would be gained or learned by sitting in an inn and thinking. He needed to approach a recruiting sergeant or someone and talk to them about an army career. He was twenty-three years old and felt he was overdue to make a serious change to his life. He had the letter of introduction. It was time he used it.

A quiet word with the landlord directed him to a doorway in a small dark alleyway. He went in and was confronted by Army, in a way that surprised and in some ways pleased him. The recruitment officer took the letter, perused it, looked Guy up and down and said 'yes.' Guy didn't even ask about pay and conditions of service, how long to sign up for, nothing. He was swept along in the whole ethos of the office, the smartness of the officer, the efficient way everything was dealt with, name, address, age, previous occupation, religion, next of kin, sign here and it was done. In a very short time a clerk had produced passes for him to travel to the coast, a ship was leaving for Flanders in a week and they wanted him to be on it.

"Go and say goodbye to the family," he was told. "You have two days to pack everything up. Four days travel to London, one to the coast and the ship to Flanders. From there on out you're in the Army and go where we tell you. And good luck!"

Head reeling, he had gone home to do just that. His mother met him at the door, ostensibly to ask if he had posted her letters but more than that, to find out how he got on in York. They stood in the hall, both knowing that something had happened on the visit to York.

"I joined the army, Mother," he told her straight out, not wanting to conceal anything from her. He saw her face drop and her eyes fill with tears and was glad he had signed up before going home, it would have been far more difficult, she would have found a hundred reasons for him not to go without even thinking about it. 'I joined the army' was a deal done. Nothing could be undone. "I'm going to Europe very soon."

"Why?"

"There is nothing here for me. I want to be free of the restrictions of being a Catholic, I want to fight for that which is right – God's will. Truly I want to be away from here. That Pulleyne nonsense might come back to haunt me and how can I prove I am not the father of her child?"

She turned and went into the parlour, sitting down on the settle and staring into the empty hearth as if it held the answer to all her questions. Guy followed her and stood by her side.

"I don't want you to go," she said finally, with a tremendous effort.

"I want to go, Mother, because my task is to be a warrior for God and His cause. I go for no other reason than that."

"You go because we are not enough for you anymore."

He knelt down beside her and put his hands on hers. "Don't think that, not for a moment! I have loved being home with you all but I need to look to my future. I cannot fight for God here, where the laws are so restricting the only way to rebel is to be arrested and perhaps executed. Would you want that? Of course not. So I need to go where people are fighting, where I will have a career, where I will be my own man. I don't wish to be subservient to rich people ever again. I had a year of it and that was enough for anyone, especially token Catholics, as they were!"

"Guy, you came back bitter and hurt from that place, but there are other houses, other families..."

"Not for me, Mother, not for me. Now, let me go and talk with Father and arrange things as best I can. I have all of today and all of tomorrow before I have to go. Don't spoil them with entreaties and tears. I signed the papers, I'm committed to go. Let's make the most of the time we have left." She nodded but her tears flowed and as he reached the door she began to sob.

Dennis looked solemn when he told him, as they walked in the garden in the cool breeze bringing the scent of honeysuckle and thyme to them. "You need to do what is best for you, Guy, but your mother will be distressed at your leaving again." *Not you, Guy noted. Not you. I am always the intruder here, getting between Mother and you. I understand that.*

"I know, but I have to go and fight, I can't stay here with the laws and the authorities and the lack of work. All these things have combined to make me see I need to go elsewhere and make a living."

"You're right, of course, about the Pulleyne thing, if you were to get a job, that girl would be on to you straight away," Dennis remarked as if it were a casual comment. "I'm surprised she's not been round here already demanding money. That tells me it isn't an honest claim, she would have come before now if it was."

It wasn't as casual a comment as it seemed on the surface. It told Guy that his stepfather still held a sneaking suspicion that it was true, that he had in fact fathered the child and absconded from his responsibilities. That hurt and was yet another spur to his determination to leave.

Parting from his family would be hard. His mother continued to use the emotional blackmail that he had not that long come back from Sussex, that she had got used to him being around and here he was, leaving again. That was not true, he told her, he had been home for a long time before the restless part of him wanted to be gone, to seek new lands, new places and new challenges. But, knowing how the days slipped by, he thought she would be surprised to know it had been almost two years since he returned.

His sisters cried and clung to him when he told them he was leaving but he knew well that he could not allow feminine ties to hold him where he was not happy. In the silence and quietness of his room, he asked God in prayer whether he would ever be truly happy and had no answer. Maybe there was no answer to that question, maybe it was something he had to find out for himself.

He walked around the estate, ate meals, spent some time in his tree, communing with the leaves as he had always done, with a sense of saying goodbye to it all. It was infinitely sad, yet exciting. A new career, a better one than he had been offered before, was on the horizon, it made him anxious to be gone but time was dragging its heels in the dust and every day felt like a week.

The night before he was due to leave he checked through his belongings, deciding what to take and what not to take. He counted his money, put some to one side to take with him and concealed the rest. He did not want to entrust it to his mother who, if times were hard, would be sure to spend it and he would come back to nothing. A loose board covered a small hollowed out space which was sufficient to take a small store of gold coins. Once it had held his boy-treasures, a blown egg, a special stone taken from the creek, a key which fitted nothing he ever discovered but he had lived in hope that one day he would find the right lock for it and his father's ring which his mother had given him, still wet with her tears. That was still in the space, he did not dare take that to Europe with him. It would not be right. It belonged here, in the house, even if he never came back to claim it again. He had no illusions about the dangers of Army life, anything could happen and probably would.

On the morning he left to get the coach into York he had to fight to disentangle his mother's arms from around his neck. She was sobbing and clinging with all her strength and he had to get Dennis to help him. "Come on, Mother, you weren't like this when I went to Midhurst!" He said it as gently as he could.

"You're going overseas, you're going where there's fighting, you're ..." she broke down again and Dennis led her away, back into the house, not stopping to shake hands with Guy, just shaking his head and mouthing "goodbye!" over her head. It was all he could do. Guy walked swiftly away, carrying a small bag, anxious to be gone.

In a repeat of his earlier journey, he took the coach to London, a journey as arduous as it had been the first time, and from there he went to Dover, where he boarded a ship for Flanders. Everything had been arranged for him, it all went smoothly, no one questioned his papers or his right to be there, to board the ship, to leave England and all he held dear. He almost felt as if someone should stop him, to tell him what he was doing was illegal, he could not leave, but no one did.

York felt a million miles away from the busy sea port, the many ships which were docked there, the strange accents and different coloured people he saw made it seem 'foreign' even before he left. Doing something as strange as going on board a sailing ship just added to the sensation of being in a different world. Guy thought he could not get enough of looking at everything, the gulls, the great tall masted ships, the goods being brought ashore or carried on board.

The ship sailed early on a bright clear day, with virtually no movement, just gentle waves slapping against the hull. The water seemed serenely blue but almost immediately the sea began to change, to look darker and fast running currents showed themselves, whilst the skies remained clear. Guy stood at the rail and watched, fascinated, as the colours and the surface of the sea changed seemingly moment by moment. The seasoned sailors manning the ship spoke of a storm to come although there was no apparent concern among any of them.

During the afternoon the Channel became a morass, no other word for it, of excited waves all intent on crashing into one another and then into the ship which tossed and turned under their impact. The ship dipped and rose, rose and dipped, seeming to swing end to end although that was possibly an illusion brought about by the fact he could not see the horizon in either direction. For all he knew they could have been on the sea for days and not made landfall. Logically he knew this was nonsense but logic had a habit of disappearing into the tumbling waves when all you had experienced was the closeness of the water and the ignoble reaction of his stomach to the tossing and turning vessel. He vomited again and again and told himself to stop thinking foolish thoughts. It didn't help.

Another wave crashed on the deck and cascaded over his boots. He hadn't bothered to try and evade it, he was already soaked through from the spray but it was better than being below decks, not seeing what was happening, just sensing the violent dips and thrusts of the small ship fighting its way through large waves.

He clung to the rail and wondered if he would see Europe at all, or whether he and the other soldiers who had embarked with him would end their days beneath this turbulent grey hungry water instead. No, God had greater plans for him than that, he was sure of it. He just had to get through the dreadful voyage that already felt as if it had lasted half his lifetime but was in truth no more than part of a day. Eventually he made his slow painful way below decks, knocking his elbows, knees and even his head at one point as the ship rolled and he fought for footing. He fell into his bunk and almost immediately fell asleep, worn out by the tensions of keeping upright and vomiting endlessly.

Somewhere in the night he was rudely woken from sleep by being tossed from his bunk onto the floor of his cabin, narrowly missing his fellow traveller who had also been unceremoniously thrown out. They scrambled back onto their bunks where they held on for dear life. The ship was rolling heavily; the promised storm had arrived with a vengeance. Overhead he heard pounding feet and shouted orders, accompanied by ropes creaking as sails were brought down as fast as possible. Guy was no sailor; he could not make sense of the commands and had to trust the captain and crew to see them safely through this turbulence.

He lay flat on his bunk in the darkness, tensing himself against another surge that would tip him out again but that seemed to have been a particularly bad wave as it didn't happen although the ship continued to roll. He muttered prayers to the Blessed Virgin for a safe voyage; he really did not wish his new career to end with the ship and everyone on it capsizing this close to home. It came as a shock to him to realise he had never learned to swim.

His companion, a bearded taciturn man about twice his age whom he had seen earlier, reached out for the lantern swinging overhead, then produced a flint and tinder box and lit the small wick. The cabin leapt into view, narrow bunks, weather-stained boards and worn planking smelling of salt, sweat and ale for some reason. The ship was far from new. Guy was aware the man was watching him as he recited his prayers and crossed himself. His travelling companion had not spoken once since he had come on board; he had stowed his bag and gone back up on deck. Guy had stood a little distance from him as England was left behind in the wake of the ship. The other soldiers sailing to Flanders had not chosen to come up on deck.

After a meal of salted pork, potatoes and hard biscuits, the two men had not seen one another until Guy returned to the cabin and they laid on their bunks, silent and apart. That was, until the storm hit and threw them, literally, into each other's company.

"Catholic, friend?" the man asked when Guy lapsed into silence.

"Yes."

"Good man. Me too. Leaving that Protestant hell-hole?"

"New career, actually. I just joined the army."

"Even better. Soldier for the faith. We can do with them."

There was a gruff friendliness beneath the somewhat abrupt sentences. Guy reached across the space between the bunks and shook hands with his companion.

"Guy Fawkes, newly enrolled soldier, late of Yorkshire."

"Edwin Thomas, merchant, late of Lancashire."

With the courtesies disposed of, the two men lay in comfortable silence, listening to the sounds of the ship as she cut through the waves with a heavy rolling gait, an elderly overweight lady struggling against the elements. More shouts, more orders, then the sound of something shifting overhead had them both look up at the cabin roof at the same time. Edwin laughed.

"Foolish, aren't we? We can't see through wood!"

"Tis natural we try to see, though."

"Of course. Foolish all the same. Where are you bound, Mr Fawkes?"

"Flanders, to take up my duties and learn my new trade."

"I wish you well. I have business in the Netherlands."

"What do you deal in, Mr. Thomas?"

"Wool, silk, all manner of materials needed to clothe people."

"A useful merchant, then."

"All merchants are useful, in their way."

Guy pondered that for a moment. "I had not thought it to be thus," he confessed after a short silence. "My father was Proctor at York Minster, whilst my stepfather – does nothing but live from rents and investments. I thought little of how the goods we use arrived."

"Few do. Think nothing of it. Many of us travel across to buy. We arrange shipment back. It is a living, of a kind."

"But my foolishness, why did I not think how the goods came to be in England? It is as if I have been blinkered."

Edwin laughed a short bark that was harsh to the ears.

"You are a young man, Mr Fawkes. I would say you are newly out into the world."

"I am. I worked for Lord Montague in his great home as footman for a year, but – came away from that employment."

The hesitation was not lost on Edwin Thomas. "I take it the Lord of the Manor did not care for you."

"No."

"Happens. Not subservient enough for him?"

A good enough supposition, thought Guy, being unwilling to reveal the true cause of his dismissal.

"I thought I was, but-"

"No, Mr Fawkes. There is a core of iron within you. One I detect. It says 'I bow willingly to no man.' I would say this. You bow willingly to the altar of God and His Blessed Lady, no other."

Guy was astonished, he did not think he could be that easily read. This must have shown on his face for the man laughed that short bark again.

"Mr Fawkes, you reveal much with your look. You have not learned yet to dissimulate. It is a good thing to learn. Conceal your thoughts. Show a blank face to the world. Let no man see your inner turmoil. Control the muscles. Allow no smile to come if it is not meant. Allow no frown to form if it misleads. Speak only when you must."

This was sensible advice and Guy stored it to think about later.

The sea appeared to quieten; the storm had obviously abated. There was less noise from the crew and the sound of creaking timbers could be heard, rhythmic and almost comforting. Guy was no sailor though, he knew he would be much happier when his boots were resting on solid earth again, no matter who the earth belonged to.

The lantern flickered and went out. Edwin Thomas spoke through the darkness.

"I trust I did not offend. I did not intend such."

"No, Mr Thomas, you did not offend. My apologies, I thought your words more than passing wise and was dwelling on them as I lay here. And on the fact I am no sailor and will be content when I am on dry land again."

There was a chuckle from the other bunk and then a companionable quiet between them. In the silence Guy found a degree of peace he did not expect. His nerves had been drawn taut by all the new experiences he had been through in the last few days: his enrolment, his new clothes, his new status in life and finally going on board ship for the first time, heading for a strange land.

Finally he slept, his sleep tormented by bizarre dreams of York, Scotton, Cowdray House and Edwin Thomas somehow all mixed up together in the strangest way, none of which he truly recalled when he woke.

Morning found the ship all but becalmed as the wind had dropped completely. Their progress was minimal. After a breakfast that resembled the meal the night before in every respect, Guy walked on deck, looking out at the smooth surface of the sea, wondering how it could change so completely. Edwin Thomas was leaning on the rail, contemplating the cold murky water.

"I was wondering," Guy began hesitantly. He wasn't at all sure of his standing with his companion and the question might have seemed a bit personal. "I was wondering why you went to Europe to buy everything yourself, rather than send someone else. Then you could stay home in comfort."

"I want quality." Edwin looked round at Guy and grinned through the beard. "You are still young, Mr. Fawkes. You will learn. There are times when 'tis best do it yourself. Leave it to others, it goes wrong. I know what I want. Another would not. I discard the not so good and buy the good. My customers rely on me."

Guy smiled at his acquaintance. "Once again you offer me great wisdom, Mr. Thomas. Right glad I am that you were on board this ship this journey."

"I am right glad to have been of use, Mr Fawkes."

The faintest smudge of darkness on the horizon showed they were approaching land. Edwin Thomas sighed and turned away. "I need to be sure I have everything. We make landfall in a few hours. Then my work begins."

"Mine too, I believe." Guy looked again at the horizon. "I think I will stand here a while longer."

"I trust I will speak to you before we disembark." Edwin Thomas walked away without another word, or a look back. Guy thought about that, too. A man who knew when to speak and when not to speak was rare; a man who said so much in a few words was even more rare, in his mind. He thought he would try it, make it part of his personality if he could. Speak little, listen much. Try not to show feelings by his expression. It seemed a tall order but with practice he thought he could do it.

A group of fellow soldiers spilled onto the deck, cheering when they realised the voyage was soon to be over. One, a tall bearded man with massive chest and arms, walked over to Guy and put a friendly arm around his shoulders. "Nearly there, nearly ready to take up arms and fight the infidel, or whoever we're sent to fight."

Guy smiled and said nothing.

"Got to get to our lodgings, then we can go out on the town. A break before we start training. Want to come?"

"Where?"

"Oh, a few inns, then on to a brothel or two."

"Not I, thank you."

The man stared at Guy with disbelief. "Young man like you not heading for the drink and women? What's wrong with you?"

"Nothing. It's not for me, that's all."

"You one of those devout believers, or something?"

"More or less."

"Your loss."

The soldier walked away, obviously disappointed. Guy considered his feelings. He had joined the army in the hope of finding some like-minded people to be friendly with, to feel part of something for once in his life, but drink and women – no. That was not for him. The occasional tankard of ale was about his limit. Anything else he considered beyond what he should do.

He realised he had put his new-found resolution into practice immediately. He had spoken fewer words to the young soldier than he had to his travelling companion. He had not confessed to being devout, he had not explained why he did not want to carouse and fraternise with women, he had simply quietly refused.

It felt good. It was strange to admit it to himself, but it felt good. Now all he had to do was learn to control his expression and his meeting with Edwin Thomas would be of tremendous benefit to him. He knew he would never forget the man who had said so much in so few words.

Chapter Nine

The journey across the Channel soon became nothing more than an unpleasant memory as Guy became absorbed in his new life.

Flanders was flat, torn by winds, tormented by rains which had nothing to stop them sweeping across the seemingly barren countryside, leaving in their wake a mass of new vegetation and bright flowers. The men, the soldiers from the ship and Guy, marched through this flat countryside under the supervision of a captain. He did not allow much time to rest, and although Guy was well able to keep up with the steady fast pace, he noticed that some of the other younger soldiers had difficulty and were falling back to the rear of the column. He wondered if he should go to their assistance, then decided that it would not be a good thing to do, as each man had to find his own pace and his own strength if he was to fight. The captain noticed this lack of stamina on the part of some of the men, and declared a halt. They were allowed to rest for half an hour or so on the side of the road, and then they were ordered back on their feet and marching on yet again.

After what seemed an eternity, with Guy's awareness of his sore feet, they reached the Army training post. They were shown their barracks, Spartan in the extreme, nothing more than a row of narrow beds and nowhere to store possessions. Each of the soldiers claimed a bed, leaving Guy to sort out one for himself. Already he was an outsider, and he had not been with them very long. There was a disappointment in this, but he had half anticipated it and the disappointment was not as deep as it would have been otherwise. A bed in the far corner had been left unclaimed, he made his way toward it and sat down. The young man sitting on the next bed looked at him. Then he held out his hand.

"Stoneley.

Guy shook hands with him. "Fawkes."

"You kept up pretty well with the walk Fawkes, have you been in the Army long?"

"This is my first time," said Guy. "But I do a lot of walking when I am at home in Yorkshire."

Another of the soldiers came over. "Miller." He too shook hands with Guy. "You seem like one of the tough ones, perhaps you can give us a hint or two."

"Well, the only thing I can say is I spent a year as a footman in the home of an aristocrat." Guy smiled. "Being on my feet from dawn to dusk, rushing around a very large home, doing this errand and that, opening the door and that, serving meals and then rushing away again, was very good exercise."

Stoneley looked at him in astonishment. "You don't seem to be the type of person to be a footman, Fawkes!"

"What sort of type is a footman?"

"More... servile... or something like that."

"Perhaps that's why I lost the job." Guy laughed with a touch of bitterness. "I could not be as subservient as they wanted, perhaps."

Miller grinned at him. He was a cheerful looking young man, with a round ruddy face and a head of ginger hair.

"It seems to me that you did not have a very good time then, Fawkes," he said. "Is that why you have chosen to try the army?"

Guy noticed that the other young men were listening intently to the conversation. He looked at them, wondering how long it would be before he learned all their names and all their likes and dislikes, and whether they would become friends, before he looked back at Miller.

"No I didn't have a good time. I found them to be not very good Catholics, they scorned the poor and the menial, they paid mere lip service to the tenets of the Gospels, and all in all it was a most unpleasant experience. But that is not the reason I am trying the Army. I came here because I wish to fight for my faith."

A most surprising thing happened then. Every one of the young soldiers began to applaud. This shocked and surprised Guy, who did not expect that reaction. One of the other men came over and stood by Miller. "I heard what you said." he looked at Guy intently. "You meant every word of it, didn't you, Fawkes? Like the rest of us you are tired of the restrictions on the Catholics in England, like the rest of us you want to fight on behalf of the true faith, and here is the only place we can be free."

Guy was overcome. If he had nursed any doubts whatsoever about coming to the continent, they had been washed away in the applause and the approbation of his fellow soldiers. For the first time in what seemed like an age he felt as if he had come home. It was a wonderful feeling.

Sir William Stanley was a tall, heavily built man with a dark chin and face as if he never shaved close enough to rid himself of the incipient beard. His eyes were dark and missed absolutely nothing. His mouth was downturned except when he laughed, which was rare. He took his soldiering and his command of the rank novice soldiers very seriously.

The first morning they gathered to hear him speak he read them his usual patriotic lecture, that they were fighting the forces of evil – for which everyone read Protestantism – and upholding the good, Catholicism. He lived his words. This soldier had been knighted for his services in Ireland for his queen, and served under Leicester, the queen's favourite, in the Netherlands. This he told them in complete honesty, he fought for the Protestant queen because at the time it had felt right to him. But he later surrendered the fortress he was manning and told everyone he was changing sides – and religion.

This brought a cheer from the novices. Guy suspected it did every time he gave the speech, it was just the right note to strike for new arrivals who were still a little uncertain of themselves, why they were there, what they were doing. To know their commanding officer had been through a change of heart, as Guy had, and possibly some of the others too, made all the difference. This was a man they could follow into any conflict and be proud to do so. Guy mentally stood back and assessed the cleverness of the speech and the effect it had. He had to admit it had reached him, although he needed no persuasion to know he had done the right thing.

Hugh Owen, Sir William's right hand man, made no secret of the fact they were both enemies of the English parliament, in parliament's view and their own. These were the men who would lead the campaign to support the claim of Archduchess Isabella, among others, to a more rightful role in the Catholic hierarchy and in government.

And then training began. They learned to fire cannon, to handle firearms, to fight with sword and dagger, to use explosives to lay charges and disrupt the enemy. It was intensive work and tiring, night after night they collapsed on their narrow beds and slept as if dead, being roused next morning to go on marches, to learn to track and ambush, to use every advantage to disrupt the enemy and score major advances for themselves.

Those who could not ride were taught until they were as proficient on horseback as any of the other men in the force. Guy enjoyed the riding, enjoyed the closeness of the contact with an animal who did his bidding so quickly and easily. It added to his skills, which was what he sought more than anything.

It seemed Sir William had a special liking for Guy, he made him an ensign fairly soon after he arrived and put him in charge of a small group. The other men didn't seem to mind Guy being promoted over them, they accepted his calculating logical mind and, although they professed disappointment that he would not go drinking and carousing with them, they respected his piety and his decision to stay alone when they went into the town to find drink and women, not necessarily in that order, as Miller said one night as they were leaving.

Guy watched them leave with only a small ache in his heart, not because he wanted either the drink or the women, but because he would have liked to be a part of a group which was friendly and somewhere he felt he might belong. But he consoled himself with the thought that they were a group when they were together, training, and that was sufficient for him.

He just wished he could believe it.

There was a good deal to think about on a daily basis. There was the novelty of being in another land, where English was spoken by some but not as a first language. The smattering of 'foreign' words soon became second nature and he began to learn more Spanish from the mercenaries who were training and working alongside him. There were duties to be learned, as well as the various ranks and the respect due to each one. That came easy to Guy, having worked at Cowdray House he had some idea of the hierarchy of the aristocracy. It just meant applying it to the ranks in the Army. As a mere foot soldier, he had a lot of walking to do, which strengthened him and the training with firearms and cannon helped broaden his chest and develop the muscles in his arms.

He was intrigued with the whole subject of explosives. The calculations of fuse to quantity, the delay to allow the person setting the fuse to get away from the resulting explosion, the way gunpowder had to be handled and stored, for fear of it decaying, all of this challenged his mind and he found he could absorb it as easily as he was absorbing the languages he heard daily.

New arrivals were coming in all the time. One of them made a determined effort to seek Guy out and introduced himself as his cousin Richard Collinge. Guy had heard much about this cousin from his mother, he knew Collinge was a Jesuit, for example, but he had never met him. There was an instant rapport between the two, Collinge having the same ideas on purity and sanctity of body and mind as Guy did. His cousin was slender and ascetic in his appearance and clipped in his speech, as if it was an effort for him to communicate. But once started on the fight for Catholicism and his whole being changed to one of the committed patriotic martyr. Guy was afraid for him, for a little nervousness helped in times of danger.

Training occupied many hours and although he didn't socialise with the rest of the group, he liked many of his associates. This combined with the freedom to practice his faith was everything; it made him realise just how restricted Catholics were in Protestant England. The cause was just and the fight ordained by God, surely it was, for the commanders were there and the men were there and, it seemed, the arms and ammunition they needed was in plentiful supply.

Sir William Stanley was a man with principles, someone who had offended the government of England, someone who wanted to fight for the Catholic cause the right way, with arms, in pitched battles. Guy felt completely secure under his command and soon began to take on the mentality of a soldier, obeying orders without thought which meant instant action, instead of delays whilst it was thought through. He and Richard Collinge spoke often of home but not in a way that brought on a nostalgic longing to return, more of the fact that they could not openly practice their faith under English law and how they both resented that fact. At least, he was not homesick when he spoke with his cousin. That seemed to come over him when he was alone and had time to think. For that reason his promotion to Ensign pleased him very much. It seemed his commanding officer had noted that Guy did not follow the others into town to get drunk and began to entrust him with tasks. Guy was proud of his new rank and more than willing to do other work, it kept him busy. Thinking, he had found, caused him a degree of heartache if he indulged in it too long. He would find waves of homesickness sweeping over him, for his family, for the comfort of the Yorkshire countryside, for time to sit and watch the wildlife go about its daily fight for survival against all the odds. How strange that when he had that time, he had become restless and unhappy, wanting to be somewhere else, experience new things, see new places.

Guy realised that he needed to belong, to be accepted and being promoted certainly made him feel much more secure in his new career. It was odd that his insistence on not being part of the 'good time' group set him apart from his fellow soldiers but was the very thing which had caught the attention of his superior officers and gained him early promotion. Life was indeed full of the strangest contradictions imaginable.

For all that he had no real friends, life was good. He had contacts through the Catholic network and was able to send a little money home to his family and news of his career which he knew would please them, especially his mother, who had been unhappy at his choice. He needed her to know it was right, that her son was content to be a fighting man and to be where he could really serve. Somehow the position of footman, prestigious though it might have been, had not been what he thought of as real service. Now he had meaning to his life.

The Spaniards he trained with called him Guido, which he quite liked. It made him sound at first different and then later part of the group. All their names seemed to end in an 'o': he made friends with Antonio, Pedro, Ignacio and others with similar sounding names. He began to speak Spanish easily and wondered why he had never tried before to learn another language, apart from Latin.

'I am known here as Guido,' he wrote to his mother in one of his irregular letters home. 'It seems to fit well with someone who is of one country whilst being a soldier in another. It is obvious to all where the name originates and yet is of Latin origin, too.

'Cousin Richard is well, training and fighting alongside me. He is quick with arms and good with knives and sword. He does well in all the training we have and has leadership qualities which I know have been noted. I think he will be promoted above me ere long. Do please tell his family how well he does. He says he does not have time to write.

'I wish there were easier ways to travel, for I would dear love to take the time and come home to visit just once, so you can see how your son prospers here. I seem to have grown taller, certainly fitter and stronger; I now have powers of endurance which I did not have before. But the crossing is arduous and expensive and I could not take the time from my company or my work here to undertake it at the moment. For now I must of necessity content myself with sending you what I can in the way of monies to help you through and to send you my dear love and the prayers of our Blessed Lady.

'Your loving son, Guido Fawkes.'

He wondered why the signature didn't look wrong to him. Was he already completely absorbed into this new life?

Chapter Ten

In the darkness, in the utter desolation of the darkness, the broken man gave way, at last, to tears. They streamed down his face, soaked his jerkin, put salt into his mouth and burned his eyelids. Racking sobs tore at his chest muscles and created additional pain. But for all the agony the tears caused, he could not stop them. A dam had been breached, whether through the memories or as a result of the unremitting agony he was suffering he did not know. The tears were a release. He welcomed them even as he hated them, viewing them as a sign of weakness. Then he asked himself, even as he cried, did it matter? Who would care? The answer was – no one.

***

There were many different currents underlying the religious politics of Europe. Guy knew it well but was not privy to any of it at any sort of diplomatic level. He was a 'mere' Ensign, albeit one with skills the company relied on. He had become an expert with explosives, his childhood clumsiness having been expunged by his work as a footman. It would not have done to spill anything on the family or their guests, or to smash the delicate plates and bowls. He had learned to be careful and it had paid off. He had a steady hand when it came to setting fuses and an analytical mind when judging how much or how little explosive or fuse to use. He was rarely wrong. At times he defied higher-ranking officers who wanted to dictate how they thought he should do something – albeit he did it politely. They soon learned that this soldier brought a single-minded dedication to everything he did, which was both unusual and praiseworthy. They began to draw him into their discussions on how the war against the Protestant regime should be waged and then asked if he would consider returning to England for a brief visit, to deliver important documents and bring papers and documents back. He agreed, with the proviso he would be permitted to visit his family whilst he was there. That was agreed. It would give the recipients of the papers time to read them thoroughly and compose their replies. For those in charge of his mission and Guy himself, it was a good arrangement.

He left Flanders and made his way across country to Calais, the sea crossing was shorter from there than anywhere else along the coast. He did not want to be at sea longer than he had to be, he wanted to be on the move, either on foot or riding if he could 'borrow' a horse and leave it with someone further along the road. Catholic supporters were more than willing to help out anyone who was fighting for the faith and he often got the chance to ride. But when he had to walk, that was no difficulty for him either, he relished the stretching of his long legs and his stride ate up the miles.

The voyage back to England was considerably less fraught than his voyage out – calm waters and no storm to tip him out of his bunk this time. He stood at the rail watching the coastline of France become smaller, wondering for a moment why he wasn't watching the coastline of England become larger and wondering too about Edwin Thomas, his companion from the earlier journey. Was he was still travelling back and forth, supervising and choosing his own purchases so as not to disappoint his customers? Guy wished for a chance to speak to him again, to thank him for some of the best advice he had ever been given. He had learned that there was so much wisdom in those few words, wisdom that he could make use of, controlling his own words, not speaking of everything that was in his mind. He had learned too not to give away anything with his expression, although that had been harder to do. He knew he had conquered it when he overheard a comment by a friend that 'no one can tell what Guido's thinking, he's so closed up.' That suited him well. His privacy, his innermost thoughts were not for everyone to know. They were between him and his God, as they had always been. That had probably contributed to the trust his superior officers had in him. He was being sent on more and more diplomatic missions, testing the water, as it were, to see if the time was right for an uprising to put the Catholic faith back where it belonged, as the legal religion of England. Yes, he had much to say to Mr Thomas and the chances were he would never see him again to tell him so. A chance meeting, a few words of wisdom and he had a new way of thinking and acting. Few people had such an opportunity, he was glad of it.

The ship docked at Dover with it usual chaotic rush of ropes flying through the air to be tied to different posts, a gangplank being secured, porters rushing on board to help unload and hapless bystanders all but shouldered out of the way. Guy picked up his bag to disembark along with the other passengers and was hit immediately with the dichotomy that he had experienced when he returned home after his year in Sussex. It was familiar and yet strange. He was back among his own people, with a language he had grown up with, but he felt like an outsider – again. He had to stop himself speaking anything but English, had to consciously think about the words before he uttered them, but then decided that was not a bad thing anyway. It fitted with his habit now of speaking few words rather than many. The difficulty he had this time was that he had been away for five years rather than one and those years had been spent in another country where he had learned another language, acquired another name, skills and a rank in the Army, none of which he had anticipated when he left home. It was good, though, he walked among the residents of Dover with a new air of confidence, combined with a new strength of body, too. The life of a soldier was not an easy one and he was lean and fit. He wondered what his mother would make of him when he got there.

That October day was bright and clear, Dover looked freshly washed and gleaming as though it had been cleaned especially for his return. He looked for and noted the coaching inn, but he had a little time before he needed to be in London. He could stroll around for a while, get some food and record some impressions, all before resuming what seemed like an endless journey. He had priorities, his first task was to deliver papers from his commanding officer to several addresses in London and tell the people he would return after a week or so for the answers. Once that was done, he would take a coach to Yorkshire, let his family see he was fit and well and hear news of his Army career, then travel back to London, collect the replies to the papers and return to Europe. It seemed simple enough. What was there in that plan that could disturb him, divert him from his pathway – he frowned. Why was he thinking like that?

No, he was wrong. His first task was to find a church and offer thanks for his safe journey across the water. He knew one thing for certain; he would never be able to board a ship and think nothing of it. Always there was the lingering fear that something would go wrong and the ship would capsize. He still had not learned to swim.

Like it or not, the only place he could go and pray was a Protestant church. He thought the Blessed Virgin would not mind: a church was a church after all. He controlled the strange feeling that he really was a traitor to his faith as he entered the first one he saw.

The simple church was deserted, which was just what he needed. He knelt, crossed himself and launched into his prayers of thanksgiving for his safe arrival. He asked for strength to continue his battle against the heathen Protestant religion, realised what he was saying in a

Protestant church, concluded his prayers and quickly left. No one took any notice of his coming or going, everyone was too busy with their own lives, but he felt as if he had CATHOLIC written clear across his forehead and that someone would demand to know what he was doing leaving a Protestant church. He chided himself for being foolish. There were other things to think of, such as finding a place to eat that did not rock as he stood or sat, nor did it resonate with the sound of waves against wood.

It was gone midday when he finally boarded the coach for London. He knew it was going to be a long time before he got into a proper bed again. Fortunately his training had taught him to sleep anywhere, no matter how hard the terrain. The coach was only half full and he had room to stretch out a little. They had scarcely cleared the outskirts of Dover before he was asleep.

They broke the journey overnight at an inn that was a copy of those he had stayed in when travelling from Yorkshire, the shared room, the watered ale, the hastily prepared breakfasts before the bone weary travellers got back on the coach for London. The journey should have been an easy one but there were problems in changing horses, then an axle appeared to be giving trouble and in all it was late when the coach finally arrived. Most inns appeared to be full and Guy decided not to bother with trying to find a room, not at that late hour. He made his way to an open grassed area and wrapped himself in his cloak to lie down under a tree. Others were doing the same thing but very likely not for the reasons he was. He used his bag as his pillow for security and was asleep before he could even think about where he had to go in the morning.

London was as busy as he remembered, as full as he remembered and as dirty. He washed his face and hands in a small stream, tidied his hair, brushed his clothes free of leaves and dirt and walked into the nearest inn to order a pint of ale and a platter of cheese and bread. His confident stance obviously made up for any lack of attention to his dress and general cleanliness, no one seemed at all bothered by his presence. They took his money and supplied him with food and ale. Once his stomach was full, he made his way on foot to Kensington village to deliver the documents.

It was a pleasant surprise: elegant homes, clean streets, the sound of birds other than the usual London sparrows and crows, made it a most desirable place. He quickly found the address he sought, knocked and was prepared to do no more than hand over the sealed papers and leave. To his great surprise he was invited in and even offered a bed for the night.

The people he had been asked to visit wanted as much news as possible of the mercenaries in Flanders, the mood of the people over there – everything that Guy could give them. If he had not been assured they were part of the Catholic network he would have been suspicious of their questions but their credentials had been assured by Sir William Stanley before he left. So he sat and talked with them, told them all they wanted to know and expressed his great thanks for their hospitality. It meant that his money would go a little further. It also meant a comfortable clean bed. Not all inns were scrupulously clean.

Next morning he left for his next port of call, where again he had to talk of life in Flanders, but he made it clear he had to move on, his time in England was limited. One more call and then, with his duty done, papers delivered and the assurance that the other sealed documents would be passed on to those in the network, Guy was free to make his way to Yorkshire and home. He was concerned he had not had a chance to let his family know he was coming – again – but was sure they would be happy to see him.

It was as well he asked the cost of the journey to York before he took his seat, the price had increased somewhat from the last time he had travelled but he consoled himself with the thought that it had been five years since he had been home and the cost of everything had increased during that time. He had saved himself two nights' accommodation, which was good.

The coach was full and the passengers seemingly indifferent to one another. Guy was able to watch the slowly changing landscape without feeling he needed to socialise, which pleased him. He had little time for the niceties of polite conversation these days, having become used to the abrupt way of Army life: give orders, receive orders, move on, get the task done. His time spent with the family in Kensington had been pleasant for a while, but then became an ordeal as he sought for things to talk about. He hoped his family would be garrulous enough to make up for any lack of conversation on his part. Half dozing, half feeling a sense of anticipation as the coach moved steadily northward, Guy surrendered himself to being back in England and thinking and speaking English again. The countryside, so familiar, worked its magic on him as it had done before. He noticed some villages had new buildings but overall there was little change out here, away from the large sprawling metropolis of London.

Fortunately, although to him his clothes were like a uniform, close fitting jerkin, tunic and breeches, it did not stand out even among the changing fashions of England. No one asked if he was a soldier, no one questioned his profession, he remained all but anonymous among the English, which suited him well. He had taken Edwin Thomas's words to heart and spoke as little as possible. It had served him well in his career and he intended to continue that way.

He slept deeply enough to dream, aspects of Flanders mixed with England, Edwin Thomas warning him to beware his words and then laughing as he faded away, shards of sunlight pinning him to the ground so he could not move, women flashing their bosoms at him and trying to tempt him, men pouring ale on the ground around him, soaking his clothes. The dream was chaotic and crazy and in some ways, disturbing. Guy woke with a start, grunted and shifted slightly, trying not to annoy or irritate his fellow travellers, who were dozing as the coach rattled over the rutted roads and through villages where the people looked and then got on with their lives.

The endless journey, marked by the changing of horses, the overnight stops in the same inns he had slept in all that time ago, had a soporific effect on him. He dozed through the days and still slept at night, no matter how many were in the room with him. No one spoke, it was as if they had all taken a vow of silence as they got on board the aged coach.

On the fourth day they finally reached the boundaries of Yorkshire. Guy sat up, straightened his jerkin and for the first time began to think about what it meant to be 'home'. He was shocked to find at that moment it meant nothing. There had to be some feeling there, some pull to his family, surely. Not his mother, his sisters? He felt empty, completely hollow. It was odd and he wondered why it had happened. And when it had happened.

He sat in stunned silence until the weary lathered horses stopped outside the coaching inn in York. He climbed down; stretching cramped confined muscles, taking in deep breaths of crisp autumn air. The sun was low in the sky but it was still bright enough and warm enough to make walking an inviting prospect. He picked up his bag, deciding in that moment to do just that, to walk to Scotton, as he had done the last time he returned home. He needed to think through why he felt so empty.

York was busier than he remembered, as London had been. Whilst he had been away business had grown, it seemed, prosperity had come to England under the Virgin Queen who had done everything possible for her people – apart from restoring the true faith. If she had done that, she would have had Guy's undying loyalty. He looked around, seeing new offices, new merchant stores opened, slightly different fashions on the street. He felt like a stranger in a city where he had spent his formative years, which added to his sense of displacement. He wondered how he would feel when he knocked on the door of his home.

There was an urgency in his need to get there which prevented him stopping in an inn for ale or food, but not that strong an urgency that he hired a horse or took a ride on another coach. He needed to walk, to think, to absorb but not to hesitate long enough to eat and drink. It meant he would be starving by the time he arrived but that too he had become used to during his time abroad. He could not pin down where this sense of hurry and need to get there had come from, it was an intuition and he had learned to trust that above all else.

The golden sense of autumn enveloped him as he walked. The drifting leaves were good to crunch beneath his boots, the feeling of everything winding down, burrowing deep for the winter, the animals storing as much fat as they could before they had to stop eating and begin their hibernation. The last of the wild flowers bloomed here and there along the roadside; darting birds sought the last of the insects. England in autumn, he thought, there could be nothing finer than that in his mind. He realised he was consciously storing memories to take back to Europe with him.

Scotton appeared to have remained unchanged. People worked in the fields, horses were pulling ploughs, winter crops were being sown, thatchers were repairing roofs ready for the winter weather. Everywhere there was the sense of winding down and deep inside him, another sense that this journey was a final one in many ways.   There was a melancholy which came with that feeling, one that fitted well with the autumn day. There was also a growing sense of apprehension that when he got to his destination he would not find all was well but he didn't know why.

Would his sisters be there or would they by now be married with their own homes and perhaps children? Would Dennis have done anything with the Hall, which was in disrepair when he left? Would his mother - and that was where his thoughts stopped.

The answers would come soon enough, he thought, as he walked through Scotton to the Hall.

The first answer was; Dennis had done nothing to the Hall. It looked even shabbier than when he departed five years earlier.   The other answers would be revealed when he got inside.

The maid who opened the door to his knock was new. She was slender, with a mass of blonde curls escaping from her cap, pretty enough but unsure of herself. She seemed flustered, as if callers were rare at the Hall.

"Mistress is-" she began and then stopped.   "I'm sorry, sir. Mister Bainbridge is at home if you wish to see him. Who do I say is calling?"

"His stepson, Guy Fawkes." He pushed his way in, closing the door after him.   The maid backed off, blushed and dropped a curtsy. "Sorry, sir, I didn't know…"

"I know. I hold no blame.   Would you be good enough to tell my mother I am here?"

"Mistress is-" Again the words were bitten off and she looked down. Guy's feeling of apprehension grew even stronger but before he could speak, he heard a voice.

"Do we have a visitor, Charity?" Guy looked up. Dennis was standing on the stairs, looking old, tired and much greyer than he had been before. His face lit up with pleasure when he saw who had arrived. "Guy! In the name of Heaven, how did you know? Come in, come in, put the bag down, please, come up at once! God in Heaven, the Virgin must have brought you!" Dennis hurried back up the stairs, calling out as he went: "Edith! Guy's here! Edith, your son's here!"

Guy felt physically sick and held on to the newel post for support. Something was terribly wrong and he had a dreadful foreboding of what it was. When he regained his strength, he took the stairs two at a time and then hesitated, afraid, before quietly walking into his mother's room.

It was in semi-darkness from the drapes drawn against the afternoon sun. There was a smell in the room, one made up of sickness, dust and decay. The coverlet was hardly mounded; the body beneath it was so thin it scarcely disturbed it. The first thing Guy thought was that the tiny, wizened, grey figure in the bed was not his mother. It was a shadow, a remnant of the buxom strong woman who had made her stand after his father died, who had moved them from York to this tiny place, who had made a successful second marriage and who was now very obviously dying. Dennis was hovering, all rumpled clothes, untidy hair and unshaven face, muttering words about food and drink and how pleased he was Guy had come home. Guy ignored him. He could eat and drink later. All that mattered was that by a miracle he had been brought back just in time to say goodbye. The grief smashed into his stomach so hard it was like a physical blow. He almost couldn't breathe for a few moments.

"Guy." The word was whispered so low, on such a small intake of breath he wondered if he had actually heard anything. He recalled his feeling when he had held her before he left, the sensation more than anything that she was not as substantial as she had been. He had wondered about it, but dismissed the thought at the time. A change of food, anything could induce a weight loss, he had lost weight working in Cowdray House. Who would have thought it was this?

"I'm here, Mother." The words almost stuck in his throat. This was not his mother; this was a skeletal mummified figure who still had the ability to talk. There was nothing familiar about her, apart from her eyes, which remained alive and full of tears. The rest of her appeared to be dead. She could not even lift her hand from the coverlet to reach for him.

"What brought you back … my son?"

He sat down on a stool by the bedside and struggled with his emotions. "Work. Important papers to deliver. I cannot stay long."

"You – look - different."

"How different?" He was fighting tears as he sat there holding a hand which felt like a starved bird's tiny body, all bones and skin and little enough of both.

"You're more of a man." Dennis spoke across his wife's ravaged body, pride in his voice and in his eyes. "You're fighting fit and very much the soldier now, Guy."

"Thank you." Guy looked down, wondering how to handle a compliment like that. "It's all the training…"

"No, it's more than that. It's confidence. You have confidence in yourself. It shows."

"Guy. Stay with me." The whisper was even quieter than before.

"I will. But first let me attend to a few things … it was a long journey."

"Of course." But the look said, don't be long, I don't have long to live.

Guy moved away from the bed toward the door and spoke quietly to Dennis.

"I need to use the-"

"Yes, yes. I'll organise some food for you. I don't suppose you stopped for anything."

"No, I didn't."

"Your room is still there for you, Guy. Go attend to everything and I'll have the food brought up for you. Edith is – I can't tell you what it means to us that you got here in time."

Guy looked away as Dennis' eyes filled with tears. It wasn't manly and it wasn't doing him a lot of good, either. He pushed past, politely, and went to the water closet, then to his room. There he quickly uncovered the secret space and, with a sense of great sadness, took out the coins and his father's ring which he had left behind. He had the strongest feeling he would not come back to Wheatley Hall again and he had no intention of leaving anything of value which he might need in the future. His father's ring was his only memento of a fine man. He wanted that to go with him this time, now he had a position, now he had standing in the army corps where he belonged.

He stopped and thought about that. The army corps where he belonged. That confirmed it. When he left the Hall it would be for the last time. He had no intention of coming back ever again. The Army was his life.

Anne came into the room just after he had covered up the space and was putting his bag on the bed. She went into his arms and wept.

"You came… We were so worried you wouldn't find out, wouldn't be back in time," she muttered through her tears. "We wrote…"

"I didn't find out," he told her, looking down on the dark curls. "No letter reached me."

"Then how did you…"

"I'm in England on business for the army. I go back tomorrow."

"If she – if Mother – if – will you stay for the funeral?"

"Anne, dear sister, I cannot. I have business in London and then I must return to the continent. There is much work and planning going on and I am needed there. I am under orders, I cannot disobey."

"Elizabeth will be here shortly."

"I wondered where she was." In truth, he hadn't, he was too emotionally shattered by what he had found but it would not do to tell the truth at such a fraught and sad time.

"Married now and a child to come. I am bound to be married and will be ere long. You were not here for her wedding and it seems you will not be here for mine, either." The words carried no bitterness, just acceptance.

Nor will Mother. Neither of them said it.

"I have a career now, you know that. Soldiers don't take time out to go home for weddings. It's important work."

"Of course. I would have liked – but no, of course you can't travel back. It's enough that you are here now."

She had matured into a stunning woman, Guy thought, looking at her as she stood back, surveying him at the same time.

"You've changed, Guy. There's something different about you."

"Father just said that. He said it was confidence."

"That's it! You hold yourself differently now, as if nothing could touch you."

Oh but it has, he thought. The feeling I had on the coach, that nothing here mattered to me, was wrong. It does. This does. One sister married, one going to be married, Mother dying and my not being here for any of it. I am now even more of an outsider than I was before.

With Anne at his side, he left his room and went back to sit by his mother's bedside. Dennis brought the food himself, obviously he did all the fetching and carrying when it came to Edith's room. He put it on a small table at Guy's side and smiled down at Edith.

"Like old times, isn't it, my dear?"

Through half closed eyes Edith watched as Guy ate his way through everything that had been provided for him, seemingly pleased at his appetite. To Guy the food was sitting leaden-like in his stomach, the grief he felt stopping it going any further. He knew he had to eat just to keep going, but it was very difficult. One of the maids stood at the door and called to Dennis. He got up and left the room. After a few moments, Elizabeth rushed in. Guy put the platter to one side and stood up to greet her.

"Guy! Father said you were here but I didn't believe it!" She flung herself into his arms, pressing her swollen body against him. "You're going to be an uncle and you didn't know about it, did you?"

"No." He held her at arm's length, again observing the maturity and beauty of his sisters. "I am so pleased for you. Are you happy?"

"Oh yes, very happy." But her eyes told a different story as she turned to the bed. "Mother?"

"Guy's here." The whisper was almost a breath.

"Yes, yes, he's here. And you're still here."

"Not for long."

Elizabeth's eyes filled with tears and she turned back to Guy. "I am so sorry we had to bring you home to this."

"I'm here on Army business, not because of Mother. I had no knowledge of this. I have to leave in the morning."

Her face betrayed the shock she felt. "We – I – we thought you would have got our letter, they said you would get it. Oh Guy, can you not stay?"

He took her hands in his. "I already spoke to Anne about this. I'm a soldier now and have orders. I cannot ignore them and stay as long as I want. I'm due back in London very shortly and then I need to take ship to Flanders once more."

She nodded. "We forget sometimes that you have commanding officers and battles to fight, Guy. It must have been important for you to come to England in the first place."

"It was, it is."

"And come home to find-"

"At least I came home. Our Blessed Virgin must have directed my actions, my journeying. I asked for permission to come but did not know why it was so important – until now."

He turned back and sat down again, holding his mother's hand lightly. "You are to become a grandmother, then!"

"Yes." The smile was radiant but distant.

Elizabeth sat down on the side of the bed and rubbed her mound. "Won't be long. This one was anxious to be born, kicking and moving around but now it is still."

"Good sign."

"Still no woman for you, Guy?" Elizabeth asked, trying to make light conversation in room of death.

"No. Never will be." He must have said it with an edge on his voice for Elizabeth looked away as if embarrassed she had asked. He was quick to soften the comment. "I only serve the Blessed Virgin."

"I think you possibly took the wrong pathway, Guy. You should have been a monk."

"Maybe you're right but monks don't fight. My need is to fight."

"My son. Fight for. True Faith."

They both turned and smiled at their mother from the depths of their love.

"Open curtains." It was an order more than a request.

Elizabeth struggled to her feet and laboriously crossed the room to tug back the drapes and allow the autumn sunlight to flood into the room. As she did so, Dennis came in and immediately went to close them again. Guy held up his hand.

"Mother just asked us to open them, Father. Please leave them."

"It's too bright for her eyes."

"Leave. Them." This time the whisper was vehement and Dennis backed away, raising both hands in surrender. "As you wish, Edith, dear one."

The room suddenly seemed filled with light stronger than the sunlight had been. Guy wondered if he was the only one who could see it but then realised his sister was staring too. In that moment, between one breath and the next, his mother's heart stopped. Everyone became aware of the silence even though the breaths had been so quiet they could hardly be heard. Their absence was loud. They were stilled by the moment, the quiet, serene passing of a life right before them. Guy raised his head and saw, for a fraction of a second, a younger, smiling mother standing in the bright light and then she - and the light – were gone. The autumn sunshine resumed its normal gold shade and the room was filled with the sound of weeping.

Anne came in, looked at them and burst into tears. Dennis went over to her, gathered her in his arms and held her close. Elizabeth went to Guy's arms for consolation. The combined grief made him, for a moment, feel completely at home.

It was doubtful that anyone in the Hall slept that night. Guy tossed and turned, consumed with grief and reproach that he should feel nothing when approaching home, only to find his heart turned inside out by his mother's – to him – sudden passing. Dennis had been able to get used to the idea, he had nursed her and cared for her and loved her to the end. He had been forced to watch the slow decline of the woman he had loved. He eventually gave up on sleep and spent the remainder of the night staring out of the window, listening to the sounds of the countryside, watching the moon and stars slowly walk their endless way across the blackness. There was an element of comfort in being aware of the inevitability of life, the universe, of death itself. It came whether anyone wanted it to or not. None could put off the moment it arrived, be they monarch or peasant. He was overwhelmed by the impulses which had sent him home just in time to see his mother's last moments, he had not had to read about it in a letter months later, or hear it third hand from someone. He had been there, he had witnessed the passing, just as he had when his father was taken all those years earlier.

There were footsteps in the halls and on the landings throughout the night as people went to get something to drink or just to be outside their room, perhaps to walk the grief out of their bodies. The servants had been subdued when they went to bed.

The morning brought more autumn sunshine. It should have been a bright cheerful day but those who appeared for breakfast came with dark ringed eyes. During their silent meal, such as it was, a messenger arrived from Elizabeth's husband with news she had been safely delivered of her child, a girl, in the early hours. Dennis was elated and shook hands with Guy across the table.

"A new Uncle!"

"A grandfather!" said Guy in return.

"Will you come with me to see the child?" Dennis was all eagerness and smiles; it was just what he needed to offset Edith's death.

"No." Guy knew he had to go, he had to get to London and then to Flanders. He did not want to see a tiny baby, to let it grab his heartstrings and not let go. He had enough to think about and endure with the loss of his mother. As far as he was concerned, the knowledge of the safe delivery was enough. "I'm sorry, Father, I must get back to London. I did say I could only stay one night. I have to collect some important papers and then go back to Flanders. There is much to do to carry on the fight."

"I would wish you could stay for the funeral, Guy, but I understand. You committed yourself to a life as a soldier and that has to come first." It was said with sincerity but his eyes betrayed the fact that he was deeply disappointed. Guy got up from the table.

"Go and see Elizabeth, Father. I will be gone by the time you return, so let me say goodbye now and give you my regrets I cannot stay for the funeral or the baptism."

There was a brief hug, another handshake and Dennis hurried from the room, once again trying to disguise the fact his eyes were full of tears. Guy went back upstairs, repacked his bag and came down again. He avoided looking into his mother's room. He had said his goodbyes to her when she slipped quietly away; he had no reason to go in there again.

No one came to bid him farewell. Dennis had gone to see Elizabeth, the servants were busy with their tasks. He was able to quietly leave without fuss and emotion. With no regrets at all he walked out of Wheatley Hall to begin the journey back to London, to Dover and the Continent. The conviction that was the last time he would see his family grew stronger as he went. He felt as if he was walking toward his destiny.

Chapter Eleven

'Oh God, when I said I would give my life for Your fight, I meant it. But God, merciful God, end it now! I cannot stand another minute, another moment, of this agony! But oh, I realise I am not speaking aloud and You cannot hear my plea. How can You answer me if You cannot hear me! Those foolish wasted tears have robbed me of a voice. I should not have cried. But in my weakness I did and now I have no voice to speak to You and ask You to release me from this agony. And so I suffer still. Can Purgatory be worse than this? I think not. I think not...'

Sailing back to the continent after so short an interval in England made Guy feel like a seasoned traveller. He had become accustomed to the motion of the ship, finding his sea legs very quickly and having no difficulty in walking about the deck despite a strong swell. The sound of the rigging and crack of sails was familiar rather than strange. He watched the fast flowing water, white capped here and there as a strong wind savaged the channel and the shipping which dared to venture onto it, speculating on his feelings. He had felt part of the family for a brief moment, when they clung to one another in their grief. But that sense of belonging disappeared the moment people broke apart to do all the necessary things, inform the household and Elizabeth, call the doctor to confirm the death, arrange for the undertaker. Suddenly the house had been full of activity, none of it concerning him, all of it concerning a body that was bereft of life. He had retreated into his shell again; knowing it was all going toward reinforcing his decision to leave first thing in the morning. He knew well that if he were a few days late in returning, his commanding officer would consider it compassionate leave. Deaths in the family were honoured, he knew that, but he had no intention of staying. He did not want to see another parent lowered into the ground, to see and hear the earth hitting the coffin, to know he would not look on their faces again until he was reunited with them in Heaven. Some things were too painful, that was one of them. He could, if he put his mind to it, dismiss the small grey shrunken figure in the bed and remember only the vigorous devoted loving woman who had run a household with ease and confidence, who had stood up for her beliefs and had brought up a good moral family. Seeing her buried would not benefit him at all.

No one was aware of his small deception in saying he had to return swiftly, apart from his conscience and Almighty God, of course, but he was a soldier in the fight for the restoration of the True Faith and God knew that. He would surely overlook the lie. It was a very minor one, after all.

London enfolded him in its busy frantic bustling arms, threw papers at him and spat him out again on a coach for Dover in what seemed like an impossibly short time. The journey to Yorkshire had seemed to take forever; the journey back was being accomplished in a much shorter time, at least, that was how it was perceived.

Maybe it was because the horses were fresher, the ground was harder, and there were no accidents or incidents to halt them. Every stop to change horses, every night they slept over in a cheap inn seemed to be mere moments in a journey that was being accomplished much faster than he had ever known it before. Maybe it was because he was leaving behind a good deal of sorrow and grief and heading for the great fight he knew was to come. Anticipation made everything speed up.

On board ship, the sense of familiarity with the way the vessel worked, where he could go and could not go, the narrow bunk and the usual seafaring meals all served to wrap around him and make him feel accepted. He was someone who knew his way around. It would not be long before he and the papers he had collected were back in Flanders, back with his commanding officer and the men in his corps, back where he felt he belonged.

Ass guy stood by the ship's rail, looking toward France rather than looking back at England, as was his won't., A brash handsome man came and stood beside him.

"I have been told you are Mr Fawkes," the man said, not quite looking at Guy, as if he was a bit nervous.

"I am indeed. Should I know you, sir?"

The man turned to him then and held out his hand. "Anthony Dutton at your service, Sir," he said with a broad smile. "I understand you are on your way back to Sir William Stanley."

"Yes I am. Sir William entrusted me with a mission in England. I am now returning to him."

"Then we have much in common, Mr Fawkes, and I trust we will become friends, for I feel we have much travelling to do together."

"It would be good. Anything I can do for the cause I will do, and if that means travelling I am well prepared to do it."

"There will be much travelling, Mr Fawkes, we have to go to Spain among other things."

"You are remarkably well-informed, Mr Dutton, if I might say so. You talk of things that no one has mentioned it to me yet."

Anthony Dutton laughed. "Believe me when I say your commanding officer knows you very well Mr Fawkes. He has every confidence in you. He contacted me some time ago and told me of your sterling service to the cause and to the corps as a whole. He said you were an exceptional man and a first class soldier."

"And you have need of me to travel with you?"

"I do indeed. It is relatively safe to travel around the continent, but I would be much happier if I had a first class soldier with me. I see and understand you are a man of few words and that is exactly what I want. To have someone with me who talks all the time might well be counter-productive to the diplomatic task on which I will be spending my time."

Guy was silent for a moment or two. The man's comments had shown him that Sir William had a tremendous faith in his abilities and that pleased him very much. It would be interesting to go to Spain with this man, to see more of the land and of cities that he had only heard of. If he was no more than bodyguard, it was a service in itself.

"If we are to travel together, Mr Dutton, please feel free to call me Guido. It is a name that some of the other soldiers have used for me, and it seems to fit somehow. I trust this is not an imposition or a vanity on my part."

His companion looked at him closely. "It is not a vanity, Guido, but an effort on your part to fit in with those with whom you soldier. It is an unusual thing to do, most men would have held on to their given name but you chose to become part of the corps. I admire this is in you. Certainly it is not an imposition and I will be pleased to use the name."

The two men shook hands again. They seemed to have reached a very good understanding between them, which boded well for the future.

***

Anthony Dutton and Guy were given horses, a backpack of food and supplies, and instructions on their diplomatic mission to the Court of Spain.

Their journey from the Spanish Netherlands to Madrid was lengthy but not tedious. The men did not speak very much, Anthony respecting Guy's manner of only speaking when he had to which in truth brought about a quiet understanding between the two of them. Guy pondered often as they rode why people talked endlessly, as some of his fellow soldiers did, about very little that in doing so often caused offence. By not speaking, he found he had never caused offence to anyone, which was something he was very proud of. He learned a little of Anthony's life but spoke so little of his own that at the end of the journey Anthony was no wiser than he was when they set out. It was precisely what I wanted. He had no intention of telling anyone about his devotion to God, the Virgin Mary, the loss of his mother, or any other of the trials and tribulations he had endured so far. The words of Edwin Thomas came back to him regularly, speak only when you need. That and the smile which should be given only when meant, and the blank face, had stood him in very good stead for a considerable time.

Spain was dust, heat, exotic plants, colourful people, whitewashed houses with red roofs, and a language he had already learned to be comfortable with. It helped their journey considerably.

The court of King Philip III heard Anthony Dutton's proposals for a diplomatic and military mission to establish the catholic faith in England with great friendliness, but Guy was very aware they were not committing themselves one way or another to anything that was being said. The beautiful white cool rooms in which they sat to talk were beautiful and he could have stayed there contented for some time. But it was obvious that their mission was going nowhere and they had to return to their commanding officer. Although Anthony believed that the English Catholics were ready for rebellion, and said so at great length, it would appear he was not fully believed. They returned to Flanders, knowing they had not succeeded, but also knowing they had done their best.

***

Orders came through for the army to move on Calais, which the Spanish king had decided he wished to claim. They set out, encumbered with cannon and supplies but lifted with the fast running rumour that Elizabeth was hesitating over whether to send men to support the French. As long as she held off from committing them to the fight, the word was Calais would be in their hands without too much of a fight. At least, that was the hope.

They set a fast pace, stopping only when they had to for the sake of the pack horses and some of the men who were carrying heavier loads. They were not stopped by any French soldiers along the way, no villagers came out to shout abuse or even encouragement. It was as if they were invisible, this noisy lengthy procession of men and animals passing through village after village, not seeing a living person. It felt strange. Perhaps the people who lived around and in Calais had become used to war and all its horrors, this was just another time when someone else held the port. Guy thought about this as he marched, wondering why his mind was veering off in such strange directions. But then, having realised that was what he is doing, he let it go.

Calais, so close to England yet a completely different world, was to be put under siege. He considered the dichotomy, a foreign port surrounded by armed men, some of them English, flying the flag of Spain. At times the world seemed to have gone mad, as if someone had taken the globe and shaken it hard to mix everything up. Other times, when he was busy with commands and obeying orders, it seemed natural. He gave up trying to sort it out; it wasn't worth the effort. All that mattered, all that should matter, was that he was a soldier with a regiment he liked under a commanding officer he trusted for a cause that was right, that of the true faith. No one could ask for more, he told himself. It was on occasions like this that all his training came into force and he could see the logic of all he had been taught to do. He also appreciated the fact that he had maintained his fitness and strength.

More than anything, though, was the underlying reason for his contentment in the situation in which he found himself. He was trusted by a man he admired. Trusted to the point of being given temporary command of a company. He, Guido Fawkes, in charge of a company! If only he could stop and write a letter … but then the realisation crashed in yet again that his mother was not there to read anything he wrote. His sisters would not be impressed; they had their husbands and their own lives to lead and as for Dennis, who knew what Dennis was doing? Doubtless still living in a mouldering house which needed so much work and money that it would never get so it would eventually fall down of its own volition.

None of that mattered any more. In truth, he had known the feeling – more a deep conviction than a feeling – that he would never go home again for a very long time. Yorkshire held nothing for him anymore. His stake in the land had been sold, his mother had gone, his sisters had their own lives and would do perfectly well without him. Dennis … well, Dennis would go on being his usual self, living off the bit of land he had and the goodwill of the family. No doubt if Guy walked in there again, he would be offered his old room if he wanted it but there was no blood tie, nothing to draw him back. Here was home. Here was family, within the regiment, within the company, in the service of the King of Spain and all that meant in the way of commitment to the true faith, to his own heart and his God. He looked down at his father's ring, which he had put on as he left for London and had not taken off since, with a strange conviction that it too would be taken from him at some time. Before then, it was his one link with his past.

Then they were there, setting up camp, hauling the cannon into position, ever watchful for the French cannon which was within range – just – and for fireballs which could do so much damage to men and supplies. All seemed quiet, unreasonably so. Surely the French knew they were there and what they were doing? The order went round, carry on setting up the camp and attending to the horses. Keep your nerve. They are withholding fire for some reason. Be calm. Be ready.

Guy found himself being pestered for decisions, everything from the siting of the canon under his responsibility to the best place to dig a latrine. Whilst rushing from one place to another to attend to the many details, it was easy enough to keep calm and hold the nerves. Nothing was happening and until the first shots were fired, it would seem like an exercise rather than an actual happening, a true siege.

Nothing happened all that night. The soldiers rested, those who were not set on watch, but no fire was exchanged, not a French soldier was seen.

It erupted next morning, with a cannonball landing close by to Guy, causing casualties and chaos. From then on battle was engaged and Guy found himself directing the removal of the dead so as not to impede the living, the range and frequency of fire, whilst coping with the sounds that threatened to burst his eardrums, the cannon's horrendous boom, the ominous crackling of fire when something had been set alight, the clashes between Spanish and French engaged in hand to hand fighting.

A taste of conflict. Guy pondered on the phrase which he had heard uttered by one of the other officers and felt it was right. There was a distinct taste, the bitterness of gunpowder, the tang of animals and of human flesh when it leaked blood, the acrid touch of whatever it was that surged through the body and gave impetus to everything, especially at a moment of crisis when a battle seemed to be going the right way, when the commands came easy to his mouth and the men obeyed instantly.

He was aware of the fact his commanding officer was watching, as much as he could, as he walked around and through the men, encouraging, sympathising, sending medics to cope with the wounded and burial details to see to the dead. There was little time for grief or sadness, every man had to take care of himself and the one next to him, if he could.

And then, within a few days, the siege of Calais ended. With no support from the English fleet, the town fell neatly and easily into Spanish hands. The soldiers celebrated, the Spanish flag was raised over the town and they spent a day carousing and eating well from the inns and bakeries of the town. The French seemed indifferent to the occupying force, as if it mattered little to them which flag fluttered in the breeze. Life went on regardless, it seemed.

They had to pack everything up and begin the journey back to Flanders, where other work awaited them. During their march back, Sir William confirmed Guy's status as Captain of a company, in light of his outstanding actions in battle. Guy was intensely pleased, if still haunted by the sights and sounds of battle, the names of the dead resonating in his mind still, as he wondered whether he could have done things differently, which would have preserved their lives. His cousin Richard Collinge was safe, Miller, Stoneley and others who had befriended him were safe, although Miller was badly wounded in the thigh and would have difficulty walking for some time to come. He was being carried on a litter and trying to make light of the pain he was suffering. Guy knew that the thoughts were insane, in a time of conflict there was no way any man could be saved from cannon fire or any other weapon if it was meant to be. Those who were left behind in the ground around Calais were proof of that. But the sadness lingered along with the thought that he should have done more. The accolades of his commanding officer said he could not and in that he sought - and found – a little consolation.

They stopped for the night to rest the wounded and those who were simply worn out. Guy walked away from the makeshift camp to find a quiet place for prayer. It was overdue.

Beneath a large tree with huge twisted roots, he found a place to sit and there gave himself over to a few moments of intense communication with his God. He gave thanks for his safety and the safety of his cousin, along with those of his company who had survived and were marching back to their base alongside him. He asked for peace and even as he asked, he heard the lilting song of a night bird and knew all was well. An owl hooted somewhere, as if in jest and he smiled. Then he went back to his men, checking on the wounded, making sure they were given sufficient food and water. As he was making the rounds, he met up with Sir William.

"Fawkes, why are you not having a rest?"

"I am checking on the men, sir. I need to be sure they are being taken care of."

Sir William nodded in approval. "I should have known. You're a very unusual young man, in my opinion. Outstanding as a soldier but with the piety of a monk. I would swear an oath that you have just come back from your prayers."

Guy flushed a little. "I have, sir. Is that wrong?"

"No. Nothing is wrong if it produces a soldier of your standing, Fawkes. It is noted, it is accepted. Thank you for all you do for your men."

Sir William walked on, making his own rounds of the men, just as Guy had been doing. Guy was left filled with an intense pleasure that he was doing something right, that he was totally accepted. No matter how many times he thought he was, he always sought that bit more confirmation. Now he had it.

Despite his pleasure at being in command of a company, Guy knew there was more work, other tasks for him, more diplomatic than military. There was little time to rest on his laurels.

Sir William Stanley kept him busy with visits here and there, people to talk to, missions to discuss. He travelled to Spain and Italy, riding through rough often dangerous countryside, sleeping rough, carrying little more than his immediate needs and letters for officials in the capital cities of both countries. He was not attacked, fortunately, but he heard of travellers being murdered for their horse or their few coins. Only once he woke in the early hours, aware of the shuffling of feet and whispers, but whoever it was ran off when he got to his feet. Villagers supplied fresh food in exchange for a coin and he was able to get fodder for his horse cheaply too.

Madrid no longer overwhelmed him, he was very much the soldier on a mission, arrive, talk with people in authority, with clerics and high ranking members of the Catholic church, arranging finance, military help, anything that needed to be brought in to fight the Protestant disease, as he saw it, then move on. Nothing mattered but the task, telling people of the sacrifice made by Margaret Clitherow, so that all would know of the extreme brutal lengths the authorities went to in England if someone was found harbouring a priest. Everyone had horror stories to tell of persecution and prosecution, of starvation in prisons and of being hounded out of homes and villages across the country. Everyone said they were prepared to join in the fight if they could. Guy saw himself as a knight in shining armour, prepared to liberate the 'lady', his faith, from the clutches of darkness, Protestantism. He wondered if anyone would understand if he described his mission thus and decided they would not. It was something to be kept between him and his God. As with many things, secrecy was best, that way no one could judge, no one could throw accusations at him. His tendency not to speak much had become an ingrained habit anyway. He was the perfect diplomat in that way, trusted, believed, committed, as well as being the perfect soldier. Every order was obeyed immediately, regardless of cost.

He knew, though, in his darkest hours, that all the talk, all the travelling, all the diplomacy was not getting him where he wanted to be, part of a campaign to restore Catholicism to the English. Everyone spoke nicely, everyone was friendly, few actually gave a handshake to confirm they would be there, guns at the ready, to launch the assault. But he had to go on trying, there was nothing else to do.

***

He was recalled to Flanders as a battle was looming between the Dutch and Spanish armies. Eventually they met at Nieuwpoort. No one told him why the two countries were battling, unless once again it was to capture land, ports and cities, for the greater glory of the winning side.

The battle lines were strictly drawn up, three lines of defence on both sides. Guy and his fellow soldiers were in the third line, fighting for the Spanish.

It was some of the fiercest fighting Guy had ever seen.

The English army were firing at them steadily, but the Spanish army broke through with pikes and actually managed to push the English from the top of the hill they were defending, though with heavy losses. They would have been all right but pikes and muskets got themselves mixed, despite the shouted orders of the officers, and their advance was slow. Reserves were sent in and the

Spanish retreated in disorder, leaving many more dead behind them.

When the battle was over, they returned to their base, somewhat disheartened, their numbers depleted, with many wounded who needed attention and a long period of recovery.

The memory of it stayed in Guy's mind for a long time, the smell of powder, men, animals, the sounds of the guns, the screaming, the dying, the orders being shouted and misheard or ignored by many.

Most of all he remembered the smell and taste of fear and hoped never to have to experience that again.

***

The treaty signed between Henry IV of France and Phillip II of Spain officially ended the troubled wars in Europe, which in turn changed the role of Sir William's regiment but the fight remained. England was not a Catholic country. There was much excitement in Europe when it was realised that Mary Queen of Scots' son would take the throne on Elizabeth's passing, it encouraged them all to continue their preparations for an invasion, should it be needed. Many believed that England was ready for this, that if they were to move in, the people would be on their side. Guy travelled extensively back and forth across Europe, acting as courier for his commanding officer, directing, supervising and discussing the practicalities of an invasion.

And there, in the court of Spain, he met up with his old friend, Kit Wright, on the same mission. In an instant he was transported into his past, into the school, the playing area, the games, the fights, the dust and chalk filled classrooms. In a moment it was as if all his sorrows and years of soldiering had been wiped away. Kit embraced him, tears in his eyes, full of obvious pleasure at meeting Guy again. The Spaniards applauded and cheered, their English compatriots were after all capable of showing emotion. It was good; it endeared them to everyone. With huge smiles and many handshakes, the two men sat down to catch up on their years apart.

The passing of an icon, of an age. Queen Elizabeth died and was buried with great ceremony and much mourning among the people of England. She had been a potent power both in her own country and in Europe for so long, it was almost impossible to believe she had actually passed on.

James I was the new king of England. Guy saw him as a militant, bringing to the throne all that he hated. Reports via the Catholic network spoke of recusant fines being rescinded but still the feeling persisted among some of them in Europe that England was ripe for an invasion, for a restoration of the true faith. For Guy it was the culmination of all that he had worked for and believed in for much of his life. His military career had done much to reinforce his belief.

The Spanish government listened to his and his compatriot Anthony Dutton's propositions that a force be raised to invade and take over the country, but no decision was made. There was considerable prevarication and they were quietly put to one side, as it were. Guy knew there were other forces at work, people trying to engineer peace when he felt they should go ahead and use strength to achieve their aim. Without backing it could not be done. That did not appear to be forthcoming, no matter how convincing their arguments were to those who gave them the time to express them.

News filtered across the channel to the regiment and to those who were working for a Catholic country again of how James was firmly Protestant, how he insisted Catholics must not 'multiply' – he meant to keep them firmly held down. He had made it clear he would not tolerate their religion. Heavy fines were imposed on anyone not attending Protestant church services. Despondency struck at the heart of every Catholic who had hoped for a degree of leniency from the new monarch who had, after all, remained totally Protestant. Nothing had changed, nothing at all. The hopes they had for leniency had disappeared like the early morning mist. Guy wondered if there was anyone in the community who was a leader, someone they could look up to, someone who could do something, offer them some hope, some way out of the impasse. There had to be someone. Surely God would not leave His people living as second rate citizens because they were not Protestant! Somewhere out there was such a man. If he was patient, he would meet him and in meeting him, would know immediately this was the one to lead his country back to the truth, to the pathway of righteousness, of Catholicism once again.

Chapter Twelve

When and how did I become deceived by the shining radiance of Catesby? When did the charm become so compelling that I was drawn in? I, who desired no man or woman, saw in him the ideal man, the leader, the prophet almost who would lead us to our victory, our great and overwhelming triumph. Where now the shining man, where now the glory we were to have – where now Guido Fawkes, broken man, hurting man, doomed man ... where now? The bowels of the Tower from whence none have emerged sane or even fully alive.

God grant me relief from the agony – it is intolerable, unbearable, endless. Blessed Mother, I ask no more than that you stop my heart in its beating right here, right now ... and still it beats. Still it beats...

***

Rumours and more rumours, no longer news, no longer reports anyone could rely on – that is, if the earlier reports could be relied on anyway. Every person newly arrived from England came with different stories of this being said and that being done. Nothing made sense, nothing was clear, except that the Protestant religion was supreme and the Catholic community were once again being persecuted for being 'different'. Guy spent hours in prayer, asking for a sign to show him the way forward, worrying he had strayed from his God given pathway. It had been a long time since a shaft of sunlight had picked him out and shown him his direct link with God. Mostly he had been operating on prayer and faith, with no divine sign to encourage him. He was not weakening but a sign would help, would lift his deflated spirits.

Guy took the introduction to Tom Wintour as that sign. Here was a man Guy could like and understand, they shared the same visions, they were both men of action and diplomatic experience, they had both been through the frustrating business of attempting to encourage the Spanish to help them with their fight, among other things. They knew the disappointment of being shown friendly faces and infinite amount of time, but receiving no help.

His talk of 'a resolution to do something to help the Catholics' was, in Guy's mind, the equivalent of the ray of sunshine. The glowing reports of the man known as Robin Catesby also fired his imagination. At last, a leader! Guy asked for release from his Army position and, despite Stanley's reluctance to let him go, he got his papers and was free for the first time in many years. He was his own man, able to go where he wished. His wish was to return to England and help in the fight.

The two men sailed for England in April, on a relatively calm sea. Tom Wintour commented on Guy's seemingly natural affinity with the ship, which pleased him very much.

"I've crossed the Channel a few times," he admitted after a while, reluctant to make anything of it. "You get to know what you can and can't do, what parts of the deck to avoid, how to keep out of everyone's way when they go aloft to tend to the sails."

"You are everything I was told you would be." Tom was open and honest. "They said you were a fine soldier, a quiet close mouthed man who knew his way around most things. You'll like Robin and there'll be a part for you to play in our new plans, for sure." He would not be drawn on any part of the discussion, saying that was for Robin Catesby to explain. Guy was intrigued but was well used to waiting for someone to admit him into whatever was going on. It was the way of Sir William and he was prepared to accept it from someone else who was also a leader, judging from the way Tom Wintour spoke of him. It was what Guy needed, someone to direct, to issue instructions, to take the fight to the authorities and do it well. Someone who would recruit more people to the cause too, which was much needed.

England seemed busier than ever to him and, oddly, smaller. That was something he had not expected. In his time abroad he had got used to the wide-open spaces of the French and Spanish countryside, the long journeys he had undertaken to get to Rome and other places. England felt almost crammed with cities and towns, with people and roads. He wondered if he would quickly adapt after being back home for a while. But then, he mused, was this really 'home'? Nowhere felt like a place where he belonged any more. He had liked living abroad, but only the regiment, only his fellow soldiers and his commanding officer felt anything like family to him. Still the outsider, he told himself, but if that is the way it is to be, then so be it. I have no doubt God wanted it that way, or He would have given me a home and a family to cherish and work for. It didn't happen so it was not for me.

He sat silent in the coach as they headed for London, listening to Tom chatting to the other travellers, making them laugh, swapping stories of disastrous journeys they had taken. That, thought Guy with sudden insight, is what I lack, the ability to talk and befriend people, to make them laugh, to share anecdotes with them. It is beyond my imagination to do that, to find the right words, to begin a story and let others listen. Look at the anticipation on their faces as they wait for the culmination of the tale, no matter how trivial it might be. It lightens their journey and gives them something to pass on to someone else. I cannot do that. Is that a failing in me?

You are what you are.

The words were silent but loud. In the seclusion of his head, he asked *what am I?*

Ours.

I don't understand.

You have no need to understand. You are what you are. Our trusted servant and faithful follower.

Ours.

Who are you?

The coach hit an obstacle, a pothole or a rock, and lurched heavily, throwing Guy against Tom.

"I am sorry," he muttered, straightening up again. "I trust I did not hurt you."

Tom smiled at him. "Stop your worrying, Guido, it happens on journeys like this."

The other passengers began their own tales of times when a coach had all but tipped over, one man recounting when he had been thrown clear of the coach and suffered a broken leg because of it. They universally blamed those in government for not spending any money on the roads, despite it being necessary for commerce generally. The talk turned to politics and then Guy became interested, interjecting a telling comment here and there. He saw surprised looks and realised that his taciturn silence had probably made them believe he had no thoughts at all about anything. In the political chatter he could, temporarily, forget the strange conversation he had held with someone – some thing – unknown. Whatever and whoever it was, they had said the one thing, the one wonderful word, he needed to hear. Just one word. Ours.

It comforted him in a way no other word could.

London: crowded and rotten with filth underfoot, was as challenging as it had always been. The complex mix of people of all races and faiths trying to work and live together in one huge metropolis created many problems in communication, understanding and acceptance. Guy could easily believe a radical change was coming, that with the right leadership this disparate group of people would rise up against a government that was persecuting a minority for no other reason than they held a different view of the Christian faith. A leader was needed. He told himself that and hoped that this Robin Catesby was that person. In many ways he regretted he was not the leadership type, knowing he was too shy, too reserved and so incapable of inspiring people. He felt he was a go-between, a diplomat with a mission, rather than a leader. In other ways he knew that suited his personality better and to throw him into the fray as a leader would not work. Leaders were born, not made.

The evening was dark, overcast with heavy clouds, making the streets a place of shadows. Tom walked confidently through Lambeth, a quiet sedate area which Guy could see had good quality houses, to Robin Catesby's elegant home.

The solid oak door spoke of security and safety, the glow of the lamps inside spoke of warmth and comfort. The servant who opened the door was well dressed, the house spoke of money and security. They stood in the hall to await their host.

He came striding out of one of the rooms along the hall, smiling and radiating confidence. From the moment Guy shook hands with him, he was lost. No matter what the outcome was, he knew this was the man who could and probably would attempt a strike at the very heart of the corrupt Government.

Robin Catesby was tall, strong of body, good-looking with a ready smile and eyes that bored into you with the intensity of his emotions. A charismatic person in every way. He radiated enthusiasm and strength; qualities Guy looked for in someone who was to share the conspiracy. No, change that, to lead the conspiracy, whatever it was. Robin invited them into his study, a cluttered, panelled room housing many books and papers. In the centre stood a table covered in yet more paper, with used quills scattered over it and new ones standing waiting to be used. In the centre was a large ceramic bowl full of fresh fruit.

"Welcome, gentlemen," he said with obvious pride, waving a hand to indicate his room. "This is my sanctuary, the place where I do my thinking. Sometimes, anyway." He pressed a corner of one of the panels and it swung open to reveal dark green bottles of spirits and an array of fine tankards. He reached for the tankards, handed one each to Tom and Guy, then took out one of the bottles and poured them a drink. It was a clear liquid with a fiery taste which Guy found quite appealing. He was finding it hard to remember he had only just met this man, it was as if he had known him forever.

"I like the secret compartment," Tom commented with a smile. Robin returned the smile and pushed the panel shut.

"It stops the servants raiding the liquor. Now, sit down, gentlemen, please."

They sat around a heavy oak table scarred with the marks of many tankards and with places here and there worn by elbows resting on it over the years. The room was warm despite the lack of a fire; it felt safe and secure.

"I mentioned servants, gentlemen. I wish to assure you this room is totally secret. No one can overhear anything. I know for I have tested it many times. I would not invite you here to talk of serious matters if I thought they would be compromised by bribes from the authorities."

Robin Catesby was nervous, it showed in the jittery way he poured the drink and then adjusted the position of the fruit bowl. Nervous and yet excited at the same time.   The atmosphere in the room was one of great anticipation.

"I am glad you brought this man to the house, Tom, that I am." He gestured to Guy with his tankard. He was still delaying, that was obvious.

"Thank you." Tom drank more of the spirit and smiled again. "Guido's a good man, Robin, the kind of person you've been needing for this plan of yours, the one you've been wanting to talk about but haven't yet said what it is."

"I needed time and I needed the right people, you see. I can't just shout this particular plan to the world. It's dangerous, very, very dangerous but in truth, I see no other way forward for the Catholics of this beleaguered country."

He took a deep breath. "I'm going to trust you both. I've only just met Guido so I am taking a chance but Tom, I doubt you would have brought him here if you had any doubts at all about his capabilities and his trustworthiness. Can I ask, though, Guido, how long have you been a Catholic?"

"From the age of fifteen, Robin. I converted at the time Margaret Clitherow was so cruelly executed. I have spoken of it across Europe to let people know how brutal our authorities are against those who hold to the true faith."

"Ah, yes, Margaret Clitherow. Should any of us ever forget that martyrdom it would be a disaster. A momentous occasion for the faith, a tragedy for her children and family. And, all the Catholics in England, too. Outrageous is not too harsh a word to use in connection with that dreadful happening. That means you have been one of us for a long time. Your faith must be rock solid, my friend. Right, I am going to say what is in my mind, what I think should happen to change the course of religious intolerance and persecution in this country. What I am about to say is treason, so believe me when I say I trust you both with my life. If I didn't, nothing would persuade me to say this. It is simply this.

"I want to get enough powder in a cellar somewhere to blow up Parliament when the king and all his officials are in it. I want to wipe them all out so we can start again. There is no longer time to talk. There must be action!"

The words hung in the air above the table, as solid and real as the fruit in the centre. It was as if they could reach out and grab one of them, rather than an apple, take it, look at it, study it and return it to its place in the sentence.

Shock registered on Tom's face, shock which changed to one of agreement. A slow smile began to work its way across his features and he nodded to show his agreement.

Guy felt a frisson of excitement that offset the stark horror of what Robin had in mind because at last, at long last, he felt someone was taking the lead, someone was prepared to do something about the situation. Robin was prepared to use violence if necessary to change the regime and allow Catholics the freedom they sought, if not restore Catholicism to its true position as the church of the English once more.

"It's treason, as I said," Robin warned them as they sat thinking about it. "Treason means the ultimate death if we fail. You know that. Hanging, drawing and quartering is the worst death a man can face. That is, if we are not tortured before that. This is something you need to think on; to be sure you can face it if you take the decision to join us. I have already decided. I am already committed to the cause. All I need is people to commit to the cause with me."

"Your faith must be deep," Guy observed with the greatest respect for his host. "You have chosen a pathway of violence and the end, if it fails, will be even more violent."

"My faith is deep, my friend." Robin looked at Tom and then at Guy. "Tom here knows of it, knows my commitment to the cause is absolute. Jack Wright is with us. I understand you know him, Guido."

"That I do!" Guy was pleased to think his old friend was involved. "Jack and his brother Kit are old friends. You can rely on them."

"I have the distinct impression I can rely on you too."

"I am committed, too," Guy said with total sincerity. "I know the consequences. I am prepared to face them. Some years ago I made a promise, a vow, to God. I said I would serve Him, even if it meant laying down my life. I will do anything to further the cause."

"Have you ever seen a hanging, drawing and quartering?"

"No. I have not seen any judicial execution, Robin, but my imagination has supplied enough details for me to fear it. Having said that, I am still with you."

"Good man! If we had more like you, the cause would have been won a long time ago."

Guy looked down, unwilling to accept compliments for something he felt was no more than his chosen destiny. God had spoken and he had obeyed. Nothing else needed to be said about it. He wondered who else would be brought into the conspiracy and a tiny thread of cold logic laced with fear asked whether those who were to come could be trusted.

"We will talk again of this plan. It is not to be discussed lightly, for it is far from being a trivial act we consider here. It is murder and that is against God's law. Murder not only of an anointed king and his ministers, but innocent people too. Unfortunately I see no other way to restore His chosen faith to this beleaguered land and to find solace for those hard pressed to follow that faith. Think on it and we will talk of it again."

The subject was closed. With relief they turned the talk to other things, the state of London at the present time, the overcrowding, the way the houses were spilling out into the countryside, how the villages would be swallowed up in the metropolis if proper control was not exerted and who would do that, when money could change hands and yet more properties were built, each moving a little further out.

It was something that concerned them all and they talked of it for some time. Beneath the talk, though, the thoughts were still churning. Guy could see that, as from time to time a sentence would trail off, a sentence would dry up in its tracks and the eyes would go blank as the thoughts turned inward. It's what we need! He thought urgently, proper action! As long as the others who come can be trusted, it can be done! He began to wonder how he could calculate how much gunpowder would be needed and what kind of fuse. He realised one of his sentences had trailed off and the other two were looking at him. They didn't seem surprised.

"My apologies. My thoughts were elsewhere for a few moments."

"My friend, it is nothing. We will do this from time to time. We have committed ourselves to an act of pure unbelievable violence, the like of which has never been seen before in this country. To remove the king and all his hangers-on in one fell swoop is beyond the imagination of most people. I have seen it as a vision. I know it can be done, with the right expert to plan the explosives and set the fuse. You come with the highest recommendations, Guido. I know you are my man. I know you are right for the task. Fear not. This will succeed and we will be victorious. The rotten heart will be removed once and for all."

Guy nodded, unable to speak. He had never been praised in such a way; it was balm and yet salt to his aching heart. He longed for acceptance, if only it didn't come at the price of many lives, some of which would be innocent. And still the thought of treachery from within nagged at him, a tiny cold worm of doubt.

That doubt seemed to be subdued when, a few weeks later, Thomas Percy was brought to the house to meet them. He was an energetic friendly man who had links to the great earl of Northumberland and a close family tie to the Wrights. He could not come with better credentials, thought Guy.

They sat around the table in Robin's sanctuary, each with their tankard of the fiery spirit, Tom, Jack Wright, Thomas Percy, Robin Catesby and Guy. There was the usual preliminary talk where they became comfortable with one another. Credentials had already been established and Guy was content to have Thomas Percy in the room with him. He had decided that was his own small 'test' of someone's reliability and trustworthiness.

The talk inevitably moved to Robin's Great Plan. Thomas was extremely enthusiastic, despite its elements of mass murder and treason. He urged action, not talk. "Talk gets nothing done," he insisted. "We could talk forever but will this government listen to our justified demands? Is it possible that our words – and others – can change the mind of this king so that he is lenient toward Catholics? I think not. Only action, gentlemen, only action, such as that our good friend Robin is proposing. I am with you, to the end!"

In what appeared to be a sudden surge of emotion, Robin got to his feet and held out his clasped hands across the table. "Join with me in a solemn oath to pursue this course to its end, gentlemen."

Guy stood and put both his hands around Robin's.

"I am with you to the end. I swear this on the blood of our Saviour and of His Holy Mother, the Blessed Virgin. I will stand strong and fight for the cause regardless of the consequences."

Tom Wintour stood to add his handclasp to theirs.

"I swear by Almighty God and His angels that I will stand true and strong to the cause regardless of the consequences."

Jack Wright, already standing, held out his hands too.

"I am with you, I declare and swear it in the name of the Holy Mother and all the saints in Heaven regardless of the consequences."

Thomas Percy pushed his chair back and put his hands around those already clasped.

"By the sacred blood of the martyrs, I stand with you in this venture come what may. I pray that God's mercy will be with us and that we will succeed."

The moment seemed to freeze into a tableau of deep emotion and commitment. The strength they radiated was almost physical to the point when it was an effort to break apart, to hide faces which might reveal unmanly emotions. When they did, they stood, hands at their sides, uncertain of their next words, their next actions.

"I believe Father Gerard awaits us in the next room." Robin finally broke the difficult moment. "If you would care to join me in the sacred Mass…"

Somehow, without it being expressed by anyone, they knew they had to keep their oath secret from Father Gerard and from anyone else who might be damaged by the knowledge. Father Gerard had problems enough just being a Catholic priest, without having knowledge of such a major event being planned. What they did not need to do was swear each other to secrecy. Their very lives were at stake by simply meeting to discuss such a devastating act; they had to rely on each other to keep close mouthed.

Heads bowed, lost in their own contemplation, they filed out of the room and into the next, where Father Gerard was at prayer. One by one they knelt to say their own prayers before the solemn Mass began.

One big problem for the group was the need for individual members to remain innocuous. The authorities were highly suspicious of any Catholic activity and so they all, without exception, needed to keep a low profile. Fortunately London was a teeming cosmopolitan city which was expanding at an alarming rate and remained a place where strangers were not always obvious. The group had the great luck and good fortune of Thomas Percy securing a promotion in the service of the Earl of Northumberland, something that could be proved if anyone asked. No one ever did but it was a comforting thought that he had a perfect alibi to be in London at that time.

The bigger problem the group had to confront was the continuing anti-Catholic legislation going through parliament. Heavy fines for those who refused to attend a Protestant church service, arrests and executions for priests and those who attended them were becoming commonplace. Priests and their associates or servants were hanged, drawn and quartered, the traditional 'traitor's' death. It brought home to the conspirators just what they faced if their plan were to fail, but it did not deter any of them from their aim. If anything it strengthened their resolve, for the clamp down on Catholics was increasing and the fervour with which it was being carried out meant that something, a dramatic happening, was called for. God is with us, they told one another when they met. Surely God cannot allow this to go on, seeing His servants dying in this way just for holding a different faith to the one the law says must be observed. And who is to tell a man what to believe, anyway? That is for his own conscience. Emotions were running high but they had to proceed with caution, they had to be patient, something that did not come easy to men who were used to action, fast and lethal action at that.

Something else reared its head - their consciences began troubling them over the death of innocents when Parliament was demolished. There were those who were stout supporters of the Catholic cause, there were others who had pleaded their commitment to the Protestant religion to retain or even gain titles and honours but who in their hearts remained true to the Catholic faith. It was a fact that in every 'atrocity', no matter who caused it, the innocent were entrapped and would lose their lives. The group discussed this many times during the months following their commitment to the plan and came up with no one answer which satisfied them all, unless it was really that a few must die for the greater good of the many.

Although the main core of the group, as Guy saw it, had sorted it in their mind, as each new person joined, they had to go through the same discussion, the same heart searching. Whilst it was easy to say 'yes, we will destroy this evil government and monarch and establish the true church as the religion of this country', to say innocent Catholic lives would be lost made it a very different proposition. But still they held true to their cause, because to do anything else would mean that the state had won and that they could not allow, under any circumstances.

Guy had greater concerns at the time. As the summer wore on and plans were endlessly discussed, he found himself wondering how and why he was involved with these people. Jack was a friend; they had been friends since schooldays. He was completely under the spell of Robin Catesby, whose charismatic personality shone so bright that if there were flaws in the plan, Guy could not see them for the light Robin cast over everything. He was convinced they were totally committed but for some reason Tom Wintour bothered him and yet he had shown no signs of being anything but trustworthy. When

Robert Keyes was recruited to the group, Guy realised his suspicions had switched to the new arrival. It was obviously his own deep-seated paranoia which was causing the problem, not any degree of trustworthiness or otherwise of his co-conspirators.

Robert Keyes had a critical role to play in the conspiracy, in that he had the care of Robin's house in Lambeth and, even more critically, was related through family to a known recusant who could obtain the gunpowder. It was all coming together.

By December, Robin's servant and trusted confidant, Thomas Bates, had joined them. Guy's paranoia had more people to encompass, without knowing why he felt that way. All he knew, deep in his innermost heart, was that one among the conspirators was likely to betray them. Surely anyone drawn into the conspiracy was there wholeheartedly? Surely they were totally committed to throwing off the yoke of Protestantism and re-establishing the Church of Rome as the only true church for England? He believed that all true thinking English people, no matter which way their faith was inclined, would join in the battle for freedom of choice in the matter of religion, that the heaviness of the fines, the imposition of many Scottish barons and lords over them, would be enough to make them fight back against the regime. He had to hold to this hope; there was no point in going on otherwise.

In some of his darkest moments, when he did not feel his usual direct link with the Lord God, when the Blessed Virgin appeared to hide her face behind black clouds, Guy wondered why he did not walk away from it all, go back to Scotton, move in with his stepfather and forget all this. Then he thought of his regiment, of his commanding officer, of the bonhomie and closeness of the group of soldiers he had worked and trained with. He imposed that picture on the group with which he was now involved and stepped back from the decision to leave. He knew if he did, he would break the oath he had made to be there when the event happened and that was not part of his personality at all. He would not be able to live with himself if he broke a sacred oath to compatriots who shared the same aim as himself, no matter his personal doubts and fears. But the doubts were there, the thought that he should turn away and go back to the depths of Yorkshire was there and he didn't know why. He would look into his heart during his quiet moments and recite his mantra:

I promised my life to God if He wanted it.

One night, as he said this, he had a response which shook him.

A voice said: *I do.*

Guy looked around the small room which he shared with a man called Watkins who had some kind of business arrangement locally. It was in an inn close to Robin Catesby's house in Lambeth. The room was shabby, although clean, with the minimum of furnishings: a table, a small cabinet, hooks to hang up clothes and two narrow beds were the limit of its offerings. There was nowhere for anyone to stand and not be seen yet the words had sounded loud enough in his head for them to have been spoken aloud, as if directly into his ear. He went down on his knees, bowing his head in prayer, knowing the voice had come from God himself. As he did so, a beam of sunlight came through the distorted glass in the window and shone directly on him, pinning him to the bare floorboards. He stared at the sunshine, smiling with relief and happiness. It was the sign he had been waiting for without realising he had been waiting for it. God had smiled on him; God had set His seal on the conspiracy. God had spoken. It was enough. No matter what delay there was, and there seemed to be one delay after another no matter how hard they tried to organise a date and time, it would go ahead.

It will happen in God's good time, he told himself. God directed this, God is in control of this. It will happen when He wishes it to, not when we wish it to. If in the meantime I still feel like an outsider, despite my commitment to the cause, that is my problem. I will deal with it as I have always done, by walking alone. Where else would I be?

If that walking alone meant walking into death as part of the fight, then so be it. If there is a traitor among us, so be it. Did not Jesus Himself face the same thing? Did He not walk to His destiny with a certainty that it would end in disaster? Did He not suffer His own moment of doubt and agonising fear and did He not bravely go to His death anyway? He had Romans to fight; I have Protestants to fight. Same enemy, different name. Anyone who tries to impose a rigid rule on those who should have freedom deserves to have the people rise up against them. With this one act of extreme violence, will we not stir the hearts of the people so that they will rise up against the government and demand their rights? They cannot fail to do otherwise! God grant them the strength and wisdom to do it when we carry out our act! We do it for them, not for ourselves! We are doing this; we are risking everything for the Catholics of England!

No more doubts, he told himself. Look for the traitor if you must, Guido Fawkes, study every person, everyone recruited to the plan, but doubt not yourself. You are there to the end, no matter what that end might be.

Chapter Thirteen

The hours of darkness and pain are as endless as the wait for the right time, for the Parliament to decide to sit, for us to put everything in place and for the plot, for such is the way we thought of it, to go ahead. Before then, oh before then, others had to come, others who did not have the true faith to go through with it. Do I blame them? Look how I suffer now, how I lie here in agony, unable to move, unable to do anything but remember. Should I blame them for not wanting to be part of it? Them. One. Him. He put us in this situation. He killed the enterprise and killed my friends, too. Dear God, Almighty Father, I want this to be over! I cannot, cannot, exist another minute and yet I live on. Why? Why? In the name of all that is holy and sacred, why?

***

Robin cautioned patience through the long Christmas festivities up to Twelfth Night. It was all right for Robin, Guy thought, feeling a little resentful at times, he has money and I have none. If it were not for the others helping me, I would have no money at all. In the end he confessed his need for help to Robin, who promptly gave him a room in his Lambeth house and scolded him for not mentioning it earlier. He was overlooking Guy's pride and independence, only in the very last resort did he ask for help.

It was with a heart full of gratitude that Guy moved his few pathetic belongings to Robin's house, where he had a small room with a small window and a sense of confinement. It didn't matter, it was rent-free and his to use as he wished. He longed to pin a crucifix to the wall, a public demonstration of his faith, but felt it would be asking for trouble. Instead he stood and made an impassioned prayer to God, to the Lord Jesus, to the

Virgin and all the saints and angels in heaven, before drawing an invisible cross on the wall over his bed. In his mind it glowed with an unearthly golden light. It was enough. He was protected and secure in his physical and spiritual body and mind.

He did his best to limit his coming and going so as not to draw attention to the house or to himself. He found employment at a local carpentry shop, helping out with deliveries and some of the heavier work, particularly lifting and carrying large pieces of wood for the craftsmen to fashion into various pieces which somehow came together to make useful items of furniture. The lesson was not lost on him. First, he was following his Lord by going to work with wood, second, disparate pieces could be fashioned in such a way that they fitted together to make something useful. That was the way he saw the group, different people from different backgrounds coming together, making their oath of allegiance to one another and committing themselves to the One Cause, the overthrow of the hated Protestant regime.

Work gave him a valid reason to be in the area. It also gave him a little money to contribute to the household and have a tankard of ale from time to time with his friends. He realised after a while he was looking for the same closeness with this group as he had found in his regiment and, to his great disappointment, it wasn't there. His lack of ability to chat on light inconsequential subjects, his failure to laugh at seemingly stupid comments or someone's misfortune in falling over or spilling something down their clothes meant he was almost unconsciously sidelined by those for whom this was second nature. He could not change his ways. He was, by his own admission, a reserved, solemn man who saw nothing humorous in innuendoes about women or such trivial happenings. Such a person was rarely a welcome part of a group but he was tolerated and, at times, that was almost enough.

It was with a sense of keen anticipation when on the first day of the New Year, Lady Day, 25th March, newcomers were admitted to the conspiracy and at the same time, a lease was taken out on a house with a cellar in the Parliament precincts. The group had grown larger. Tom Wintour's older brother, Robert, had joined them, Kit Wright came to be with his brother Jack and a man named John Grant, brother-in-law to the Wintours, added his considerable knowledge to the enterprise. Guy was pleased with be with Kit again. John Grant was someone Guy could associate with, a taciturn man with strong feelings. He owned Norbrook, a large house that regularly sheltered priests and recusants. This made it an obvious target for the authorities, but such was the power of John Grant's personality and his known rages, the men commissioned to track down priests and others had begun to hold back from instigating searches in the house. This meant many could remain there in total safety.

It also meant Norbrook was another sanctuary for Catholics. The conspirators had homes across the country, known to the network, every one of which was vital to the Catholic community and to the conspirators themselves. They in turn were interlocked by marriage, making them a family group. Even on this point Guy was the outsider. He was there by reputation and experience, chosen for his steadfastness, his commitment and his experience with explosives. The others were there because of family ties as well as their combined commitment to the overthrow of the Protestant regime. The family ties were strong, almost as strong as the determination they brought to their desire to succeed. Guy envied them their familial ties and wondered if they realised how much he felt like the odd man out. It was not something he could confess to them, they wouldn't have understood it. The nearest he came to feeling accepted was having his own room in Robin Catesby's home. It was his sanctuary; it felt more like home than his room in Wheatley Hall.

Plans were being discussed to kidnap the young Princess Elizabeth, on the basis that after the destruction of most of the royal family and the government, they would need a figurehead for a new regime. It made sense but Guy could not get involved wholeheartedly in that side of it. He felt that any royal person would be an affront to the Catholics who had suffered so long under the regimes imposed by monarch after monarch. He soon realised that this would not be a popular point of view so he found reasons to stay out of it and let the others deal with that knotty problem.

The discussions seemed to go on endlessly, who would be the Princess's guardian after the event, who could they nominate, was it right to eliminate the innocent: theological and philosophical discussions which got them nowhere, for every one of them held different views. What was at stake was the future religion of England, all else was incidental. If there were deaths of innocents, then so be it; they were martyrs to the cause. If it was for the greater good, it had to be. It seemed every time Guy walked into the study, someone was discussing one or other of these topics, turning them over and around and inside out. If he had to stay, he would sit quietly, not wanting to contribute an opinion, for he felt it to be almost heretical when he heard the deep thoughts the others expressed. It was also a deeper thing than that, his thoughts were his own. They were for him and his God to understand and appreciate, not others.

His lack of contribution somehow made him feel even more of an outsider. If anyone noticed he did not join in, they did not mention it. He was not invited to say what he thought or felt. Maybe they knew, he thought, maybe they understood he did not want to be part of that. It was enough that he had a role, he was the explosives expert, it was enough for him that he was part of this group in that way, even if it did seem incidental at times. He knew well it was a critical role and that in truth the entire enterprise rested on his ability and knowledge of gunpowder. He had that, if nothing else.

He had another problem. Robin's house was comfortable, secluded and staffed with servants he insisted could be trusted. That surely went without saying, for Robin would not launch such a traitorous campaign if he could not trust those who served him, people who might conceivably overhear something, no matter how careful they were. That was not the problem, as before it was Guy's total lack of interest in anything sexual.

One of the maidservants, a pretty woman named Susanna, someone who had long curling black hair that refused to stay under a cap but trailed tantalisingly round her face, was making an all-out effort to seduce him. He found her loitering outside his room, coincidentally going up the stairs when he was coming down so that he was forced to push past her, inevitably brushing against her arm or shoulder as she contrived to get in his way. She leaned over him at mealtimes, pressing her full breasts into him as she did so. She smiled, flaunting her ankles with lifted swirling skirts as he walked past. He invariably ignored her or turned away deliberately, so he could not see what she had on offer. He was aware of her scowls when he did that and knew he had made an enemy when her advances continued to be spurned but it was not something he could help, nor did he intend to explain himself. It was a personal thing and that was not a topic for discussion with anyone other than God Himself. It had been bad enough speaking of it to his mother and stepfather when he was thrown out of the position at Cowdray Hall. He just hoped her enmity would not affect his role in the conspiracy.

A small house was found, one which had a cellar cluttered with wood, coal and debris. As far as the conspirators were concerned, it could not be better sited. The cellar was directly under the House of Lords, once part of the old kitchens belonging to the palace of Westminster. It had ornate arches and beautiful brickwork, none of which had been looked at for a good many years. It all contributed to make it an exceptional place for their plans. The cellar was unbelievably dirty, neglect and ignorance of its original function, combined with its ongoing use as some kind of storeroom for the 'house' above it had rendered it nothing more than a place fit for coal and wood. And gunpowder, it was the perfect site for gunpowder.

The house itself was small, too small for more than one person to sleep there. It was decided that Guy would move in, under an alias, and carry on going to work from there as any normal tenant would. He was asked and of course he agreed. In truth he had no choice.

It was with a sense of loss that he gave up the room in Robin's house. He had been happy there, or rather, content, for Guy realised he did not know the meaning of the word happiness. He moved his few possessions into the property and began using the name John Johnson to anyone who asked.

Surprisingly, he felt good, even though he had been unhappy to make the move. He was even more an essential part of the conspiracy now, he was the one who was in the property which would house the gunpowder, he was at the centre of the whole thing. No one could ignore him. He berated himself for what he saw as a childish thought, a longing to be accepted, whilst acknowledging it was a deep-seated part of his persona and hard to ignore. He vowed to spend more time in prayer to overcome it.

What it did do was remove him from Susanna's constant attentions, which was a good thing. He hoped that she would turn her attentions to someone else once he was no longer in the house.

Guy returned from work one evening, his clothes thick with sawdust, his throat raw from coughing and his body in need of food. He was clutching a meat pie bought from a street vendor and a flask of fine ale bought from an inn near the carpenter's. Tired, ready for food and rest, he thought nothing of the fact his door appeared to be open slightly. He pushed it ajar and went in.

Susanna was sitting in the only chair by the cold hearth. His heart leapt into his mouth when he saw her; he had no idea she knew where he lived.

"Guido." She stood, smiling her enticing but menacing smile that tore at his heart. He wanted but did not want to be involved with this sensual exciting woman. She had been a torment to him at Robin's house and now she had invaded this sanctuary. He was angry but tried not to show it. He put the food and ale down on the table and stood, hands at his side, staring at her.

"Have you nothing to say to me, Guido? You leave the Master's house without so much as a goodbye and thank you for everything? You ignored all I had to offer you and walked away? I think not, Guido Fawkes!"

Before he knew what was happening, she had enfolded him in her strong arms, her full red lips were pressed against his, the softness of her breasts crushed against his chest, her pelvic bones ground against his. He did not hold her, he did not return the kiss, he did not even speak.

She grabbed at his groin and he let her, knowing what she would find.

"Susanna, leave me alone." The words came from the depths of his very being, loaded with desperation and bitterness. "I have no room in my life for a woman."

"No." She stood back, disappointment writ clear on her face. "No man has stayed limp when I kissed him. I see you are incapable. No wonder you turned away from me."

"I turned away from you not for that reason. I turned away because-" he hesitated for a moment and then decided on the truth. "I committed myself to the Blessed Virgin many years ago. I vowed to stay chaste and serve only Her for the remainder of my life, no matter how long or short that life may be. I have lain with no woman at any time. I am not going to do so now, not with you or anyone."

"I came to give you one more chance. I came because I wanted you. I now find you are incapable. Forget the stupid oath, Guido! That has nothing to do with the fact you can't do it! God in heaven, what a waste!"

The anger welled up and burst out of him, a combination of hatred of all things sexual and her invasion of his privacy.

"Get out of my life, Susanna! Let me do what I have to do for your Master and his friends! I need no woman to complicate matters." The words came out cold and hard, sharper than he intended but they had the desired effect. She snatched up her shawl and stalked toward the door.

"MISTER Johnson," she said loudly, as if anyone could hear her, "I will do just that. I will be gone out of your life, for now. But be sure of this; if I can find a way to repay you for all I have suffered, then I will."

"I have had nothing to do with your suffering, woman! You chose to try and tempt me, I did not encourage you!"

"No, that's the truth, for sure. But no woman will stand being scorned. Not one, no matter how they look or what their bodies are like. I know I am desirable, many have said so. Your rejection hurts. Remember that!"

With those final cutting words she was gone, her wooden clogs clattering down the street, heading toward the Catesby house, temper written in every line of her body. Guy sighed, closed the door and went to eat his food. No matter what she said, what he felt, he had to be strong for what was to come. Food and drink were needed, so was sleep, but he had the distinct feeling sleep would be hard to come by that night. Susanna had touched a deep core in him. He had known for a long time he was 'incapable,' as she so indelicately put it. The 'problem' had not troubled him before but she had used it to make him feel less of a man. He could do without that hurt. The food stuck in his throat, his anger unabated. Damn all women for their contriving sensuous ways! Why couldn't they leave a man be when he makes it clear he doesn't want them? Surely there were enough other men out there to turn their wiles onto with better effect? He drained the ale and sat cursing quietly. Women, bane of his life. Staring at him, trying to catch his attention, pulling at his heartstrings. It was one of the reasons he had made up his mind not to go home again, he knew his sisters would do their best to keep him there, to get him married to some local girl and start a family. The thought was abhorrent to him. He needed freedom from all ties to be God's fighting man. Go do your worst, Susanna, he thought, biting savagely into the now cold pie, go do your worst. If God is with me, then He will help me win.

Gunpowder. Packed in old barrels, firkins or hogsheads, whatever would hold the volatile material. Loads of it. A small boat was used to bring it across from Robin's home in Lambeth, which as it happened was directly opposite the house Guy was living in, on the other side of the Thames.

During that summer Guy began to really believe they were going ahead with the plot, that it was not just a group of friends sitting around fantasising about what they could do, given the right men, the right place and the right opportunity. To sleep at night, knowing the barrels were below him in the dusty dirty cellar where no one would ever think of looking, gave him a thrill, a sense of importance, a conviction that God was with them and their audacious plan would succeed. The House of Lords and everyone in it would be blown sky high and the government of England would change in that second.

He wondered how much of a sound it would make. Thirty-six barrels was a considerable amount of explosive, but they dared not do half a job. That would be worse than not doing anything at all. Sleepless nights were enlivened by the thought of the great building being blown apart to the accompaniment of an ear bursting, earth-shattering boom! Indicating to all Catholics that the overthrow of the hated regime had begun at last. And not a moment too soon, either.

He was asked to travel to Flanders once more, to use his influence and contacts to raise help for the cause from the Spanish. The small group which had planned the assassinations was insufficient to manage a complete take-over, they needed a regiment of well-trained Catholic mercenaries and fighters to do that. He agreed to go, it was better than hanging around in London whilst talk went on and on and on about this small point or that. The carpenter agreed to his taking a break from work to go to Europe 'on business for Mr Catesby' and it was all arranged with the minimum of fuss.

The journey was a familiar one to Guy, the coach to the coast, the long tedious journey across to the continent, the capricious weather which created havoc with so-called sailing schedules. After a most uncomfortable journey, he arrived once again on foreign soil, this time with a different aim and a different standing. He had letters of recommendation to high-ranking officials which would give him access to offices he would not otherwise have been able reach. He had no doubt that somewhere his name had been recorded by Government spies, no one who crossed the Channel to meet up with soldiers could expect to remain entirely incognito but that did not worry him. Before too long, the Government which had registered his name would not exist anymore.

As had happened many times before, he was greeted with great friendliness, wined, dined, given a comfortable room for his stay but every request was met with evasive answers, wrapped up in diplomatic talk which said much and said nothing. Disappointed, he returned to England with the news, became John Johnson again and caught up on the happenings of the conspirators.

It was with some dismay he heard that yet more people were to be added to the group. Robin did not seem to think it was a problem but the more that came, the more chance there was of betrayal. Guy had not told Robin, or anyone else, of Susanna's visit and veiled threats. It was not something he could discuss with anyone without a good deal of embarrassment. Some things were best left unsaid, he told himself, whilst nursing a nagging worry that he should tell someone about it.

The biggest problem he found when he returned to England was not the talk of extra conspirators being brought in but the fact that the gunpowder had decayed and was useless. Yet more had to be brought across the river, along with a quantity of firewood to conceal its progress and its storage. The whole thing was fraught with danger for they had no legitimate reason to store gunpowder.

It was done right under the noses of the authorities who, for their own reasons, were poking around the dockyards, checking shipments. No one had a good reason for this going on, unless a rumour had begun to circulate. Robin denied that anyone had spoken to any other about the plot, but people were uncertain and restless. The checking of inventories and cargoes was not a good sign, but on the night of the lunar eclipse, when the superstitious remained indoors for fear of dire consequences, a boat slipped quietly across from the Lambeth side of the Thames and unloaded a further quantity of gunpowder. Willing hands quickly transferred the barrels to the cellar, standing them apart from the decayed powder so there could be no mistake when the time came.

Just when all seemed settled, Robin brought in three more people. Ambrose Rookwood, on the surface, was a good recruit, he was rich, had contacts and was a devout Catholic, but they had managed without those attributes up to that moment. What he did have was a considerable stable of fine horses and the ability to rent another property in the Midlands which the conspirators could visit, knowing there were horses stabled there they could use if needed. Rookwood used the known builder of secret bolt-holes, Little John, to construct a cellar and tunnel leading away from the property, Clopton House. Maybe, Guy mused, he did have his uses. The next recruit he did doubt from the start, though.

Robin's cousin, Francis Tresham, became part of the group. His father had died and Francis had become the tenant of a large estate which was saddled with many debts. Whether he would benefit from the overthrow of a government in such a violent manner was subject to speculation but he had, for his own reasons, decided to join the conspirators, even if he did immediately bring in a note of discord. He had doubts about the moral aspect of the act, as others had, but he voiced his with great authority.

Guy wondered why he was there, why he was risking so much whilst he did not seem to be totally committed to the overthrow of the government and the monarchy. What drove this man? Was he in league with the authorities? Guy wished many times he had the ability to see into another man's heart. There was definitely something wrong there and he did not know what it was. He only knew he was unhappy with Tresham being in the group.

Sir Everard Digby, another person of imposing height, personality and demeanour, was drawn in. His task was to rent yet another property in the midlands where he could arrange a meeting and possibly take charge of the Princess Elizabeth after the event.

Guy was doubtful about the need for all these new conspirators, but went along with Robin's demands that he had to have them to encompass the great scope of the plot. Guy really had no choice; he was just a member of the group, not the leader himself. If it had been he who was leading this plot, he would have kept the number of conspirators to an absolute minimum. It could have been done, he told himself as night after night he went over the plans in his head. Whilst he did not find them wanting in any way, apart from the fact he felt there were too many people, there was always the human element and in that lie the ultimate danger – discovery.

Chapter Fourteen

Just a few weeks to go and still so many plans to make. But so close to the day of destruction! So close I must be now to the end. God grant it be so for I have not had a moment of relief. But they, they who inflicted the pain, are surely at their rest or their food or their comforts or with their companions. They surely are not giving a thought to those of us who lie here in total darkness and who would scream out our agony and despair if we had but voice to do it.

***

The plans were finalised over many meetings both in London and the midlands. Occasionally they took time out for dinner or supper parties, inviting non-conspirators to join them so no one would doubt their gatherings then and at other times but mostly they talked and talked until their heads were spinning. Nothing had ever been planned like this before, it was such a huge undertaking and there were so many imponderables, so many places where something could, and probably would, go wrong. Guy knew precisely how much fuse to lay and then light in the cellar and then how and where he could escape across the Thames. His task then was take a horse and ride to the coast where he would cross to Europe as soon as he could, leaving the devastation behind but carrying the news - and the reason for it – to the Spanish royal family and government. They had to realise it was the only way, that innocents had to be sacrificed for the greater good. Everyone believed they would understand and be with the conspirators in their great, almost momentous, undertaking.

In the middle of all the apprehensive tension, the repetitive recital of the plans for the event, with nerves stretched taut by the worries and concerns of the whole thing, Robin was informed of betrayal. Someone, one of their number or someone associated with them, had sent a letter to Lord Monteagle, warning him not to be in Parliament in the next session for fear of violence and he in turn had taken it immediately to Lord Salisbury, a leading Catholic peer in London. One of Lord Monteagle's servants was linked to the Wright family and passed on the information as soon as he became aware of it.

For some reason, suspicion immediately fell on Francis Tresham as the instigator or even the author of the letter. Robin and Tom Wintour cornered Francis, demanding to know the truth. He swore vehemently that he was not guilty, although he persisted in his attempts to get them to drop the plan and escape to the country before any retribution could be brought down on them. Guy was told of this soon after. It immediately brought back all his paranoia about Francis Tresham, someone he had doubted from the start. He didn't say this to anyone, as always, he kept his own counsel about these things, but he held the feeling close. One day, he thought, one day I will find out the truth and then – and then I will be able to do something about it, God willing. 'Vengeance is mine, saith the Lord' came into his mind and he smiled although it was a reluctant smile. Maybe. He would have to make up his mind about that when it happened.

Fierce debate raged among the conspirators. How much had been revealed, how much did Monteagle or Salisbury – or both – know of the plot? Who had written the letter and why? Was it a fake, a plant, to persuade the authorities to take seriously something that was already known? Had someone said something in confidence to a priest and it had been passed on? Guy longed to say out loud at these discussions 'you took too many people into the plot, Robin!' but the words were never said. They would have been traitorous. It was Robin's great plan, his dream to destroy a corrupt government and ruling royal family and replace it with a government sympathetic to the Catholic faith. Who was he, a mere explosives expert, to criticise who he had as part of the group? He held no rank, as some of the others did, no land holdings, no homes or horses that could be used. All he had was his skills and his devotion to the cause.

After endless discussion, they decided as a group to go ahead anyway. Too much had been risked already, it was agreed, too much had been committed for them to draw back now.

Following his instructions, Guy inspected the gunpowder and fuse on the 30th October, knowing members of the group were travelling to and from various locations to be in the right place at the right time – when the fuse was lit. For all his fears, as he worked with the explosive, he felt calm, oddly satisfied in his own mind. Something was at last being done and he was involved in that 'something'. He would be part of history in the making.

The days passed slowly, time dragging its feet, with the only cloud to be seen the fact of the letter to Lord Monteagle, with hardly anyone knowing at that time if it had been acted upon, or even taken seriously in the first place. If the authorities were aware, they were keeping very much to themselves. No untoward activity was discovered, no one seemed to be doing anything differently, no searches were being made of the Parliament building, for nothing had been disturbed in the cellar. Guy made a point of checking from time to time. His fears were running wild, like rats over a dung heap. He could hardly rest and sleep was out of the question. He had to play his part to perfection. Everything rested on him. The weight of responsibility was greater than any he had ever carried. It was almost too much.

Somehow it became the 4th, the day before it was all to happen. Guy was ill, sick to his stomach through lack of food and weary beyond belief because he had been unable to sleep for more than a few minutes at a time before jerking awake, shivering or burning with fever as his mind replayed every possibility, every variation on the gunpowder not firing, the whole thing going disastrously wrong, he not being able to escape after the gunpowder was fired and being crushed under the weight of the stonework, or the authorities discovering the plot and arresting him. That last scenario had him in such a state of terror he wondered if he could function when the time came.

Restless and unhappy, he wrapped in a warm cloak against the chill November day and went down into the basement of the Houses of Parliament. His intention was to check his escape route, but as he walked through, he heard the sound of boots and muttered voices. Quickly he walked back the way he had come, as if he had been on an errand of some kind. He turned his face away from the men when he passed them. No one spoke to him; no one asked why he was there. He hurried down a small side passage he had noted on earlier visits and waited in the darkness until he heard them leave. What were they doing? Searching for someone? Searching for – explosives? Were they taking the letter seriously after all? With a sense of rising panic he went back upstairs and tried quieten his mind. It didn't work. He waited for the time to go by, until he heard the watch call the hour of ten, when he left to go to Robert Keye's house as arranged previously to collect a watch Thomas Percy had left there for him, the better to time the fuse. Then he returned to his house and went down into the cellar to prepare the gunpowder for the greatest event ever in the history of England, the complete destruction of the House of Lords, royal family and all the counsellors who had so brutally oppressed the English Catholics. His heart was pounding loud enough that he was sure it could be heard right through the cellar, which was as silent as the grave. He wondered why he had chosen that as his simile, it could have been as silent as a – no, nothing else would do. He set the fuse carefully and was counting down the time under his breath when he heard the voices and stamp of feet. They were not deviating, they were not searching, they were heading for him. There was no doubt of it. They knew where they were going. What in the name of heaven had he or anyone else done to spark their suspicions? It was too late, too late, too late…

As the men walked in, triumphant looks on their faces, satisfaction in every line of their bodies, he felt his own traitorous insides betray him and everything was voided. They laughed and pointed, holding their noses, embarrassing and humiliating him.

They were rough, pushing him from one to other, punching him, kicking him, trying to get him to cry out in pain. He bit his lips and did not give them that satisfaction. They had to be content with making snide comments about the condition of his breeches. Then they tied him up, too tight to allow a single movement of his arms and hands, and marched him out of the cellar.

He did not get a chance to glance back at the source of all the hopes and dreams of a new regime. It was over. The nightmare had begun.

They asked many questions. Many faces leered at him, demanding the truth, who was with him in the plot to blow up Parliament. They wanted names, they wanted villains to execute, to expose to the world as the despicable people who would even contemplate let alone attempt to do such a thing.

They talked of the grace of God preventing the outrage, they spoke of the intervention of angels.

It was all Guy could do not to shout at them that it was God's plan they were carrying out, that it was not God's grace which had intervened, but the treachery of one of the conspirators.

He said nothing of this. "I am John Johnson," he told them, "a Catholic." He averred that the devil, not God, was responsible for the discovery of the plot.

He spoke directly to the king, the man he despised, that his regret was that he had not succeeded.

Guy was ice cold by then, rigid with fear but filled with righteous anger and a sense of overwhelming destiny, far greater than anything he had experienced previously in his life. He insisted Guy Fawkes was an alias, not his name. There was no indication they believed him. He took the chance to rant at the Scots, saying he wished he could blow them all back to Scotland.

In some ways they seemed impressed by his fortitude, in other ways they merely laughed at his attempts to justify the deaths of innocents for a cause.

When the king left the chamber, they scorned him, spat on him, beat him with their fists until he fell to the ground, all but unconscious. But he held on, giving nothing else away, no names, no addresses, to award his friends time to escape. He knew the escape plans, the horses that would be awaiting them to carry them to safety, he hoped.

Then they took him to the Tower and he knew everything was coming to an end.

Chapter Fifteen

Did they escape? Did I give them enough time? Who told them to come back? Was that Tresham, was that the evil woman taking her revenge for my lack of ability? Did she pressure Tresham? I know not. I know nothing but the pain I am in, the suffering I am enduring, the loneliness that is worse than the pain, the darkness that is even worse than the loneliness for in the darkness are demons and devils, tormenting and burning and cackling their evil laughter and in them I see a foretaste of what awaits me if the great God decides He did not direct my actions after all, that the sunshine and the voices were not from Him but from the Devil himself. Now I doubt. I doubt after all these years of belief. But who would not doubt, being here, awaiting -

***

Did they anticipate his fighting them tooth and nail or did they normally make a habit of sending four men to bring one prisoner out of his cell? Guy said nothing, did nothing to stop them as he was marched out of the dark damp place where he had been thrown the night before and ushered along interminable corridors of cold dark stone which made their boots sound ominous with every step they took. The men walked in step which made the noise even louder. No one spoke. It was a co-ordinated effort and obviously well-practised, too.

The corridors reeked of damp and fear. Guy knew he smelled bad, knew that no one cared about that, or anything concerning him, not his feelings or his life. He was nothing. A body, something to be carried or walked here and there and tortured and left and tortured again. He had no illusions about that. His fear was such that his throat was tight and it was hard to breathe, his stomach and bowels rebelled, wanting to discharge yet again all he had within him. His hands shook and his eyes watered, although he wasn't crying. He tried to blank his mind from all that lie ahead of him – and failed.

They stopped so suddenly he was rocked back on his heels. A door was flung back against the wall with a resounding clang that appeared to echo from every brick in the place. Still silent, the men lifted him up, locked his wrists into manacles dangling from the wall, locked his ankles into others and then walked out, clanging the door shut behind them. If he had been able, he would have shouted after them to at least leave him a light.

Almost immediately the pain set in. His joints began to complain, his tendons stretched, his shoulders felt as if they were being dislocated. And he knew it was just the start. The entire weight of his body was being held by the manacles holding his wrists. The iron dug into the flesh, causing its own pain, obstructing the blood flow in his veins by the pressure of the metal against his skin.

The cold of the cell was insistent, carrying claws in its invisible body, claws that sunk into exposed flesh and raked it, causing additional pain to that already there in skin and bone being dragged beyond endurance. By his reckoning the men had hardly had time to reach the end of the corridor and already he was ready to scream in agony. The chains were just long enough that he could not quite touch the floor but left it within a breath of his toes. If only he could stretch his arms a fraction and gain a little relief but it was not to be. Every movement sent every nerve flashing its message of agony to his brain. His mouth opened but the shriek which emerged was silent. It was more than his pride could stand to actually make a sound.

It was a lifetime of pain before they returned. Again, no one said a word. He was taken, shivering and ashamed for his body had betrayed him again and his breeches were soaking wet, before a man he had never seen before.

"Name?" the individual barked through a greying, roughly trimmed beard and lips that were too red for a normal person. The eyes were cruel in the extreme, not a shadow or hint of compassion in them.

Guy remained silent.

"Hang him up again." The order was given as casually as someone being requested to close a door. The men marched Guy away, back to the same cell, the same manacles, the same screaming agony but this time it set in even as they clamped the first wrist to the wall and left him dangling while they secured the other. He bit through his lower lip in an effort to maintain his dignity before the cold-hearted men. Only when the door slammed behind them did he begin to scream, tasting his own blood in his mouth.

He was thrown into a cold empty cell at night, left to suffer his agonising pains and his resolve to hold out. They were long, eternal nights of stifling darkness and unbelievable pain. It was hard to think it could get worse but he knew, if he did not tell them what they wanted to know, it would get worse

The next day Guy was hung on the wall, taken down, marched - as best he could – before the surly individual, saying little, admitting to no more than being a Catholic. The same thing at night, thrown into a cell, left for dead, collected in the morning and once again hung on the wall for eternity.

For two days his entire body shrieked at him to give in, to give them what they wanted and end the agony, but his pride refused to let him. Not only his pride but his conviction that what they had tried – and failed – to do was right and so that his friends, for he still thought of them as such, had time to get away. If he had to bear the brunt of the law for them, so be it. His body complained, his mind held out. There was the dichotomy, the difficulty, the serious state in which he found himself. The moment they fastened the manacles to the wall his mouth opened to shout the words they wanted to hear, the names of his friends, the facts behind the conspiracy, the moment they left he wished he had spoken but the interval between opening his mouth and the men leaving was the interval in which his mind clamped down on the physical act of speaking.

The red hot iron shoes were a different matter.

The third day he was taken from his cell and carried to another room, another place of torture. Here there were braziers and different instruments of torture, some he could not divine their purpose until they were used. He saw the iron being heated but could not comprehend its use until they brought it over to him, dragged off his boots and rammed the burning hot 'boots' onto his feet. His entire body and mind went into shock, his nostrils filled with his own burning flesh, his screams filling the dungeon and leaving the men unmoved. They had heard it all before. They would hear it again, many times.

It was then he told them he was not 'John Johnston', the name he had given when he was arrested, but Guido Fawkes, otherwise known as Guy, late of Yorkshire via Sussex and Europe and that he was a Roman Catholic. And still, even with horrendously burned blistered feet and his state of shock, he could not bring himself to reveal the name of his co-conspirators. It was as if something was blocking him. He longed for death, pleaded with God to take him, to end the misery. He prayed all night in his empty lonely freezing cell and was sobbing with misery when they came for him in the morning because he was still alive.

Still alive and capable of being tortured.

For their amusement, the torturers got him to sign his name. He did, proudly, firmly, an educated man in an uneducated world of men who were nothing but brutes

231

of the lowest order, there to inflict maximum pain on another human being without thought of what they were really doing. "Just doing what we're told," they said as if proud of it. Proud of breaking a man on the orders of someone higher than themselves, proud of wrecking a proud man and bringing him down to the grovelling level of a mentally retarded child. Bringing him down to the level where he could do little more than sob, was no more than a mass of screaming agonised flesh.

And they had only just started.

He endured a day and a night of nothing, no attention, no words, no food, no light. He wondered, during the endless hours when he could not stand on his blistered burned feet or sit because his back refused to support him for some reason he could not define, why he had given the name Guido. It was as if his time in Europe had changed him from an Englishman to a European, as if his allegiance had been transferred to another place entirely.

It was in the darkness that he came to the realisation that those who had called him Guido were the ones who had accepted him, who, for the first time in his entire life, had not made him feel like an outsider. In his moment of duress, and what greater duress could there be than your torturers demanding a signature, just for fun, for they had no reason to ask for it, that you sign a name that was not your birthright but a name adopted in another place for another group of people.

I miss them all, he mourned. I miss them more than I miss my family. What will they think of me, that I failed in our great scheme? Will they despise my memory? I did my best but you can do nothing when you are betrayed.

Oh sacred Lord Jesus, You too were betrayed. Now I know how it feels. It is a pain deeper than that they are inflicting on my body. A man I trusted gave the information to others. He of all of them gave us into the hands of the torturers. He knew what he was doing. He caused this agony, this despair.

Where are the others? Are they in other cells, being tortured even as I am? Are they screaming in agony, are they giving all the information I tried not to give? How many got away? Why is no one prepared to speak to me about this? Why is no one prepared to speak to me?

He recalled the time when he had returned from Sussex to his home, how his thoughts had seemed squirrel-like to him, leaping from topic to topic, from one thing to the other. He was doing it again, but he was helpless to stop himself from doing it.

After all, there was nothing else to do but think.

They came the next morning, different men, same faces, same determination, same coldness. They dragged him to a different cell, or dungeon, what did they call it, he wondered idly, until he saw what was in the middle of the room.

The rack. It was nothing more than wood and ropes, handles and cogs, a piece of machinery which could do anything, but what it did was draw a man's joints out of their place and leave the tendons twice as long as they were and the man himself in so much agony he loses the ability to breathe, let alone scream.

Guy found this out very quickly. He had thought hanging from the wall was bad but nothing had prepared him for this new agony. He could not stand and the men had no difficulty in securing him to the machinery. He could do nothing but let them. Fighting was out of the question, outside the scope of his diminished strength and already partly broken mind. He had held out as long as he could. His feet were blistered and raw, his shoulders already damaged probably beyond any chance of being healed and now his other joints were to be stretched beyond what was human.

The man who seemed to be in charge stood by and watched. Then he raised a hand as a signal and the cogs began to move. The agony, threefold, fourfold, fivefold, began.

"Speak." The voice was cold, no hint of compassion. There never would be. He had a job to do, he would do it.

Guy could not, even if he wanted to and at that moment he did want to. The pain was such his voice was snatched from his throat and no sound issued but the harshest of breaths, each laboured and torn from his lungs as if they were themselves being racked.

"Speak."

It went on for an entire day.

Guy had no food, no water, no respite. When the cogs were not turning they stayed where they were, he was not allowed a moment for any part of his body to begin to return to normal. When he did not speak enough in those intervals he would see the cogs begin to turn and know that the agony was to increase yet again when he felt there could be no higher – or lower – level it could reach.

He spoke, when he could, in gasps and stuttered words, gave his name and those of the conspirators.

They left him all night, in the rack. They left him stretched and tormented and tortured and screaming silently into the dark dungeon which smelled of fear and sweat, of urine and excreta and of quiet satisfaction on the part of the torturers that once again the terrible machinery had achieved its aim.

They began again the next day.

They had all the names, all the information, all they needed for a trial, mockery though it might be. They had it all and still they racked and still they tortured and called him names for what he had tried to do, still they taunted him that they would make him half as tall again

as he was. Only when there was no sound left to issue
from the parched lips, the raw throat, the ruined body,
were the ropes removed and a demand made that he sign
his name once again. He did and did not recognise the
hand which scrawled the letters or the letters which he
had written.

They carried him, two men, one under each broken,
destroyed shoulder, to a cell where they laid him on
straw and slammed the door on the darkness that was
within and without.

Chapter Sixteen

In the darkness he turned and moved first one leg, then the other. By a miracle his limbs could still obey his brain, how, he did not know. The mind cannot retain pain, it registered only that he was experiencing right then, the pain that the rack had inflicted was relegated to the total darkness, to the part of his mind he had shut off completely. All he had left, all, he thought with derision, was the screaming of his nerves in the stretched tendons which would never ever be right again, no matter what. Oh let it end soon, he prayed silently. Let it be over soon.

But there was the mockery of the trial to come first, to satisfy those who insisted that 'justice' be seen to be done. What justice was there to be found in information given under such extreme circumstances and cruelty? But it would be given that it was 'necessary.' Would it have made any difference if he had spoken out the moment he was arrested? He thought not, for they had no reason to rack him the entire second day, only that they wanted to spite him, repay him for what they knew he had tried to do, as if his execution would not be enough. He knew well the fate for traitors. It did not bear thinking about.

***

The main part of the hall in Westminster was packed with onlookers, men with coarse features and rough voices, women with hard faces and even harder voices, yelling and screaming obscenities as they fought for a place in the crush. They were drawn there by the notoriety of the accused, by the crime for which they were to be tried. They were avidly awaiting the sure verdict of death, seemingly impatient with the preliminaries of the trial yet wanting to hear it all so that they could relay it to their friends and family and be noted for having heard it themselves. The noise of so many people talking at once, shuffling, pushing, arguing, edging their way forward for a better view, was deafening. Guy could hear it even as he was carried along the corridor to the hall.

He was the only one being carried. His co-conspirators were walking, albeit with extreme difficulty, but they were still recognisable as human beings with the ability to move by themselves. He was not. Their heads were bowed, he could not see their faces and try and recognise the signs of agony. Had they been tortured too? Probably, but not as badly as Guy himself.

As the accused were led in or, in Guy's case, carried in, the tone of the spectators' voices changed. They began yelling obscenities and oaths, screaming for their heads, their bodies, anything. These people, thought Guy, these people who had no time for the monarch and his family were still ready to tear to pieces those who tried to dispose of them. How strange was the mind of the uneducated.

Each of the accused came in accompanied by a gaoler and shackled with heavy chains, despite the fact they would not have managed to run more than a yard before being torn apart by the mob even now baying for their blood.

He felt small, almost insignificant in the splendour of the hall, with its sweeping vaulted roof and towering walls. It was difficult to remember that the entire majesty of the place was being dwarfed by the very trial in which he was a central part.

Guy's mind was wavering from conscious to unconscious; everything fading in and out, going black. One of the men supporting him found a chair and pushed him into it, tying him to the back with a piece of rough rope. It seemed harsh but it was a kindness, it stopped him having to fight to remain upright. He slumped against the rope the moment it was fastened and closed his eyes. He might have imagined the words which were whispered in his ear as the rope was tied but he doubted it: "wish you had succeeded." It was enough to give him courage, despite the incredible pain he was suffering, to endure the trial. It became something he repeated over and over to himself whilst the court was silenced and the indictment was read.

"Wish you had succeeded." He was not alone.

The court officials somehow restored order and the business of trying the 'treasonable people' began.

Before the justices, the defendants, the prosecutors and the packed onlookers, the indictment was read out, that they collectively had endeavoured to end the life of the King, the Queen, the royal family and as many officials of the parliament as they could, because they were all heretics and heretics could not hold the throne or high office in the land. Guy listened, half abstracted, to the fancy legal words which he condensed to those few in his head. He only reacted when he heard that Kit and Jack had been killed. They were the lucky ones, he decided, even as he felt intense sadness at their deaths. Tresham, he heard, was dead – lies! His mind screamed at him. Lies! No, Tresham was not dead; Tresham had bought his way out as he bought his way in, he being responsible for the treachery that had brought them all to this, suffering and death. Tresham, who smooth talked and charmed and –

Forget it. A voice spoke clearly to him through the tumult of the pain he was enduring, through the many sounds that came between him and the court, creaking of timbers, voices, feet shuffling, robes swishing, people coughing and restlessly moving. A cacophony that all but rendered him deaf to that which was going on. He should concentrate, this was his fate, his future, his life – but that was all but over. He knew that and he craved it, reaching out for the bony arms of Death itself to come and take him, right now, as he sat there enduring the misery of knowing his friends were dead. The traitor, he knew it deep within him, was not dead but walking freely somewhere, safe, unrecognised, unknown. Alive and well. Not a pain, not a hurt and no doubt not a twinge of conscience either, if he knew the man. God knew that he had fought against bringing him in on the plot but none would listen to him. Fools! Too late for rancour, too late for sorrow and regret. Too late for anything but wishing himself dead.

Forget it, the voice said. Not easy to forget the person who brought the authorities onto them, who stopped the whole plot and doomed the country to having a Protestant monarchy as far as he could see.

Forget it. There was logic in the words, for at this point of his life/death, there was no point in hanging on to resentment. Sooner rather than later he would be meeting his God and would have to account for his thoughts and actions.

The rope dug into his ribs and gave him additional pain but without it he would be on the floor, under the feet of the gaolers and his co-conspirators, those that were left. Dignity had to be maintained. He was, after all, named as Guy Fawkes, Gent, in the indictment. Gentlemen did not give way.

Oh but he had. He had given way, he had given their names to the torturers, he had betrayed them, he had been too weak to hold out against the racking and the burning and the pain. Too late to say 'anyone would have given way, you held out long enough'; the truth was he didn't hold out long enough. He should have let them kill him in the torture chamber, but he didn't. Large tears began to trickle down his face and he raised a cautious careful hand to dash them away before they were seen. Even that movement all but took his breath away.

None of his co-conspirators had as much as looked at him. He did not exist in their eyes. He wondered if he had ever really existed in their eyes, other than someone who knew how to place a fuse. Apart from Kit and Jack - and even they he doubted were true friends – who was really a friend out of all of them?

We are accused of assenting to the Jesuit plan. We are accused of trying to put a superstitious religion in place. God knows it is not that long since the country believed that the 'superstitious Popish' religion was the right one. How contrary are the views of men when they are dictated by the monarch and that monarch not able to see clearly which is the True Faith. As the official droned on, Guy asked himself if he would not have been conscious stricken to have the many deaths as a stain on his soul if the plot had gone ahead. The answer, he knew, was no. The True Faith should have been restored. Now it was too late and it would never happen again, for no one would be foolish enough to make another attempt.

How many times can they say my name? If nothing else, that will be in the court records, along with the others, all the others, those whose names I gave because I had no choice, those whose names will go down on the record as traitors.

Are we? Are we not patriots and martyrs, fighting for that which we believe? Margaret Clitherow died for her faith. I am going to die for mine.

Random foolish thoughts ran through his mind, around and around, up and down, once again likened to a squirrel darting from one branch to another, sometimes dropping a nut to the ground. How many hours had he spent watching the wildlife going about its daily lives, how many times had he wished he could have used the knowledge he had gained in such a way rather than the knowledge he had acquired, arms, explosives and true and false friends and how to tell the difference. Would that the others had listened to him about Tresham!

Does the way we went about it need to be spelled out in such tedious detail? The facts are known, we could not dig a tunnel, we never attempted to dig a tunnel, no one is that foolish, for where would the earth have been taken had we tried it and how long would we have had to dig? Until the next monarch took over? No, bring in the gunpowder and set it to go. What else could anyone do to rid the country of heretics?

I want to die now. Let me die now. I cannot stand the pain another moment. I crave food, I crave water, I crave something to take away the pain. If that be Death itself then He can come and take me. I do not wish to be here.

But still the court droned on and still the onlookers shrieked and yelled and whistled and stamped, much to the annoyance of the officials trying to keep a semblance of order.

So we brought gunpowder in. How else do you destroy a building of that magnitude and solid masonry? Blowing it up was the only way. And we would have done it. Be assured of that, we would have done it if we had not been betrayed.

Yes we rented a cellar, yes we brought in twenty barrels of gunpowder. I do not know even now if that was enough, would have been enough, but it was dangerous just getting hold of that amount. Dangerous. How stupid to think of that now, when I am here, a broken man with a broken body and almost a broken mind, how dangerous could it be?

What's that smell? It's disgusting. It's —

Everything I have voided over the past few days. I am shamed.

I am starved. How stupid to think of being starved when I want to die. How stupid to long for water when I want no more than to quit this life.

How stupid to even try and concentrate. I cannot. There is no need anyway; the outcome is a foregone conclusion. This trial is for those in power to say it was done properly, that we were legally tried and found guilty. The court knows that. I know that. Those who stand trial here with me know that. What are they thinking, feeling, suffering right now? Certain knowledge of being executed? Are they terrified to their very entrails, which will be dragged out and burned before their eyes? Are they ready to void their bodies at the thought? Would they have given my name had it been them on the rack? They who were hanged from the wall, they who were burned with the red hot boots? They who were thrown in a dungeon and left to rot, no one to attend to their pains? They who were left on the rack all night? All night. A night that lasted for eternity. An eternity stamped forever in my mind by pain, every second a different pain, every minute an hour of suffering. Thank the Blessed Virgin that this existence will be over before too long, then I can go to my home and rest and be mended and visit the great God Himself. I can bow down before the Blessed Virgin and her Son and ask forgiveness for all I tried – and failed – to do to bring the True Faith back to England.

I am not old enough to die.

But I am ready to die.

They have broken me and there is no way on this earth I can be mended.

Life is done.

" … Henry Garnet, Oswald Tesmond, John Gerrard, and other Jesuits, Thomas Winter, Guy Fawkes, Robert Keyes and Thomas Bates, together with the said Robert Catesby, Thomas Percy, John Wright, and Christopher Wright traitorously did meet with Robert Winter, John Grant, and Ambrose Rookwood, and Francis Tresham, Esquires; and traitorously open Rebellion against our said Sovereign Lord the King; and to that end did publish divers feigned and false Rumours, that the Papists Throats should have been cut; and that thereupon divers Papists were in Arms, and in open, publick, and actual Rebellion against our said Sovereign Lord the King, in divers Parts of this Realm of *England*. To this Indictment they all pleaded, Not guilty; and put themselves upon God and the Country."

Guy slumped against the rope holding him up, unable to take any more. His mind was drifting, his body failing fast. His heart was beating slower than usual; he fought for breath even as he longed for death.

The words of Sir Edward Philips, Sergeant at Law, flowed over him almost unheeded.

"The matter that is now to be offered to you, my Lords the Commissioners, and to the Trial of you the Knights and Gentlemen of the Jury, is Matter of Treason; but of such Horror, and monstrous Nature, that before now, the tongue of man never delivered, the ear of man never heard, the heart of man never conceited, nor the malice of hellish or earthly Devil ever practised. For, if it be abominable to murder the least; if to touch God's Anointed be to oppose themselves against God; If (by Blood) to subvert Princes, states and kingdoms, be hateful to God and Man, as all true Christians must acknowledge: then, how much more than too monstrous shall all Christian Hearts judge the horror of this treason; to murder and subvert such a King, such a Queen, such a Prince, such a Progeny, such a State, such a Government, so complete and absolute, that God approves, the world admires, all true English hearts honour and reverence, the Pope and his disciples only envies and maligns?"

Guy heard part of it, scorned what he heard, slipped back into unconsciousness. He did not hear the full charges, he did not need to. He knew what he had tried – and failed – to do and that was all that mattered.

For a long time he heard nothing, the murmur of voices was no more to him than the sound of the ocean lapping against a quiet beach. The fact they spoke of him and his 'crime' was not enough to bring him back to consciousness, for there was nothing to say. They would ask why he had pleaded and he would tell them. If he could. They would ignore it anyway, the trial was pre-judged and decided long before they even took him into the torture chamber.

His one-time friends shuffled their feet, their manacles clanging and chinking against the wooden floor. His one-time friends continued to ignore him, not so much as a whisper of encouragement or thanks for holding out for so long against such overwhelming pain. Nothing. Did he really expect it? Well, yes, in a deep dark untouched corner of his still functioning mind, yes, he did. Just to show they cared a little. Obviously they didn't or were they horrified by the sight of his broken body? If they did not speak he would not know.

He told himself it didn't matter.

He didn't believe it even as he thought it.

The trial was interminable. A stage show, a performance in which he had a reluctant part. And only part of him was aware of it, anyway. The remainder was drifting on a dark sea that would eventually take him to Heaven and away from all this.

In the murmur of voices a thought came to him, one he had not properly considered through all his agony, his intense loneliness, his sense of loss and fear. Mother. She would be devastated by the news, for surely someone would tell her. Someone within the Catholic community would carry the news back to Scotton, back to a mother who stood for the faith, who had been so pleased when he had converted, had been so proud when he had left for his first job, a footman, no less, she had said to all who would listen, a footman way down south in a big house with a rich family!

Not so rich, Mother, and not so big after all. Nothing was as it seemed in this world, nothing seemed to be right in the sight of God. How could He let these heretics take the throne, be responsible for governing this country, the place he loved, how could that government kill an innocent woman and leave her children motherless because of a priest? A holy man of God, for God's sake and even as he thought it, he almost smiled.

Whatever Mother thought it was too late to ask for forgiveness. It was too late for anything, because even as he thought it, they pronounced their fate. The traitor's death, hanging, drawing and quartering.

Fool. Mother was long gone. His mind was wandering, lost, buried in the past still, where it could find refuge from all that he had endured and what was still to come.

It could not be worse than he had already endured. Could it?

The court was being cleared of cheering, yelling, stamping, shrieking, blood mad spectators. Cleared with difficulty for each one there was set fair to ensure the traitors, for so they were now named, heard their venom. He wanted to shout, it doesn't matter, you fools! It doesn't matter, you are under the Protestant yoke and until you fight back for religious freedom, there you will stay! But speech was beyond him. Living was beyond him but so far Death had refused to reach out and take him into those bony arms which right then and there would be a welcome relief.

There was comparative silence in the hall now.

"We have to get you out of here." The voice sounded stern and yet beneath it was a note of compassion Guy noticed immediately and decided to take a chance.

"Can't walk." He was annoyed that his words slurred, as if he was drunk.

"I know. We'll carry you. Like before."

But it was not like before. Not men under each damaged ravaged shoulder. Four of them hefted him, still tied to the chair. They lifted it, tilted it deliberately, banged him against the wall as they made their way out of the hall, jarring every part of him. At least no effort was required of him, he only had to endure and that was something he had done for the past four days anyway. He lolled against the rope, praying it would not give way and allow him to fall, for he knew he would not survive that. Then, as before, he wondered why he thought that, when death would end the suffering. He raged at himself silently for being so stupid.

The journey down to the dungeons seemed interminable, even the air passing over his body felt as if it was burning his skin. He tried to take notice of the surroundings but blackness swept over him again, the only way his mind could find release from the incessant pain of his useless body.

Nothing was said. Boots resounded on the flagstones, breathing was laboured from the effort of carrying his weight and the chair, his manacles clanked mournfully, or so it seemed to him in the brief moments he was conscious. Even curses would have been better than the seemingly total indifference to the fact they were carrying a shattered man.

Finally they arrived at a cell. One of the men kicked the door open, it banged against the wall and came back to hit the chair as they manoeuvred him in. The shock was tremendous, but then someone sliced through the rope so he collapsed on the floor with a scream of pure agony that rebounded from the stones. That was far, far worse. The men laughed and stomped out, leaving him in the darkness of his own pain.

Guy woke, or regained consciousness, he wasn't entirely sure which, to find a lantern burning beside some stale bread and lukewarm water. The temperature didn't matter; it was water, something he had not had for some days. The temptation was to drink it all, senses said no, take it a sip at a time. He moistened the bread with the water to make it easier to eat and wondered again why he was bothering. Why not lie back on the cold floor and allow Death to walk in and claim him? Why allow them to put him through the traitor's death, the most awful death imaginable – although he was trying very hard not to imagine it. But somehow his heart insisted on going on beating, his stomach demanded something to fill it, his mouth knew he was in desperate need of water and he gave in to the silent demands, even as every movement made him want to shriek aloud.

The lantern went out before he was through but he had the bread in his hand and the water by his side and the darkness no longer troubled him. He had walked in its silent comforting presence many times in the previous few days, both real and in his mind. It held no fears for him anymore.

Suddenly tears began to spurt from his eyes as the realisation of his friends being truly dead hit home. Jack, Kit, gone. Gone from earth already. Would they have been able to withstand the inquisition he had suffered? He thought Jack might, he was a strong man, but the rack would break the strongest man in England. No pain existed like it. Being burned to death, that was what everyone said was the worst pain of all, but no, it wasn't. Being burned to death meant there was an end to it. Being racked meant there was no end to it – until they decided to make it end, by which time you were useless. Nothing could be mended after that. Nothing.

No one came near him for what seemed like days. He heard sounds: boots, chains, screams, but his door did not open. He slept as best he could, waking often when the pain became too much. There was no way to keep track of the hours, it could be time for them to come for him or it could be days away, he did not know. When awake he prayed endlessly for deliverance, for mercy, for divine intervention to prevent him having the further ordeal of the awful death sentence and then begged forgiveness for asking for it to be taken from him when the Blessed Virgin's son had endured so much more – for his sake. Then he recalled once again that the Virgin's son had asked for the cup to be taken from Him, so he felt a little better about asking. Thoughts jumbled in his mind, pain confusing his rational sensible side and allowing hallucinations to take over. He thought he saw an angel standing in the corner of the cell, one who beckoned to him and told him it would soon be over and that he would be home with the Father. Another time he thought he saw a devil, evil personified in its grinning features, taunting him that he had days to go, days of suffering before even more suffering. This caused him to break down in helpless unmanly tears which made him feel even worse. Nothing else moved in the cell, not even a rat explored his wasted flesh. It was truly as if he was nothing. No longer a man, no longer a person of any note. No longer a person. Nothing. Ignored. Left to rot. Self-pity consumed him and he began to rant against his imprisonment.

He could not decide what was the most difficult to endure, the pain which consumed him or the bitter cold which burned him. For the first time in his life he began to believe that Hell was not a place of endless heat, flames and vile demons, but the empty lonely coldness of a dungeon when the body which was of necessity lying on the ice cold floor had been racked beyond endurance. He clung to life for no reason that he could rationalise in his pain-swamped mind. Again he asked himself, why not let go, deprive them of their show piece execution, of their taunting and their smug satisfaction that another traitor had been dealt with? Why not give himself into the hands of the great God who surely awaited him in Heaven? Ah, he thought, groaning as another wave of intense pain swept him from head to foot, ah, if only it were possible to still the heart by a thought! If it were, he would do it in an instant but no matter how hard he tried, he remained alive – just.

Was it night or was it already day? Would they come for him soon, to carry him to the traitor's death that he knew awaited him? He had lost all sense of time for the Tower was a dark place of endless torment and suffering. All he knew was that he hurt and that it would soon all be over.

He heard footsteps on the cold stone, a jangle of ice as chains rattled and keys knocked against one another. He heard a curse as the lock refused to give under the hand of the person trying to gain access.

The door opened, a light shone into his eyes. He painfully raised an arm to shield himself from the beam.

"It lives." Someone spat into the dungeon. "We will be back for you tomorrow, scum. Be ready to meet thy Maker."

The door slammed, the mechanism protested but finally moved, locking him in, as if they believed the broken man could get up, open the heavy door and walk out. Fools, he thought with intense bitterness. Fools. I could no more raise a hand to them than I could fly through these walls and disappear forever.

Guy subsided onto the cold stone. Tomorrow. What day was tomorrow? And then wondered why it mattered. Tomorrow it would be over.

With a tremendous effort he forced his shattered body to its knees and began the prayers that would last until they came for him.

Chapter Seventeen

Almost there, the voice told him, almost there. Be a man. You cannot stand but you can be proud, you can show them you are not broken. If you do that, they have not won.

The racked man felt strength come into his damaged body, felt a burning that was not of pain but of restoration. Someone, some-thing, had entered his cell and was giving him what he needed, respite from pain and a surge of pride. His prayers had been answered. Why had he ever doubted they would not be?

***

Only two men came for him the next morning. Guy briefly wondered why he would have assumed there would be more than that. He was detaching himself from his body, slowly but surely, allowing the lifeless marionette that was once him to be dragged, pulled, bound, secured to some kind of harness leading from the back of a horse. His feet were in the air, his head banging on the cobbles and stones. It didn't matter anymore. The bitter coldness of the January morn did not matter, either. He looked once at the men handling him and then closed his eyes, never to open them again. He did not wish to see the faces of those convicted with him, did not wish to see their terror or their stoicism or their mouths moving as they murmured prayers that would no longer help. The Lord God knew their crime and their intention, He had already decided their fate once they walked through the door marked Death. Guy did not wish to see their contempt or their pity. It was enough that he felt it in what was left of his mind.

The horse shifted as Guy's bulk was attached. The animal released a shower of manure which spattered him. As with everything else, it did not matter. His clothes stank anyway of his own ordure, what mattered a little more? Someone sniggered but the sound died in the morning chill.

More horses' hooves, more hustle and bustle. Strange sounds he could not identify and could not bring himself to think on anyway. More protests and groans from the condemned men and the excited muttering of the crowd which had gathered. To see what? Men bound to harness to be dragged through the streets? What entertainment was there in that? But then, what was there to observe, unless it was a morbid interest in what was contained inside a man's body when it was cut free and held up for its owner to see.

It was all speculation. Nothing mattered now. It was as if he hovered outside his body, looking down on the broken wreck and wondering why he had clung to it for so long.

Nothing mattered any more. No family, no friends, no plot, no conviction, nothing. Empty of thought, empty of emotion, empty of anything but a strange light that seemed to fill him.

"Go!" The horses moved off. The convicted men's heads bounced from the cobbles, raising shrieks and cries. Not from him. There was nothing left in him to protest about.

The journey was endless and yet, for those about to suffer, over too soon. The scaffold was ready, the nooses dangling, the executioner in his place. Guy knew this without opening his physical eyes; his spirit could see it all clearly. He needed nothing more than that.

He was carried to the rope.

Someone read out his name and his crime, the verdict and the sentence. A great cheer went up from the crowd, standing many deep around the platform. The blood lust was as evident there as it had been in Westminster Hall during the trial. He made no speech; he had nothing to say to the crowd. What could he say at that point, the point of death, that would make any difference to anyone?

The rope was rough on skin that no longer felt anything. Someone's breath touched a face that no longer carried any expression. Someone's voice said, so softly that none could hear it but the dead man himself, "twill all be over in a moment. Fear not. I will pull a little too…"

In his last lucid moments, Guy found himself wondering if anyone would remember his name.

Epilogue

Guy Fawkes did not suffer the traitor's death of hanging, drawing and quartering; he was killed by the sympathetic executioner before that part of the sentence could be carried out. Someone decided he had suffered enough.

Guy and I have endured endless comments such as 'explosive stuff' and 'it will take off like a rocket' during the writing of this book. Guy has heard all this and more during his time as a spirit. The hope is that after reading this book, people will take him – and the 'Gunpowder Plot' - more seriously.

He has been both shocked and pleased by his ongoing recognition, outside of the annual burning of his effigy, that is. He has seen, on the Internet, Isla Guy Fawkes (also known as Guy Fawkes Island) a collection of two crescent shaped islands and two small rocks north-west of Santa Cruz Island, in the Galápagos Islands, part of Ecuador.

There is a Guy Fawkes River in northern New South Wales, Australia. It runs from the south to north along the valley of the Demon Fault Line in the Guy Fawkes River National Park. It was named by the explorers who camped there on November 5th.

There have been racehorses called Guy Fawkes, as well as the many places in and around York, all named for this famous man. It ensures that his name will live forever, not only in England but around the world. The ongoing subversive joke, that he was the only man who went to Parliament with honourable intentions, has lingered to this day, despite some of the great leaders we have had since his time. (Sir Winston Churchill comes to mind immediately.)

You may well decide not to believe that this is a channelled book direct from spirit, that I am a good author who wrote an interesting work of fiction, in which case I hope you enjoyed your read. If you choose to believe that I channelled the work, then you will have had an insight into a period of history usually only seen through the distorted eyes of historians. There are more such insights to come from a great variety of people who have approached me with the same request, to tell their story and put the truth before the world.

Thank you for buying this book and for reading it to the end. If nothing else, you should have a different opinion on the man known as Guy Fawkes, which is what we set out to achieve.

Dorothy Davies,
Isle of Wight, 2009

Grateful thanks go to:

Mary Holliday, devoted friend;

Lynne Mulrooney for the portrait of Guy and her reading;

Terry Wakelin because he is Terry Wakelin, my rock and my anchor as always;

To my inner Circle for support, love, guidance, laughter and for always being there.

We must mention, with gratitude, D.B. who willingly responded to our appeal for help. Guy needed a 'ghost' writer to help turn what was in his mind into a readable book. He admits that without help from the spirit side of life this book would not have been half as good as it is. Our grateful thanks to D.B. for becoming part of the project. Both Guy and I agree it was a pleasure to work with such a good author. (We are aware of the 'oddity' of a spirit being asked to be a 'ghost' writer…)

We wish to mention all the people who have researched and built websites in Guy's memory or mentioned him on other sites in connection with various times of his life.

Guy says: Your assumptions may be wrong at times but your hearts are in the right place. I thank you.

A percentage of the royalties from this book will be sent to Amnesty International. It is a fitting charity for this compassionate man.

My friend Mary and I sit together most Monday nights for spiritual development and invariably say, 'is there anyone who wants to come and talk to us?' One particular night in October 2005 someone did come. We sensed a presence but we had no idea who the person was and we could not persuade them to talk. In the end, Mary left the room to make tea. It was then Guy spoke to me, told me who he was and asked if it was all right to stay for a while. His innate shyness was then - and is still - an essential and charming part of his personality.

I began writing to my close and trusted friend Gene Stewart about Guy and then found he was writing back as if to Guy rather than me. It was obvious there was a bond between them and, after much discussion and a few visits, Guy said he would like to go, to share Gene's life and be part of his team. We both shed a lot of tears at the parting but if it was right for him to experience another land, another lifestyle, it was something I had to accept.

I received messages from Guy from time to time and sent mine in return. A year or more passed and then, for reasons personal to them both, Gene and Guy parted. He packed his belongings and returned to be part of my team. It was as if a part of me had been restored; a part I had not appreciated was actually missing. It was a strange feeling but a good one. There being no such thing as coincidence, a fortnight before this happened one of my team members said his task with me was complete and he would be moving on. He commented that the rooms he had occupied were needed by someone else. Guy moved in to that suite.

Guy has remained with me ever since. He has taken on the task of building a group of people who counsel those who have been tortured, helping them to return to full spirit life. They aim to help each person to come to terms with the appalling experiences of that particular incarnation. It is difficult, often heart wrenching work but he does it. The choice of charity for this book's royalty percentage is his. The dreadful end he went through in his incarnation as Guy Fawkes is bestowing its rewards on both sides of life.

I am honoured to have Guy both as friend and close companion. I acknowledge and appreciate the work he does and I am grateful to have had the chance of giving his story to the world.

You may well decide not to believe that this is a channelled book direct from spirit, that I am a good author and wrote an interesting work of fiction, in which case I hope you enjoyed your read. If you choose to believe that I channelled the work, then you will have had an insight into a period of history usually only seen through the distorted eyes of historians. There are more such insights to come from a great variety of people who have approached me with the same request, to tell their story and put the truth in front of the world.

Thank you for buying this book and for reading it to the end. If nothing else, you should have a different opinion on the misunderstood man known as Guy Fawkes, which is what we set out to achieve.

Dorothy Davies,
Isle of Wight, 2010

Notes on the name "Guy"

The name arrived in England with the Normans. It appears in some Latin records as Guido. It is the same name in a different language. The name disappeared for about two hundred years after the Gunpowder Plot as the population of England chose not to use the name because of its connections. Whilst thinking on Guy's reputation -

It is stated by several sources that a Head Boy at Guy's old school commented that their most famous ex-pupil was 'not exactly a role model.' One wonders what was in that person's mind at the time. To do what Guy did meant total commitment to his faith, his friends and the cause, regardless of the consequences. He knew that if he were caught, it would be considered treason and that accordingly the traitor's death of hanging, drawing and quartering would be his fate. To go ahead knowing that possibility was in front of him shows fortitude of mind and character that many of the school's pupils would do well to emulate. I would politely request that in future, the school - and its Head Boys - think twice before commenting adversely on such a famous ex-pupil. Guy Fawkes has a reputation which has lasted for centuries. His story has been told in many books. Even in today's world he is often regarded as the one of the few men to enter Parliament with honourable intentions. It is to be asked how many of St Peter's School pupils will be remembered in 400 years' time...